The Winter Wedding

*Lisa,
Thank you for being an inspiration!
Rhonda McKnight*

Rhonda McKnight

Copyright 2019 Rhonda McKnight

Elevated Press
P.O. Box 164
Morrow, GA 30260

All rights reserved. No part of this book may be reproduced in any form or by any means without prior consent of the author, excepting brief quotes used in reviews.
This is a work of fiction. Any references or similarities to actual events, real people, living or dead, or to real locales are intended to give the story a sense of reality. Any similarity in other names, characters, places and incidents is entirely coincidental.

ISBN-13: 978-0-9843660-2-6

Unless otherwise noted, all scripture quotations taken from the King James Version of the Bible.
Scripture taken from the New King James Version®. Copyright © 1982 by Thomas Nelson. Used by permission. All rights reserved. Scripture quotations marked (NIV) are taken from the Holy Bible, New International Version®, NIV®. Copyright © 1973, 1978, 1984, 2011 by Biblica, Inc.™ Used by permission of Zondervan. All rights reserved worldwide. www.zondervan.com The "NIV" and "New International Version" are trademarks registered in the United States Patent and Trademark Office by Biblica, Inc.™

Also by Rhonda McKnight

Restoration Series
The Winter Reunion
The Winter Baby – Coming Dec 2019

Samaritan Woman Series
An Inconvenient Friend
What Kind of Fool
Righteous Ways
Almost There
Shame On You – Coming May 2019

Jordan Family Series
Give A Little Love
Live A Little
Love A Little

Second Chances Series
Breaking All The Rules
Unbreak My Heart

Other
When She Loves
A Woman's Revenge
Secrets and Lies

Table of Contents

Dedication 7
Acknowledgments 9
Prologue 15
Chapter 1 21
Chapter 2 32
Chapter 3 35
Chapter 4 44
Chapter 5 48
Chapter 6 70
Chapter 7 79
Chapter 8 86
Chapter 9 96
Chapter 10 105
Chapter 11 107
Chapter 12 109
Chapter 13 114
Chapter 14 122
Chapter 15 128
Chapter 16 137
Chapter 17 141
Chapter 18 149
Chapter 19 158
Chapter 20 167
Chapter 21 173
Chapter 22 185
Chapter 23 205
Chapter 24 209
Chapter 25 212
Chapter 26 219
Chapter 27 230
Chapter 28 237
Chapter 29 254

Chapter 30	265
Chapter 31	278
Chapter 32	284
Chapter 33	291
Chapter 34	295
Chapter 35	300
Chapter 36	306
Chapter 37	315
Chapter 38	320
Chapter 39	339
Chapter 40	347
Chapter 41	353
Chapter 42	357
Chapter 43	362
Chapter 44	371
Chapter 45	379
Chapter 46	384
Chapter 47	391
Chapter 48	393
Chapter 49	397
Chapter 50	399
Reader Discussion Guide	404
Scriptures On Healing	406
The Winter Reunion	407
About the Author	413

Dedication

For My Aunt Delores Burgess
…because you've been good to me and you read my
books and I love you!

Acknowledgments

My Readers Rock! Thank you for inspiring me to write another story. I couldn't do this without you cheering me on. Special thanks to the ladies in my Facebook Group Rhonda McKnight Readers. You especially bless me with our daily conversations and fun interactions.

My destiny-sisters, **Tia McCollors** and **Sherri L. Lewis**, y'all the best. You know how I feel. I couldn't do this without you. Thank you for holding me accountable and being my help and my sounding board. You two are the best friends and accountability partners a person could pray for. But for real tho'…do you guys even read these? LOL. Hugs!

My sister-writer-friends at **Black Christian Reads** (www.BlackChristianReads.com) love and hugs for the sisterhood. You are a blessing to me. Thanks to Jacquelin Thomas for a lending an endless listening ear ALL THE Time and

Special Thanks to **Liesha Ann Barnett** for helping me with the medical research on Stephen's knee. I appreciate you sharing your story, your hardships, and your thoughts about what someone would be feeling during the recovery from a tough injury. You helped me with the emotional aspect of Stephen's situation as well as the physical. I pray God continue to heel you in miraculous ways and I wish you every success with your business venture.

My sons, **Aaron and Micah**...you love me and overlook much as I write. You inspire me to be my personal best. Thank you!

My parents, **Bessie and Jimmie McKnight**, and siblings, **Cynthia and Kenneth McKnight**...thank you for the encouragement, love, and support!

Everybody else...love you too!!!

'Fear not, for I *am* with you; Be not dismayed, for I *am* your God. I will strengthen you. Yes, I will help you. I will uphold you with My righteous right hand.'
~ Isaiah 41:10

The Winter Wedding

Prologue

Run!

Adrenaline laced with fear propelled Tamar through the parking lot. Snow crunched under the weight of her boots. Barely breaking her fall with the side of someone's car, she slid across a sheet of ice.

Slow down, girl. She wouldn't have to deal with this problem if she killed herself.

Suddenly she paused. She had to try, again, to remember what her car looked like. It was silly. She'd been driving it for months and still, the sleek, silver Range Rover was foreign to her. It was a gift from Stephen that she wished she'd never accepted. In the end, she kept it, because she couldn't explain why she wouldn't accept it. NFL players with forty-five million-dollar contracts gave their women big gifts.

Tamar fished around in her handbag for her keys. She pushed the alarm for the car and followed the noise two rows over and pushed the button to stop the noise. Her cell rang. She removed it from the bag as she slid in behind the steering wheel.

"Mrs. Pierce, this is Vehicle security."

Annoyance. "I'm fine. I couldn't locate my car."

"Would you please give us your personal security code?"

Tamar provided the code and answered the other two security questions. Once they were done, she slid her cell into the special slot that was cut into the dashboard for it and started the car. The doors locked around her. The automated voice welcomed her to the vehicle and asked her if she needed GPS.

Tamar clutched the steering wheel. *You need to run.* She closed her eyes and blinked hard against burning tears. She had to talk to Stephen. She had to tell him before the reporter did.

"You know better than anyone that you need to get in front of this story." The cocky jerk opened his notebook. *"A few questions can sway the direction I'll take it."*

In the quiet of the car, she cried, "What does he know?"

"Good Afternoon, Mrs. Pierce." The automated voice from the dashboard speakers stated.

Mrs. Pierce. She was not Mrs. Pierce. She would never be Mrs. Pierce. She thought back to the day he gave it to her.

"This car is too much, Stephen. I told you I didn't want you spending money on me."

"I've spoiled myself and my mother. I don't have any kids. Who am I going to spend it on?" he'd asked. *"You have no idea how much I'm looking forward to spoiling you."*

Tamar pushed the ignition button. Within seconds, a voice greeted her with the words, "Please put on your seatbelt, Mrs. Pierce. Will you be needing GPS assistance?"

Tamar turned toward Stephen and cocked an eyebrow.

"You might as well get used to hearing yourself be called Mrs. Pierce." He leaned in and kissed her. "You'll be my wife soon enough."

Feigning indignation, Tamar snatched back her head. "Who said I was going to change my name?"

Stephen chuckled. "You make a compelling argument for not changing it, and I won't utter a word about you keeping Johnson."

Tamar pursed her lips. She had only been teasing him. "Really."

"I don't care what other people call you. I just need you to know who you are."

"I wouldn't dream of keeping my name."

"Good," Stephen said. "I was kidding."

Tamar slapped him playfully.

She felt the blood in her veins surge. How had she gotten here? "How did I let it get this far?"

She removed her gloves, reached for her phone, swiped the screen, and scrolled through her contacts for Escape Travel Agency. She pressed the phone against her chest and dropped her head back. She couldn't run. She had responsibilities. Besides running was hard. You were never really going anywhere. You were only trying to get away from your past and the past ran harder and faster than she'd ever been able to, because her past was in her mind, memories, and heart. There was no escaping that. But as hard as it had been to disappear the first time, disappearing…again, was preferable to explaining herself.

Stephen's face came into view. It wasn't his good looks that haunted her right now; it was his heart that she saw. A heart she was going to be responsible for breaking. She opened her eyes and sighed.

You want to get in front of this.

Tamar reached into her pocket for his business card. She read the contact information again. Roy Cray, Feature Reporter, *The City Standard*. She was a writer. Some folks would say she herself was a reporter. In any event, she knew how this worked. The clock was ticking. If Roy didn't get a quote from her soon, it would be too late to give him one.

Tamar sighed and dialed his number.

"This is Cray."

Uneasiness clutched her stomach as she spoke. "This is Tamar Johnson."

Silence for a moment and then, "Ms. Johnson. I haven't gotten far. Can we meet?"

"I'm not sure I want to meet."

"I have a story."

Solid.

Definitive.

Sure.

When a reporter's tone carried confidence, they weren't bluffing.

Irritated, she replied, "Stephen has told his side of the story a hundred times already. We don't have anything else to say."

"This isn't about Stephen."

Tamar closed her eyes. She'd known it, felt it when he stopped her. She fought to keep a tremble out of her voice. "What is it?"

"I'm sure you know." A beat of silence and then, "It's about what happened after the video."

Fear crept up her spine. She masked it by keeping the irritated tone in her voice. "A lot of things happened after the video."

"Okay, then let me be more specific. You dropped out of school. I know what you were doing. I'd like a quote or two before we go to press."

Tamar swallowed bile. "I had to change colleges because of people like you."

"Ms. Johnson. I'm almost done with my research. I need to hear from you in 24 hours or…"

Tamar pressed the button to end the call. "Or you'll write it anyway."

Run!

She closed her eyes. Running was cowardly. She wasn't eighteen years old this time. She was a grown woman who had to face up to this situation. This truth was coming out. This story had to be told. This wrong had to be righted.

Stephen will hate me.

"Mrs. Pierce, do you need GPS assistance?"

Tamar banged on the steering wheel and yelled with the same intensity. "Home!"

"We are searching for the location, Mrs. Pierce."

She checked her mirrors. The tires screamed as she backed out of the parking space. She was not Mrs. Pierce and after she had this conversation with Stephen, she for sure never would be.

"Cancel Home."

"Do you want to go to another location, Mrs. Pierce?"

She hesitated before saying, "The airport."

Chapter 1

Four months earlier...

Stephen Pierce was persistent. I pushed the "reject call" button and sent him to voicemail for the third time this morning. I couldn't talk to him. Not right now. Right now, all I wanted to do was disappear.

Returning to Pine, Pennsylvania had more implications than I'd anticipated. The journey to my high school reunion had been difficult. I'd spent most of the time agonizing over my reunion with my ex-boyfriend, Stephen Pierce. The tremble in my gut was about him and my feelings for him – unforgiveness mixed with an unrelenting, heartsick love that was like the milk and rum in the season's eggnog. But now that I had forgiven him, all that was left was the love. That was up until this morning, when reality came crushing down and I realized, love wasn't all I had. The unforgiveness had been replaced with fear.

My phone rang again. Relieved to see it wasn't him, I pushed the "talk" button and greeted my Aunt Josephine.

"Hey, Auntie. Belated Merry Christmas."

"Hey, Tamar. I see you called me a few times yesterday. I'm sorry I didn't get a chance to get back to you." Aunt Joe coughed. "Hold on." The phone went silent, but I didn't lose the connection, so I waited. Then I heard background noise again. "I'm sorry for that."

"Do you still have that cold?" The answer was obviously yes, but I still asked.

"Cold, flu, something had me down for a few days."

"Were you out yesterday?" I already knew the answer was yes. Aunt Joe was in charge of a large toy drive run by her church. On Christmas Day, the toys were delivered to various shelters and families all over the county.

"You know we do the toy delivery." She coughed a few more times. "It's my ministry. I have to lead it no matter how I feel."

"I hope you rested when you got home."

Aunt Joe took her time answering. "We didn't get home until ten last night. Deacon invited us to his house for dinner. I hadn't cooked, so I wasn't passing up a plate. They played spades and some other games. The kids had a video game contest and a dance contest. I sat in the corner with my sweet potato pie and let Isaiah play to his heart's content."

"Mama, is that Cousin Tamar?" I heard Isaiah's voice above the television noise in the background. "Tell her thank you for the new games."

"Did you hear him?" Aunt Joe asked. "I would give him the phone, but I done put germs all over it."

I shook my head. "That's fine. He's the most grateful child I know."

"He's in his room with one of friends anyway. All they care about is those games."

"I thought I heard a little base slip in and out on a crack. Is his voice changing?"

Aunt Joe spoke on winded words. "It's about that time." She coughed a few times more times.

I tried to keep the concern out of my voice. This sickness hadn't been for a few days. Now that I thought about it, Aunt Joe had been sick shortly after Thanksgiving.

"Tell him I said he's welcome."

"Oh, Tamar, I've got a call coming through from my doctor."

The line went dead. At least she was seeking medical care for the cough or flu or whatever it was she had.

I sighed and put the phone down. Aunt Joe and I were going to have to have a real conversation soon. Sooner than she probably would like.

"Tamar." I heard my father's voice rise from the foyer. I hopped off the bed, pulled my door open, and looked down the stairwell. Stephen was standing there.

**

"I've been calling all morning."

Tamar took slow steps down the stairs. Her father wandered off toward the back of the house.

"I know, and I was about to call you back."

I wasn't convinced of that. Her demeanor said otherwise. "Is there a reason I can't get you on the phone? I mean, if you called me, I'd be hitting the green light on my phone post haste."

"I woke up late." She looked bothered and sounded annoyed. "I had to get my story in." She stopped on the third step from the bottom and crossed her arms. She avoided my eyes. I couldn't help but feel like she wasn't being completely honest.

"I thought your story was going to be the feature on me." I reached for her hand and tugged until she came down a few more steps.

"That's the next story," she said. "And now that it's gotten to be a bigger story. I have more time to write it."

I nodded. Tamar was in town to interview me for the magazine she worked for, but I flipped the direction of the piece when I went live on SportsCenter with my confession. I pushed that from my mind. I didn't want to talk about our past. I wanted to talk about our today and our tomorrow.

I was face-to-face with her now. I wished her eyes held a smile, but they didn't. She was closed and moody, but I leaned in and kissed her anyway. "Happy Boxing Day."

A slight hint of a smile pursed her lips.

"Uh, huh," I teased. I knew she remembered the

middle school Christmas play we'd been in. We were Jamaican characters that celebrated Boxing Day, December 26th as a big holiday. We'd always wished each other a Happy Boxing Day ever since and swore one year we'd go to Jamaica for the holiday.

"You're silly." Tamar shook her head. Her eyes warmed.

"I miss you." I looked backward toward the kitchen to make sure her father wasn't in our line of sight. I kissed her again.

"You saw me like eight hours ago."

"It's been twelve. Twelve hours is too long to be away from you."

The light went out of her eyes. She pulled her hand from mine and side-stepped me to get down the remaining steps. I reached for her hand as she passed, but she didn't let me have it. Instead, she walked into the living room.

I peeled my coat off. Like a lovesick puppy, I followed her. I was going to lose my mind if this woman didn't want me, so I pushed the thought out of my head.

"The reason I needed to get in touch with you so desperately this morning is because I have to go back to Jersey. I have practice tomorrow. You know we play Sunday."

Tamar waited for me to continue.

"Anyway, I was hoping you would come back with me. Go to the game."

Tamar hesitated. "I wanted to spend some time

with my dad. I haven't had a chance."

This was true. Tamar had been estranged from her father for the last twelve years – the same twelve years she'd been estranged from me. She'd only been in town for four days and most of those were spent at our reunion and then with me. "Yeah, I guess you do."

Tamar looked relieved, but I pressed. "What about the game?"

She shrugged. "I'm not that into football anymore, but I guess I can come watch you play."

"Guess." I swallowed frustration. She didn't even sound remotely playful or interested. This was weird. She and I had spent the earlier part of yesterday with the kids from my youth foundation and then had dinner at her father's girlfriend, Dell Mayweather's, house. We visited my parents and then cozied up in front of my fireplace until the wee hours of the morning, getting reacquainted with each other. But now she was acting like I was a nuisance, distancing herself by claiming a seat in a wing chair when there were several other pieces of furniture in the room that would have brought us closer. "Tay, did I do something?"

She hesitated before speaking. "I'm fine. I'm just, trying to wrap my head around everything, Stephen. I've been really isolated and private for the past twelve years. Being home, seeing my dad, seeing you and your parents. I think I'm overwhelmed."

I regretted my role in that. Denying I was the guy in the "Losing Her Virginity" video had kept us apart – painfully so. It had only been two days since I'd confessed. I'd been taking calls and giving interviews to the media the entire time. I'd made a public statement on Christmas Eve admitting I was the guy in the video, and reporters were all over it. I hadn't thought about how the resurgence of the press would affect her. I just wanted to prove to her that I was willing to tell the truth. I wanted to earn her trust again.

"This is all bad timing," I said. "This isn't a big story. It'll die down."

Tamar frowned. "It appears to be a big story." She reached for a throw pillow and placed it in front of her body. I felt like she'd put up a wall between us. I couldn't help focusing on her lack of enthusiasm for my visit. It chilled the room.

"It's not. In a few days, they'll be done with it. That's why I'm taking all the calls. The sooner they talk to me, the sooner they'll be done with me."

Tamar shrugged again.

"You sure that's it?" I asked.

She played with the tassels on the edge of the pillow. "I was on the phone with my aunt a few minutes ago. When you arrived. She's sick, and I'm a little worried about her."

"Which aunt?" I finally took a seat.

"My mother's sister. Joe."

"The one in Georgia."

Tamar hesitated for a moment before saying yes.

"So, when you say sick?"

She stood and walked to the windows. She pulled the drapes back and looked out. "I don't know, Stephen. She's had a bug for a month. I think I need to go check on her and since I have to go back to Atlanta for work, I don't think I'll actually make it to this game." She emphasized the word *this*.

I nodded understanding because I did understand, but I was disappointed. She hadn't been to one of my games since high school. I stood. "No problem. Take care of your aunt. I just…" I took the steps necessary to close the space between us. I pulled her into my arms. "I'm sorry. I'm doing too much. I know."

Tamar shook her head. "You're not."

"No, I actually am," I said. "I'm acting like we don't have the rest of our lives to spend together."

Tamar's eyes got that strange look again. She swallowed like she was uncomfortable with what I'd said.

"Because we do."

"It's not that," she said. "Two days ago, I was living a different life. Like I said, I need to wrap my head around the idea of a relationship."

"Maybe I need to date you."

Tamar laughed. "Well, I'm sure whatever you could muster would be an improvement over the low budget dates we had in high school."

I nodded, and spoke teasingly, "I seem to remember you enjoying those dates."

Tamar tossed her head back. The warmth I loved filled her onyx colored eyes.

I rubbed my hand down her arm. "My season will be over soon and then I have a huge break before I start training in the summer."

Tamar smirked. "You have fifty-leven things on your calendar for your foundation."

"I'm going to pare all that back. I need to spend time with you. I'll come to Atlanta if that's what it takes."

Tamar managed to crack a smile, but again, the light went out of her eyes. I pushed the negative energy from that down into my belly. This woman did not want to talk about the future. It was triggering her.

Change the subject, Pierce.

"Have you had lunch? Can I take you out or cook for you? I can cook."

Tamar frowned. "I heard you could not."

"I have a few things I can do and look, I can warm up like nobody's business. Dorsey keeps meals in the freezer for me," I said, referring to my houseman.

"I really want to spend the day with my dad. He's probably in there fixing something for us right now."

I nodded again. I was getting none of her time today. That gut punch to my stomach pushed the wind right out of me.

"Okay," I said. "Well, I'll uh, just go on and get on the road and head back. I need to rest up anyway.

"Championship game in a few days." She stepped toward the door faster than I would have wanted her to.

I picked up my coat and slid it on. I leaned in for one more kiss. When I released her, her eyes seemed misty like she was on the verge of tears. Maybe her aunt really was sick.

"Babe, let me know if there's something I can do for you. Do you need a flight? My assistant can get you exactly what you need."

She pulled door open. "I appreciate that, but I've been pretty good at getting around. I'm sure I'll manage."

"But the point is, you don't have to manage. You're my woman now, and I'm Stephen Pierce."

Tamar looked away, but I could see a playful smile had formed on her lips. She turned back to me. "I don't remember consenting to be your anything."

"I felt a little consenting happening over the past two days." I pulled her close again. "I know this is new, again, but Tamar Johnson, I'm never letting you go, so you can just get used to me."

"Never is a long time." Those iffy words slipped from her lips way too easy. They were like this entire visit. Awkward.

"Yeah, it is, but forever is our story. It has been since we were kids."

Tamar cleared her throat. "I'll talk to you later."

"You'll take my calls?"

"Man, stop trippin'. I was about to call you back when I got off with my aunt."

I could tell she was teasing, but her voice didn't reassure me. "I hope so." I felt my own voice tremble.

God, I was begging.

"I love you, Tay."

She didn't reply. I was liberal with my love you's. She was not.

Something was off. I wish I had time to figure out what it was, but she wasn't giving it to me. I leaned forward, kissed her cheek again, and stepped through the door.

Tamar stood in the door as I backed out of the driveway. I waved one more time, and she waved back. I had the sudden revelation that I did not have her, not like I thought I did. Tamar and I had some painful years behind us.

I was gripped by the eerie thought that we had some painful times ahead of us as well.

Chapter 2

My father was disappointed. It was clear from the expression on his face. Team Stephen Pierce as always, he gave me a disapproving look. "Don't begin this thing with lies."

My father was leaving town in a few hours to go to Florida to prepare to preach the eulogy of a pastor friend of his, so I was not spending the day with him. I sighed. "I need space."

Daddy cocked an eyebrow. "Tell him that."

I turned and walked into the living room. "I did, but he won't give me any."

My father followed. "Still, no reason to lie."

I went back to the windows. I pulled the drapes again. I wasn't sure what I was looking for. I guess my peace, because that's what the snow gave me and that's all I could really see from this view. "I don't want to get swept up in the whirlwind of Stephen."

Daddy nodded understanding. "You sure that's it?"

I shrugged. "I'm under a lot of pressure."

"To love someone."

"To be in a relationship like that." I snapped my fingers. "It doesn't even happen like this."

Daddy didn't seem convinced. He was no more convinced than Stephen had been, but I wasn't ready to tell either of them my truth.

"You seem a little sad. Anxious even."

I sank into the comfortable chair that had been my mother's favorite. I looked around the room. I realized very little had changed. How difficult that must be for Daddy's friend, Dell. I wondered if he entertained her in this room with my mother's pictures on the fireplace mantle. I wasn't the only one having problems letting go of the past.

"The idea of my life becoming public again is scary. This morning, I had ten emails from reporters, and I know my voicemail at work is full." I pulled my knees to my chest. "I've been in hiding for so long that I don't really know how to live in the open."

Concern wore heavy on my father. "I can ask Bishop Wilson to go in my place."

I popped out of the chair and approached him. I took his hand. "No. You've loved Pastor Norman from the time I was a child. Mom loved his family. Please, go do this for his wife."

"You're welcome to join me. They'd love to see you. It's been a long time."

I swallowed heavy emotions. "I'm not ready for a funeral at Christmas. I know that's selfish, but I just can't if I don't have to."

Daddy nodded. "Your mother is smiling in

heaven because you're back in our house." He pulled me into a hug. "I'm going to pack. I have a car coming to take me to the airport."

My father left. I was alone again. Alone with my anxiety over my aunt. Alone with my angst about Stephen. My aunt probably had a virus, but the secret I kept from Stephen was not a bug that would go away. It was a festering disease that was going to eat away at any chance we had at the forever Stephen talked about.

Chapter 3

His name was Dr. Butler. He was tall, good looking, divorced and Aunt Joe's age, which was why she was all made up and dressed up for her doctor's appointment.

I stayed in the room while he did a thorough exam. Aunt Joe and he made all kinds of chatty, low-key flirty talk while he examined her. This was the first time I'd ever seen her as anything other than an aunt and a mother to Isaiah. She was a woman who desired a man. She'd been ignoring that part of her life.

All I knew of any romantic history was that Aunt Joe had a boyfriend when I showed up on her doorstep twelve years ago. My drama encroached on her relationship and her man left right after helping to assemble Isaiah's crib. Aunt Joe was hurt by his leaving, but she said he was kind of triflin' anyway. I was hurt by Stephen. We'd formed an unspoken pact to swear off men – until now. Stephen was back in my life and now this man was curiously interested in his patient.

"I'll send the bloodwork to the lab, but for now we're going to treat you for a respiratory infection." Dr. Butler made notes on a digital tablet. "I know you're tired, Joe, so I'll let you rest overnight. I want you to get a chest X-ray tomorrow."

"Is that necessary?" Aunt Joe asked. "Can I get the medicine in my system and see if I need one on Monday?"

He took Aunt Joe's hand in his and nodded. "I'll call you tomorrow. We'll talk about it." He winked at her and left the room.

After picking up the prescription paperwork at the desk, we exited the office.

"Scandalous," I teased.

Aunt Joe hit me playfully. "Mind your business."

"I was minding my business when all of the sudden, I felt like I was being pulled into a romantic drama flick in 3-D." I raised my hands to my eyes and made mock glasses.

Aunt Joe blushed. "I've been waiting for him to ask me out. As soon as he does, I'm getting a new doctor."

"Why do you need a new one? He seems like a good doctor." I helped her into her coat.

"Chile, you're still young and thin. I don't want my man to know how much I weigh and all my vital stats."

I laughed. "I guess you have a point there, but uh, he already knows, and you've lost weight anyway. Whatever the diet is you're on has been working."

We took an elevator down to the main level of the multi-office building and swirled around in the revolving door to exit. As soon as the cold air hit us, Aunt Joe began to cough uncontrollably. She sounded horrible. I'd never heard a cough this bad.

"Maybe you should wait inside until I warm up the car." I removed tissues from my bag and handed them to her. She looked weaker than I'd ever seen her. I was glad they'd ruled out the flu, but I was hoping the doctor wasn't being conservative in not admitting her to the hospital and giving her a day of IV antibiotics or something.

Aunt Joe stepped back into the building. I helped her down onto a bench and left to go to my car. My phone rang as I was getting inside. I'd assigned a ringtone to Stephen and even though I'd promised I would take his calls, he would have to wait.

I sent him a text message to let him know I was busy with my aunt at the doctor's office, and he texted back that he would pray for her. I was happy to have him on the mainline to Jesus, because that cough needed intercession.

I started the car and let it run for a few minutes before pulling out of the parking space. Aunt Joe exited the building. I hopped out and opened the door for her.

"Tamar, I'm not dying. I can get in a car by myself," she fussed, sliding onto the seat.

I closed the door behind her and climbed in on my side. "Is your pharmacy fast?" I asked, knowing she used a small, family-run drug store that was owned by a member of her church.

"They'll get it ready for me as fast as they can, but I think I need to get in the bed. If you don't mind, I want to go home."

I nodded. "I know you've been feeling bad for a while, but has it been this bad?"

"I think I done took a turn for the worse. Probably all that cold air on Christmas." She closed her eyes and rested her head against the window.

If I was honest, the real reason I was here was to talk to her about Stephen. I needed to tell her he was back in my life. Only she knew the complications that came with that. Aunt Joe had been my strength during the scandal twelve years ago. She'd been the person I'd run to when I left home. She'd lied to my father about my not being with her. Aunt Joe was the keeper of my secrets. But this was not a good time for my issues. She needed her full strength before I started with all my "what to do" and "what if" and "what now" questions.

We arrived at her house, and I helped her out of her clothes and into bed. After giving her a few choices for drinks, I rushed back out to the pharmacy. She needed to get started on those antibiotics. As expected, at rush hour during cold and flu season, the small parking lot was jammed with cars and the drive-thru line was long, so I decided to go inside.

After waiting more than twenty minutes in line, I was able to get the attention of a woman I recognized as a member of Aunt Joe's church to request the prescriptions, but even with expediting the service, the wait was thirty minutes. Since I had time, I decided to call Stephen.

He answered. I could tell he'd been sleeping. He was in Seattle. It was a little after 2 p.m. there.

"Sleepy much?" I teased.

"We worked hard this morning. Dinner is at six. I need some rest before I have to get ready."

"You're probably jet-lagged too. The time difference."

"All that," he said. "I'll be in bed way before curfew tonight."

A smirk peppered my tone. "Before 10:30 on a Friday night?"

"Girl, I'm the same homebody you knew back in the day, but nobody on the team is hanging out in Seattle tonight. We came to win this game."

"I hear you. Let me let you get your nap."

"No. I'm always glad to hear from you. I'm not sleeping yet. How's your aunt?"

I filled him in on her visit. He whistled. "That infection hit her hard. She's not that old, is she?"

"She's in her mid-50's, but I think she needed to get to the doctor a few weeks ago."

"She'll be all right. We've got her covered in prayer, and you're picking up the drugs," Stephen said. "You were right to go check on her. It sounds like she needed you."

"Thanks for understanding."

"Baby, family first always. I'm nowhere near retirement. You and I can fall asleep before curfew in Seattle next year."

I cocked an eyebrow. "You and I fall asleep?"

"Yeah, we'll be married by next season."

I sighed. Lord, this man had not changed. He always said what was on his mind no matter how much

I did or didn't want to hear it.

"You're quiet, Tay."

"I told you I need some time. I came to the reunion for work, not all of this."

"All of this is love."

"I know that, but I didn't come for love. I didn't even come voluntarily," I added, gently reminding him of how he'd smoked me out of hiding with his social media posts. "Being involved with an NFL player is a big deal. You know I've been incognito."

Stephen sighed. "I'm sorry. You're right. I forget how big my world can be. As long as you promise me that you and I will spend some quality time together, I can be patient."

I had to push the lie through my teeth. "I promise."

"And there's no other man, like, for real, that you need to go break up with."

I laughed. "I've told you. Not a soul."

Stephen chuckled. "Well, that makes two of us."

"One-Person-Pierce, right?"

He was teased with that nickname in high school. None of his friends could understand why he was committed to one girl when so many of the girls from our school and neighboring schools were interested in him.

"One-Person-Pierce forever. That's never going to change." Heaviness reentered his voice.

"I'll let you go. I know you need your nap."

"I'm not ready to let you go and you're waiting, so let's talk until I fall off."

I frowned. "Talk about what?"

"Anything. Everything."

I paused. My life was boring. I hadn't done anything exciting in years, so I went back to when I was a little happy and told him about the time I spent in South Africa after college. I'd gone on a writing fellowship. I taught writing to the children in the village and worked on my first novel.

Stephen listened to me for almost fifteen minutes and then I heard light snoring. I pressed the button to end our call. A few minutes later, I was in the line picking up my aunt's prescriptions. I received a text message from Stephen that said:

Thanks, babe. Best naptime story ever.

I texted him:

Don't oversleep.

He texted back:

I'm going to dream about you. I won't want to wake up.

And then before I could respond.

I won't tell you I love you because I know you need space.

He added several romantic emojis.

Once, I returned to the house, I gave Aunt Joe her medication. Just as I was about to walk across the street to the neighbor's to get Isaiah for dinner, I heard Aunt Joe call my name. I entered her room. She was sitting on the side of the bed, coughing up blood. A lot of blood.

***

I didn't wait for an ambulance. I helped Aunt Joe dress and rushed her to the hospital. She was taken into one of the E.R. rooms and Dr. Butler was phoned by the internist on duty. They drew blood, started an IV and sent her for a chest X-ray stat. I felt like I'd been waiting for days when the nurse came in and stated Dr. Butler had requested a CT scan, and they were taking her for the test.

"Does she have pneumonia?" I pressed for details. If they were ordering a more invasive imaging test, they had to have the results of the first one. "I thought you could see that with an X-ray?"

Aunt Joe interrupted me. "Tamar, let the people do whatever they have to do to get me out of here. I feel better since they gave me these IV drugs, so I want to go home in the morning."

But she didn't go home in the morning, or afternoon, or at all the next day. There were more tests and finally Dr. Butler came in to tell us that Aunt Joe did not have a respiratory infection. His eyes were sad and weary, his cheerful, but professional bedside manner not what it had been.

His voice cracked when he said, "I'm sorry to tell you this Joe, you have a mass in your lung that is highly suspicious for cancer. You need a biopsy."

Chapter 4

I hadn't expected my world to be turned upside down like this. Two weeks ago, I was sitting in my cubicle, working under my deceased mother's name and hiding from the world. Now, I was receiving text messages with heart emojis from my long, lost love, and I was sitting in an oncologist's office with my beloved aunt. The reintroduction of Stephen had my head swirling, but this situation with my aunt had me completely shook.

The new doctor was not tall, dark, or handsome like Dr. Butler. First of all, the new doctor was a she. Dr. Mowry was her name. She was a white woman, young – probably not more than forty – with a seriously decorated resume, noted by the wall of achievement behind her. Dr. Butler insisted she was the best oncologist around and hard to get an appointment with, but he'd called and smoothed the way for us to get in without a wait.

"You have Stage 2, non-small cell carcinoma. Which means the cancer has spread to the lymph nodes inside the lung, but it has not spread to any other organs."

I held my breath, assuming "not spread" was good news.

"The treatment?" Aunt Joe asked.

"Radiation, surgery, more radiation and probably chemotherapy. The addition of chemo will depend on how the disease responds to radiation."

Aunt Joe let out a long, exhausted breath. "It sounds like a lot."

Dr. Mowry folded her hands together on her desk and offered a sympathetic response. "It is. I'm not going to tell you it's not, but we need to be aggressive. Lung cancer can be difficult to treat. I also don't like the growth pattern of the tumor. I want to give you the best chance I can."

"To get about a 30-60% survival rate," Aunt Joe replied, quoting the numbers the doctor had stated earlier.

"Yes." Dr. Mowry picked up a pen and looked down at a calendar in front of her. "The treatment plan would include radiation first because I'd like to shrink the tumor before we operate."

I tried to stay focused as she spoke about the size of the tumor and the different types of chemo and PET scans and all the other medical jargon, I was hoping I'd never have to understand. But it was hard to stay focused. My heart was broken. My aunt's fear was like a heat radiating off her body. The energy of it permeated the entire room, and I'd listened to her cry for days. I'd cried myself. We'd worn ourselves out just getting here.

We left the office and made the trip home without uttering a word between us. Aunt Joe gripped the straps of her handbag. She closed her eyes and prayed and then opened them again and then closed them for more prayer.

Finally, once we had pulled up in front of the house, she spoke.

"Do you know why I stopped smoking fifteen years ago?"

I turned my head in Aunt Joe's direction and waited for the answer.

"Because I didn't want to get lung cancer." She raised a hand to her face and covered her mouth. "I'm most concerned about Isaiah." She looked at me. "I wish I didn't have to tell him this."

"He's smart. He already knows something is wrong with you."

Aunt Joe closed her eyes, made a fist and pushed it into her other palm.

"Auntie, you can't put it off anymore."

"I know that, Tamar," she snapped. "Don't you think, I know?"

I waited before speaking again. When I was sure she wasn't going to say anything, I asked, "Do you want me to help you tell him?" Aunt Joe had already told me she wanted to tell Isaiah alone.

"I told you no. If I add you to the conversation, it'll make it a bigger deal. He'll be scared."

"He's going to be scared anyway."

"More scared." She pulled the door handle and pushed the door open. "I'll tell him this weekend." She climbed out of the car and dragged her tired body into the house.

Aunt Joe kept her word. Isaiah and she had the conversation in the living room. I overheard bits and pieces of it from the guest room which had officially become my bedroom now that I was staying with her. Choosing Monday and Friday as telework days, I made the drive from Atlanta every Thursday evening after work and back on Monday evenings.

I pressed my ear flush against the door and listened. Isaiah asked a few questions. I didn't hear much of Aunt Joe's answers. Her voice was weaker these days, but I did hear when he broke down and began to cry. "I don't want you to die, Mama." And then promises from Aunt Joe that she would not leave him.

Tears ran down my face. I could feel his pain. I wanted to comfort him through this. With respect to Isaiah, I had always allowed Aunt Joe to tell me what I could and could not do and should and should not feel. I'd always been lighthearted and fun, Cousin Tamar to him. I came to visit just long enough to bring gifts and take him out to restaurants my aunt did not frequent on her single-parent, para professional teacher's salary.

But in this moment when he was experiencing the worst heartache he'd ever encountered in his life, I wanted to be more. I wanted to comfort him and wipe his tears. I wanted to take the pain away, because I wasn't just Cousin Tamar. Isaiah was my son.

Chapter 5

The last NFL championship game was happening in Atlanta. I was on my way home for it. Before I left Aunt Joe's house, I had to tell her I was back with Stephen. She followed football. The chances we might be photographed together, or something was too great for me not to.

Aunt Joe shrugged. "It's your life, baby. If you think you can trust him..." She let the question hang in the air.

"I don't know what I think. It's early."

She grunted. "You know you're going to have to tell him about Isaiah."

I nodded.

Aunt Joe's brow wrinkled. "When are you planning to do it?"

This time it was me who shrugged. "After football season is over. He doesn't need the distraction right now."

Aunt Joe nodded agreement. "How do you think he'll react?"

"Honestly, I think he's probably going to hate me

for it."

Aunt Joe took my hand. She squeezed it. "How do you feel about him?"

I was slow to respond. I didn't want to admit how I felt to myself, so admitting it to someone else was difficult. "I still have feelings for him."

"You mean you love him. That's what I thought."

Her reaction surprised me. "I expected you to be upset."

Aunt Joe released my hands and waved away my words. She chuckled with no joy. "Baby, I have bigger problems than what's going on with you and Stephen."

"I was also holding off because I was thinking you needed time. I don't want you to worry about Isaiah."

She frowned. "Why would I worry about Isaiah? He's my son."

"I know, but you're going through a lot right now."

"Don't worry about me. Whatever comes of this happens, but Isaiah will always be my child. He may gain a father. That's not a bad thing. Not at his age. And if Stephen Pierce is who he appears to be—"

"He is," I interrupted her. Happiness and sadness swirled in my spirit about that truth. Who he was was what I loved about him, but it also scared me.

"Well, then do it." Aunt Joe put a finger under my lowered chin. "He will understand."

I gave my aunt a weak smile and nodded, but my

heart...my heart said he would not.

Aunt Joe released my hand. "I'll be praying for you. You go on and get on the road."

Aunt Joe's words about Isaiah gaining a father were on my mind the entire time I was driving back to Atlanta. After I told Stephen, it would be good for Isaiah. It might even be good for Aunt Joe. She'd have the male help she needed.

Stephen also had money. Money opened doors for everyone. I wanted Isaiah to have the opportunities having a rich father would afford him. The only person it wouldn't be good for was me. Isaiah would be angry with me. Stephen would be angry with me. I was back to feeling like that eighteen-year-old pregnant girl who thought her baby was going to ruin her life.

And as much as Aunt Joe tried to put up a brave front, this was not a good time for her. She didn't need stress. The doctor told us that, so I needed to keep the stress to a minimum, at least until she recovered from surgery.

I exited I-75 at Stockbridge and made my way to my best friend, Kim's, hair salon. I entered the shop and approached the booth Kim was working at.

"You have time for one more head?" I asked, looking around at the packed waiting room.

Kim smiled. "Now you know it's Friday, and I can't fit anybody in."

She wiped her hands on a towel and gave me a hug. I needed that hug, because I was seconds away from crying again. "Well, if you can't curl my hair, do you have time to talk?"

Kim grunted. "Your face looks worse than that mop on your head. You're seeing Stephen tonight? I might have to fit you in."

"Yeah, yeah, yeah," I said. "A quick wash n' go and I'll be good. Ain't nobody got time for all this waiting."

Kim surveyed my head and then walked around me to look at the back. "Nothing a little water, curl cream and oil can't fix. Give me fifteen minutes and I'll meet you next door."

I left the salon and went to the coffee shop.

I placed latte orders for Kim and I. I found a table. I took my phone out of my bag and went to Instagram. I didn't have a page. I was social media skittish and would remain that way, but I kept up with Stephen on a daily basis by visiting his. He'd posted a group of pictures earlier this morning with the message:

Hello Atlanta! Grateful to God for a safe flight. I believe and expect a blessing. #FinishStrong

The day prior, he'd posted a pic taken of him catching the ball. The caption read:

I'm ready to meet my fans in Atlanta.

The day before that he'd posted a picture of a heart with the caption:

I have it for the game and her. #2loves #MyQueen #forever

I swallowed something that felt like regretful anticipation and closed the IG app.

Five minutes, later Kim entered the coffee shop.

She rushed to my table and sat. "I have three heads under the dryer and one in the sink. What's up?"

Suddenly I didn't want to talk anymore. She was in a rush. What I had to say would take time, so I simply said, "I missed you."

"You did not come all the way over here because you missed me." Kim picked up the latte I'd ordered for her and took a sip.

"I was coming from Aunt Joe's. I'm on the way home so it's, you know, on the way." Attempting to hide my face, I raised my cup and took a sip, too.

"You look like you've got something to say."

"It's my aunt."

I'd updated Kim on Aunt Joe last night so there was nothing new to share.

"How's Stephen?"

"He's great."

"You don't seem too excited about that."

I shook my head and dropped it back. How was I going to tell Stephen when I couldn't even get up the nerve to tell my best friend?

"Kim, have you ever done something you really regretted? I mean it was the right thing at the time, but now it doesn't feel so right anymore?"

"Like the tattoo of my ex's name on my shoulder?"

I laughed. "Girl."

"I'll get it off as soon as I meet the right man."

Kim took another sip of her coffee. "But what are you talking about? You got a tat on your behind or something?"

I laughed at her silliness. She knew better than that. "No. I have something that can't be erased."

"Okay, I see I'm going to have to pull it out of you," she said. "The answer to the question is, of course. I haven't always been this marvelously in love with Jesus. I've made some mistakes."

I hesitated a moment and then let the words I'd been holding back slip from my lips. "Stephen and I have another secret between us."

Kim cocked an eyebrow and settled back in her seat for the audio version of the movie playing in my head.

When I was done telling her about Isaiah, I asked, "Aren't you going to say something?"

Her jaw was locked open. "I don't know what to say except you continue to surprise me, Tamar Anne Ferguson."

I released a sigh and took a sip of my coffee. "You being wordless is not helping."

"I'm shocked," she cried. "Do you have any more secrets?"

I chuckled through the pain in my chest. "No. I'm done. I couldn't top that one if I tried."

"What are you going to do?"

"I'm going to eventually tell him, but I can't right now. Not with Auntie being so sick. She says it's okay, but I don't want to add stress. Her doctors say no stress."

Kim sighed. "So, you have a son. I can't believe it. What's he like?"

"He's sweet. Well mannered. Smart and funny as he can be. A good student. He's perfect." I shrugged. "No thanks to me."

Kim reached for her coffee cup. "I'm sure he would have been the same child if you had raised him."

I shook my head. "I doubt it. My aunt is a special woman."

Kim sighed again. "God works in mysterious ways."

I wasn't sure what she meant. "You're not saying it's in God's plans for my aunt to die, are you?"

"Of course not. Aunt Joe will live to be a hundred. I mean everything. You and Stephen hooking back up after all these years, possibly when your son might need you both."

I was still confused about what she was saying. "My aunt will get better."

"I'm not saying she won't, but is it possible that she needs to be focused on herself right now instead of trying to bear the weight of being a single mother? That's what I mean by you and Stephen being available."

I didn't want God to reconcile anything this way. "I want to take care of her. She's got help from her church until I get back. It's a small town and they seem to be falling over each other coming to her aid. I can hardly talk to her on the phone for all the company she has when I call."

"Having help taking care of her is a blessing. What's the problem with you being the one though?"

"I'm worried that if I keep going to Yancy, someone might find out about Isaiah. You know how the media is. Our son looks like Stephen." I scrolled through my phone and found a pic of Isaiah. Kim had seen pictures of him before, but now she would be looking at him as my son and as Stephen's.

An eyebrow went up as Kim eyed the picture. "He's grown so much. And he does look like his father."

That was what I thought. "It wouldn't be hard for people to put two and two together if they saw me with him."

Kim frowned. "That's something to consider. You need to stay put until you tell Stephen." Kim cocked her head a little. "When is that going to be?"

"After surgery and maybe the first round of chemo. When Aunt Joe gets some of her strength back."

"Are you sure she's the one that needs it?"

"I've got to put some distance between my emotions and that conversation. He's going to hate me. I don't want to feel it. I'm already emotional."

Kim groaned. "He's not going to hate you." Her phone buzzed. "It's the shop." She threw up a finger and took the call. "What do you mean? Don't touch her. I'm coming." Kim ended the call and stood. "I feel like firing my entire staff. Finish your latte and then come on and let me put your head in the sink. I'll have you out in an hour."

I clapped like an excited child. Kim rolled her eyes and flew out of the shop.

My phone buzzed with a text message from Stephen:

Dinner at five.

I texted him back:

I'll see you there.

He replied:

Can't wait to see you. He added a few heart emojis.

After Kim finished my hair, I went by my apartment, showered and changed into a cream, silk crepe, capri-length jumpsuit and a pair of ankle-high suede boots Kim had given to me for Christmas last year. I'd rarely worn them because even though it was the right season for them, boots made my feet sweat in the temperate Atlanta winters. I was used to real cold and the need for real boots.

As Stephen instructed, I valet parked my car using the team code that was reserved for family and friends. I entered the Omni CNN hotel and was given directions to the Giant's dinner.

Moving an NFL team around was a big deal. Inclusive of the fifty players and just as many coaches, medical staff, owners, video crew and others, the Giants traveled with almost 150 people.

I met security at the door of the restaurant and

showed my driver's license. I was escorted in by another security person. He took me directly to Stephen's table. Stephen stood, took my hand, and kissed me on the cheek. "Not a moment too soon."

The team members at his table extended greetings, but then quickly resumed their prior activities which included talking to their own guest, swiping cell phones, and chatting with each other.

I slid my jacket off into Stephen's waiting hand. He passed it to the security person, and it was carted to a coat check area at the back of the room.

"You look great. Have I told you I like your hair like that?" Stephen kissed my cheek again. "I didn't realize how much I missed you until you arrived at this table."

I appreciated his admiration. Stephen was wearing a dark gray, single-breasted, three button, peak collar designer suit with a steel gray mock turtleneck. The cross he never took off hung around his neck in full view. The entire team was dressed in suits. They all looked like the professionals they were.

"You look nice, too," I said. "You're pretty handsome in a suit."

"I'm glad you like." Stephen smiled and popped his collar. "This is me two to three days a week. I'm not always in athletic wear." He took my hand and squeezed it. "I know it was hard for you to leave your aunt, babe. I appreciate you being here for the weekend."

"My boss had a little to do with it." She'd assigned me to cover the inside social aspects of the championship game being held in Atlanta this weekend. That was an assignment I only got because of my relationship with Stephen.

"I want to meet that boss of yours one day. She's been working on my behalf for a minute."

I deadpanned him. "Eva doesn't wake up in the morning willing to do good. Trust me on that. Besides, you were two minutes from getting on a plane and coming to South Georgia. I couldn't let you do that."

Stephen took a deep breath. "I'm not sure I understand why. I mean, you're the caregiver in this scenario."

"You're in one of the most important playoff seasons of your career. You have to stay hashtag focused," I teased.

Stephen chuckled. "True, but you ever think that maybe I want to meet your aunt? The only family I know is your father and your relatives from his side. I don't know anyone from your mother's side."

"You know my mother's family is tiny. I've met my cousins and an uncle, but my aunt is really the only person my mother seemed to care about. They talked on the phone every day."

"You love her because your mom did. I love her because you love her. It'd be nice to meet her."

I was saved from having to respond to his statement because noise filled the dining room. A group of about forty servers with rolling buffets entered. Two of them pulled up to our table and filled the center with dishes of food. They plated our meat and vegetable choices. Once all the tables had been served, the team chaplain said grace.

I was an introvert with social anxiety. Coupled with my love for writing, I was comfortable observing and not making small talk. The men talked about the game. The few women at the table talked about their kids and stuff. I said nothing, but I enjoyed observing Stephen in his environment. He was confident and warm. There wasn't a brutish bone in his body which always stood in contrast to my thoughts about the game and what it took to play it.

Stereotypes. I was guilty of stereotyping athletes. When had I started doing that? Maybe it was when the one sitting next to me broke my heart. But I'd forgiven him. I really had. The distance between us had nothing to do with him and everything to do with me. He had a lull in conversation, so he took my hand. His eyes met mine like he needed the touch.

"One more game," I said, distracting him from his romantic thoughts.

Stephen smiled. "One." He raised my hand to his lips and kissed it. "You're good luck. We haven't been to the Super Bowl in years."

"I thought you didn't believe in luck," I said, remembering he hadn't in high school.

He squinted. "I don't really, but you're all things good."

Stephen always told me I was better with words, but he was impressive himself.

"I'm trying not to think beyond the game, but I can't help it. We've been so busy. I feel like I need to do something to put us on solid ground."

Busying my hands, I picked up a bottled water I'd been served and opened it. "We're taking it slow, remember?"

He smiled. "I'm trying, but I'm fast on the field and in life. Slow don't work for me."

All the conversation in the room stopped when one of the coaches took the mic. Dessert was served. Speeches were made. Afterward, we attended a service at a make-shift chapel. Stephen had team meetings that took an hour. I went to a reception room with the other women and family members. I made some light conversation with a few people, but for the most part, I tried to keep to myself. I wasn't used to the bustle of celebrity and fandom. I preferred to sit in the corner and either observe or read a book on my Kindle app.

"Tamar Johnson."

I turned to find a woman standing behind me.

As usual, I was suspicious of unknown human beings. "You are?"

"Alicia Lyons. I'm a friend of Coach Nye. I'm also a writer." She did a quick scan of me from head to toe. "You're a reporter, right?"

I was not a reporter, and I didn't like being called one. "I'm a writer. Features for a small magazine."

"And the woman who has Stephen Pierce's heart. In person and on Instagram." She paused before adding, "But she's a mystery. No one knows anything about her or what she's been doing for the past twelve years."

I stankfaced her. "Not like it's anyone's business."

I cocked my head. "I know you're not trying to get a quote."

She laughed. "No. It's not like that. I'm just in search of another smart girl. I don't want to talk about shopping and vacations."

I nodded, but I didn't feed into the way she'd insulted the other women.

"Anyway, I know you're glad the talk about that old video scandal has died down."

"I can't imagine a scenario in which a person wouldn't be glad a scandal died down."

"Honey, please, some folks build their entire career on scandal. Who would the Kardashians be without it?"

I chuckled. "You got me there. Branding trouble is a thing, but they're on another level."

"Everyone has to start somewhere. Kim started with a tape."

I frowned.

"Relax. I'm not even trying to suggest you use it in that way," she said. "But I am thinking you must have a story that would make a good book."

My frown deepened. "A book about the worst time in my life? I couldn't fill a book about a 10-minute video."

"The video is nothing. The story is the aftermath. That was years." Alicia reached into her pocket and removed a card. "I ghostwrite, but I also consult. Think about it. I'm sure there's a story you could tell that matters."

I took her card. She gave me one more visual sweep. It was the kind of look you gave a woman when you were trying to assess if she was good enough for her man. I knew the look. I'd been getting it a lot lately. She walked away. I glanced at the card and shoved it in my clutch.

There was a rustle of noise and the doors to the conference room where the team was meeting opened. The men came in and the women and family members went to greet them. I made my way to Stephen.

"You weren't too bored?"

"Not at all."

"Good." He took my hand. "We have a lounge. We can go there." I fell into step with him.

We entered the lounge and found a sofa in a low-lit corner. Snacks were brought in. I couldn't imagine that anyone could eat another thing. The dinner was enormous, and all of the players had plates stacked with protein. But I guess that was an hour ago.

I watched as they ate more wings, sliders, and fajitas. I helped myself to a fruit cup just to have something to do with my hands. Stephen wouldn't stop staring at me. I felt like he was looking right down into my belly where my secrets were locked away. Or was that my guilt?

He reached into his pocket for his phone. "Let's play a game."

I stretched my neck to see what he had in mind.

"It's a couple's thing." He opened an app.

"You're serious."

"It's conversational. We need to do something. I'm trying to keep my mind off your body in that jumpsuit."

I slapped his arm.

"You think I'm kidding?" He chuckled. "Here's the first question. What would you change about your personality?"

I frowned. There was so much.

Stephen said, "I'll go first. I'd make myself wittier."

"Wittier? You're pretty funny."

"Yeah, but I'm not good with clapbacks. I need a little help in that area."

"I can't tell."

"Trust me, I'm slow. What about you?"

"I probably would not want to be as cautious as I am."

"Cautious. Okay. I mean we know there are some reasons for that."

I made a little buzzer sound. "Next?"

Stephen shook his head and chuckled. "You're silly. Okay, do you consider yourself to be a calm person?"

We both had affirmative answers to that.

The third question was, "Do you think a lot in the past?"

We both took deep breaths. I had to agree that I did. Stephen said, "Only about you. I was obsessing, but now I'm set free."

"Next, let's see. Do you think it's okay to keep a secret from your mate?"

Stephen shook his head. "Definitely not. Total honesty and transparency is what's up."

He looked at me. I was a little tongue tied, but I nodded. "I uh, wouldn't know really. I haven't had a mate since I was eighteen."

"You answer the question instinctively."

I shrugged. "Okay, then of course not. People shouldn't have secrets."

Stephen cocked an eyebrow. "I can see I'm going to have to watch you."

I smirked and reached for my fruit cup.

We played a little longer and then slipped into conversation about other things from politics to the Bible.

Then Stephen, flanked by security escorted me to the valet parking area.

"Did you enjoy yourself at any level?" he asked.

I laughed. "I had a good time. I'm surprised your parents aren't here."

Stephen chuckled. "I told them to stay home. Mom was angry, but I wanted to spend time with you. They'll be at the game."

I nodded. "This is all pretty intense."

"This is my life on the road during the season. I love it. I love this game, and I'm good with whatever I have to do to play it."

He pulled me into his arms and gave me a peck on the lips. "I miss you already, and you're not even gone."

I smiled. I raised a hand to his mouth and wiped off my lipstick. "I'll see you tomorrow."

A silver Range Rover with a large red bow attached to the hood stopped next to us. A man climbed out. He was not the valet.

"Ms. Johnson, I'm John Hobbs from Hobbs Range Rover of Atlanta." He swept a hand in the direction of the car. "I present to you a gift from Stephen Pierce."

Oxygen left my lungs. I raised a hand to cover my mouth.

The shine in Stephen's eyes matched the gleam from the SUV. "It looks even better at night."

"I can't accept a car as a gift."

Stephen opened the passenger side door. "Yes, you can."

I stared. Total disbelief paralyzed me. "I can't."

"You have to, or you'll have to call an Uber to get home. Yours is already gone."

"Stephen," I said, slapping his arm. "You can't buy me a car."

"Why not? You're my woman. I want you to ride nice."

"But I love my car. That was my first new car."

Stephen smirked. "It was your first new car a long time ago. Mr. Hobbs is going to drive you home. He'll show you all the bells and whistles on this one."

Mr. Hobbs talked, and I stared. I couldn't believe Stephen had bought me a Range Rover.

"Tamar, this has happened, so get in."

I did as I was told. Stephen closed the door and pushed his head inside the window. "You still have your other car. I had it taken back to your place. Maybe you can donate it or something."

I ran my fingers across the cool, buttery leather and then the glossy, woodgrain dash.

"It's nice, right? I remember you used to talk about how you wanted a Range Rover when we were in high school. You look good in it."

I opened my mouth to offer one last, weak protest and he pressed a finger against my lips.

"We'll talk about this later," I mumbled under his finger.

"It's done. All we can talk about now is the color or something." He smiled and stepped back from the vehicle. "Call me when you get home."

Mr. Hobbs got in on the driver's side. He put the car in drive and an automated voice rang out from the speakers. "We are proceeding to your home, Mrs. Pierce. There is no traffic. We should arrive in 25 minutes."

Mrs. Pierce. I shook my head. I took one last look

at Stephen. He smiled and blew me a kiss. My heart swelled. I blew him a kiss back.

The vehicle surged forward and out of the parking lot. As we rode, Mr. Hobbs told me about the features and the warranty. We arrived at my apartment complex. Mr. Hobbs pulled in front of one of the garages.

"Mr. Pierce has rented a garage for you, ma'am," he said. He pushed a button and the door opened. He drove the vehicle inside. After a few more instructions and tips, he got out of the car. Another vehicle was idling outside of my garage. Mr. Hobbs went to the vehicle and returned with my keys. He let me know where my car was parked, and then he joined his colleague for their departure.

I stepped out of the garage and pushed the hand clicker he'd given me to put the garage door down. The entrance to my building was mere steps away. Convenient. I was sure Stephen's money had secured this spot as well.

I took the elevator to my floor and entered my unit. I was overwhelmed by everything that had happened tonight. I'd enjoyed Stephen's company. Even though we'd spent our time in an open and populated area, being with him was nice. Conversation was so easy. Easy like it'd always been.

I closed my eyes and released a long sigh. It would be so nice to slide into his world – a world where a man loved me. Stephen had received many a head nod from his team members who were obviously happy to see him with me.

I was enjoying my thoughts, but then I realized,

everything about this night was temporary. I was Cinderella at the ball. It wouldn't be long before the fairytale was over, and everyone was disappointed for him.

I undressed, showered, and crawled into my bed. The phone rang with a call from Stephen. I let it go to voicemail and sent him a text that I was on the phone with my aunt. He texted for me to call him when I was done.

Honesty and transparency. That's what he wanted. But he wouldn't get it from me. In addition to avoidance, all I had were secrets and lies, and when I eventually told him the truth, it was going to break his heart. The aftermath of that video was messing up my life, again. I looked at my phone. He'd texted:

Call me back.

The message was followed by two heart emojis and one sleepy head. I rolled over in bed, away from the phone. Away from my temptation to do what he asked – call him for whispered, sleepy words that lovers exchanged when they were apart from each other, or maybe more catching up on each other's stories. There were lots of gaps to fill in. We were enjoying filling them in.

I let the thought drift through my mind that I could keep my secret. I toyed with the idea of not telling him about Isaiah. After all, he wasn't legally his son.

But who was I kidding? I could never keep such a thing. Secrets had a way of coming out. Stephen wanted children. I'd have to confess to an O.B. doctor that I'd had another pregnancy.

And then, what about Isaiah? Didn't he deserve to know that a famous, successful, good man like Stephen Pierce was his father? I was going down a rabbit hole with my thoughts. The imagination of the writer. I had a penchant for the dramatic. I knew I had to do what was right, but wrong was tempting.

I stretched my hand to the nightstand for my clutch and removed the business card I'd gotten tonight from the writer, Alicia Lyons.

"Tell your story," she'd said. "It'll be great," she'd said.

My story was not unique. What was special about a virgin getting pregnant on prom night? Who wanted to read that?

I put Alicia's card on the nightstand. I wouldn't throw it away, because no writer worth their salt ever tossed a business card, but I wasn't going to write. My story would be another American tragedy.

I rolled over again and found myself face-to-face with my cell phone and the call to Stephen. I swiped the screen and let my finger hover over his name.

I thought about those whispered, sleepy words he'd utter in his deep, velvety voice and pulled my finger back. I wanted to hear those words, but I had to protect my heart.

I put the phone on the nightstand, turned off the light, and pulled the comforter over my head.

"Sorry, babe."

Chapter 6

The football went up, spun, and Stephen lunged for it.

I closed my eyes for a moment. The ever-present fear that he would get hurt doing all those acrobatics on the field was always with me. Men from the other team were coming from everywhere. Stephen held out his arm and blocked a big guy. He was flying across the field in the zig-zag pattern he'd perfected.

The fans were on their feet, hollering, cheering, and screaming as he ran the final seventy yards into the end zone for a touchdown. The crowd went insane. I stood with everyone else and clapped. The Giants needed those points.

Stephen dropped to one knee and prayed for a few seconds. He stood, kissed the ball, and danced in a circle for the fans. When he was done the members of his team that were nearby hugged him, gave him pounds, and slaps on the back.

Waving to fans as he moved, he started a slow jog in my direction. I looked around to see what he was coming for, but when he stopped directly in front of me, I realized he'd been coming for me. He removed his helmet. The Giants didn't have an official mascot, but a man dressed in a bobble-head Giant's costume was at his side. He handed Stephen a small box.

My heart froze. I stuttered, "What are you doing?"

His face was flush with perspiration and excitement. It was red on one side from the pounding he'd taken in the last play where a linebacker had landed on his head. He dropped to one knee again.

All of his movements appeared to be happening in slow motion. Stephen removed a ring, took my hand and said, "Tamar Johnson, I love you. Will you marry me?"

The crowd went insane again. Everyone cheered. I glanced up at the big screen. The words, "Say yes!" scrolled in flashing red and pink lights and hearts. A thunderous chant came from the stands on both sides. "Say yes! Say yes!"

The bobble head waved his arms and kicked his feet to get the crowd riled up.

I looked into Stephen's eyes. "A public proposal?"

"I've had this ring for two weeks. I've been waiting for you to come to a game. I was also hoping I'd get a touchdown." He kissed my fingers. "So, what's it going to be?"

My heart cracked as loudly as my voice. "I love you."

"I love you too, babe." His eyes were as wet as the perspiration that framed his face.

I nodded and wiggled my finger.

"Is that a yes?" He smiled a sensational, gorgeous smile that sucked the answer out of me.

"Yes."

Stephen slid the enormous ring up my finger.

The crowd went insane again. He stood, pulling me with him. He cupped my face and kissed me. "I promise to make you happy."

He spun around to the crowd and pumped his fist. The big screen read: She said yes!

Stephen picked up his helmet and ran back onto the field.

The people around and behind my seat congratulated me. I was still in shock. I dropped into my seat and stared at my finger. I was blinded by the sparkle. It was a square diamond, but it was different. I didn't even know what the cut was, but I knew it had to be five or more carats. It was obscenely huge.

"It's gorgeous," the woman next me said, appreciating it with me.

I swallowed the emotion stuck in my throat and nodded agreement I could not verbalize. The dread I'd been pushing down into my belly was back. He'd made this big show of asking me to marry him. How was I going to break his heart now?

***

Stephen and I climbed into one of the twenty, stretch limos that lined the street on both sides outside the Giants Training Center. After a short celebration in Atlanta, we boarded planes to Newark. Stephen and I changed at his house and then met the team and staff for a proper celebration in New York City.

"Are we riding with anyone else?" I asked. "This is a lot of room."

"No, I asked for my own car. I had the winning touchdown, so it was easy to get what I wanted, plus they loved the publicity I got for them today. The proposal. They owe me this car."

"Speaking of that…"

"Yes," Stephen said, taking my hand. He looked at the ring.

"You shouldn't have."

"The ring or the limo?" he teased.

"The ring, Stephen." I was serious and he knew it, but he silenced me with a quick peck on the lips.

"This is nothing. If you're going to stay in Atlanta, we have to get you out of that apartment, babe. You can't keep this kind of jewelry in a place that's not that secure."

I frowned. He kissed me again. This time the kiss was long and tender. When he pulled back, my heart was racing, but I managed to protest. "I like my apartment."

"You dislike change," he chastised me. "Having the good things in life is a part of being in my world, Tay. Get used to it." His dreamy eyes were filled with love, adoration, and happiness.

I melted under his gaze. He was so content and happy right now. I relaxed. I couldn't argue with him. He took my hand, raised my palm to his lips and kissed it. "This is one of the best days of my life."

"Winning the NFC championship is a lot to be proud of," I said. "Getting that touchdown was a boss move."

"The touchdown was great, but knowing I had the ring and hearing you say yes… I don't know, it was like the icing on the cake."

"Such a cliché." I smirked. "But seriously, Stephen. Why did you do that?"

"Because I love you."

"We've been back together for a half hour. You can't propose."

"I can, and I did though." He paused for a moment and said, "Tamar, I knew when we were kids I was going to spend my life with you, otherwise, I wouldn't have accepted something as precious as your virginity. But then things went left, and you disappeared. I convinced myself that I was wrong. As I got older, I felt the Lord pressing me about you. I kept running from it. Too much time. Too much pain. Failure on my part. I had been successful in every area in my life, but I had failed the one person I wanted to win for. All I had was football."

"But it's too soon. You have to know we aren't here yet."

He took my hand and raised it between us, so the ring was visible. "This is a symbol of my love. It's about my intentions toward you. I failed you publicly, Tay. I

The Winter Wedding

had to make it right publicly. I don't want you as my girlfriend or my bae or boo. My desire is for you to be my wife. I know you think it's soon, but it's not for me. I'm ready. I'm waiting for you." He let go of my hand. "I'm here as long as it takes. I'm already at forever and happily ever after."

Stephen's words were romantic, but they made no sense. "It's not possible for you to be thinking about forever."

Stephen smirked. "You know me. I've been thinking about forever since I was six."

I smiled through the tightness in my chest. He was right. He'd always had eternity in his sights from a spiritual and natural perspective, but I never expected him to do this before I had a chance to…

"Tay." Stephen cut off my thoughts. "Baby, you just flew like ten thousand miles away. I didn't say marry me tomorrow. Stop stressing."

His phone rang. He raised a finger and took the call. Whoever it was, was talking about the game. He and his teammates had to be running on pure adrenaline. They'd already partied post game in the locker room and now they were headed into NYC to the Hudson Terrace where the celebrating would continue.

Parties. I hated them. Between last night and tonight, I'd already had enough of people.

I let my attention drift to the view outside the window of the limo. I couldn't believe Stephen had proposed like that. On national television. Now he would have to reconcile our breakup with the entire world.

I squeezed my eyes shut. Such was life with us, right? We couldn't help but live our lives out loud for the world.

Stephen ended his call. "Clyde. I'm up for contract renewal next year. He can't stop thinking about money."

He smiled again, and I saw the eternity of his happiness in his eyes. He should be happy, but his joy overwhelmed me. He thought I was a part of his peace. He had no idea I was not.

"I know you don't like parties, but this is the job." He must have been guessing why I was such a Solemn Sally. "I appreciate you stepping up."

"I'm working, remember. I'm proud of you. I'm happy for your team."

"Happy for us. I'm about to get paid."

The driver announced we'd arrived, but we had to wait in line. The limo slowed.

Stephen reached for my hand again. He touched the ring. His forehead creased, eyebrows raised. "If you don't like this one, you know we can exchange it."

I pressed my lips together. If only my life was about simple choices right now, like the only thing on my mind was a ring. I had to fight tears. If I looked at him right now, I'd cry. I looked down at the ring. Focused on the stone and the band until I could keep the tears from wetting my eyes, keep the croak out of my voice. I shook my head. "There isn't a reasonable woman on the planet who wouldn't like this ring."

"All women aren't reasonable. Trust me. That's what makes you special."

I raised my eyes to meet his. I chuckled. "The fact that I'm reasonable. That's what you were looking for in a wife?"

He shrugged. "One quality. There's a whole lot more to you, Tamar Johnson." He winked. "Anyway, I'm glad you like it."

I twisted it on my finger. It was a perfect fit. I didn't even have to get it sized. I wasn't going to ask him how he managed that. It would just be more Stephen Pierce magic.

"Stephen, what if I hurt you?" I blurted the question out before I even realized I had.

He frowned. "Why would you do that?"

I wasn't prepared to explain why I was asking him. I wanted to take the question back. "Not on purpose, but what if?"

"People hurt each other. We know that better than anyone, but we're not kids anymore. We'd talk it out until we worked it out."

"Are you sure…I mean, there are limits, you know?"

"Baby, you are bone of my bone. Flesh of my flesh. I know that's deep, but that's the way I see it. I see it the way God describes it in the Word. There's nothing you could do to run me away."

What about something I've done?

The limo rolled forward and stopped again. The

driver came around to open the door on Stephen's side.

Stephen paused before he stepped out. "So, you have something in your past you haven't shared. Tay, it's been twelve years. You've been living your life. You can tell me or not tell me, but I promise you, whatever it is, it won't matter. I love you. I'll love you no matter what. I hope you feel the same way about me, or at least you will someday. Like I said, I'm willing to wait. Until then, call it a promise ring."

He stepped out of the car and extended a hand to me. I took it. I felt that tingle in my belly that happened every time we touched each other. Bone of his bone. Flesh of his flesh. He had no idea how deep that flesh and bone went for me.

I'd really stepped in doo-doo with the relationship. What had I been thinking when I'd allowed him to push his way into my life? Too bad I loved him. Too bad he loved me. Too bad this ring would never be more than a promise.

Chapter 7

"When?"

I raised an eyebrow. Stephen's voice still had that thick, sultry, sleepy morning sound. It was warm and inviting. Intoxicating.

"When?" I pulled my blouse over my head. "Sir, you said I had time."

"I think I'm changing my mind. I'm ready to wake up to my wife. Like, we can fly to Vegas, or Miami, or wherever you want to go and do it today."

"Don't you want a wedding?" I asked putting my earrings in.

"I want you."

My heart fluttered and ached at the same time. "You have practice this week. You know there's this little thing called the Super Bowl."

"But today's my day off." He yawned loud and long.

"Well, sir, it is not my day off. I have one foot in a shoe and my hand on the Keurig. I have to get to work."

Stephen groaned. "When are you going to quit

that job?"

I rolled my neck like he could see me. "I'm not."

"Not?"

"This is my career. I know you're a big, rich football player, but I'm only your wife in the Range Rover. I'm a girlfriend recently turned a potential fiancé. What would it look like if I quit my job?"

"It would look like you were ready to become Mrs. Pierce. You know you could move to New Jersey so I could see you more often. You could plan the wedding."

"The wedding I'm not sure I want to have yet?"

"That's semantics. You gonna be mad in love with me before Easter. Wedding planning is a future Mrs. Pierce worthy activity."

Now I rolled my eyes.

Stephen continued. "If it's money you're concerned about, I'll call my accountant today and have them cut a pre-marital check for you."

"Yeah, is that going to come with the pre-nup?"

Stephen chuckled. "Baby, we will not have a pre-nup. You and I are going to be married until God separates us."

I sighed and released a long breath.

"That's not a happy sound," Stephen said. "I would think no pre-nup was a good thing."

"Maybe I'm planning to be richer than you one day."

Stephen laughed. Loud. "You know what. I can see that, so if you need me to sign a pre-nup, by all means have one drawn up. I'll do whatever you want me to do."

I shook my head. "I bet you would."

"It won't matter anyway," Stephen said. "No divorce. We don't believe in it."

"Sometimes I don't know what I believe."

"I believe it enough for both of us."

"Well, we'll have to get married first and to do that I need to actually agree to marry you for real. This is a promise ring, remember?"

Stephen was quiet on that point.

"I have to go."

"Cool, Clyde just called me. He probably wants to talk Super Bowl stuff." He hesitated again. "Tay."

"Hmmm."

"Thank you."

I searched my memory for what I might have done. "For what?"

"For saying yes and not embarrassing me in front of the entire world."

My heart pinched some more. "I'd be a fool not to, right?"

"You said that. Girl, nobody is ever going to love you the way I do. No point holding out for another brother."

I had no doubt that was true. "Have a blessed

day."

Stephen's voice deepened. "Already blessed." He ended the call.

I reached into the freezer for a microwave dinner and dropped it and an apple in my lunch bag.

My phone rang again.

Stephen had a habit of calling back. The man was doing his best to try to manipulate me out of my job. I swiped to take the call.

"Tamar." The connection was poor, but it was Kim's voice coming through the speaker.

"My phone. Who else?"

"You okay?" This time her voice cracked.

"Okay?" I stopped moving. "Why wouldn't I be okay?"

"You haven't listened to the radio or looked at the blogs this morning?"

"No. I'm running late. I have a big meeting this morning. What is it?"

Kim sighed. "It's probably a bunch of lies, but there's a story out about Stephen."

I frowned. "What kind of story?"

"I'm sure it's not true."

"Kim, I don't have time to pull it out of you."

"Okay. Brace yourself. It's a story about De—"

The phone went dead. I looked at it and realized we lost our connection.

I dialed her back, but the call went to voicemail.

I decided to check the blogs, but my WiFi was acting janky. I moved around the apartment to get a better signal but couldn't, so I gave up.

I put my coffee in a travel mug, grabbed my bag and laptop, and ran out the door. I made my way down the elevator and out to my garage. The 30-degree blast of cold punched me in the chest as I exited the building.

My heart was already pounding. The idea that a story was circulating about Stephen was causing my anxiety and blood pressure to tick up. Headlines came to my memory in a flood of visions, like newspaper clippings filtering across my face.

Stephen Pierce is a liar!

Stephen Pierce not a real Christian!

What else is Stephen Pierce hiding?

I climbed into the Range Rover, turned the ignition on and pushed the button to silence the automated voice that would soon be calling me Mrs. Pierce. My cell phone was ringing again. I saw Stephen's face flashing on the screen. I reached for it, but it slid across the seat onto the floor.

I swore under my breath, put the car in reverse and backed out of the garage. He'd have to wait. I had to get to the highway before it got jammed.

But an expedient exit out of the gated parking lot was not to be so. Once I exited the lot, I met a small army of reporters. They rushed the SUV, sticking microphones at the window, and against the glass.

I cracked the window just enough to hear what they were asking.

"Ms. Johnson, do you have a statement about…"

"Have you and Stephen engaged in sexual relations?"

"Has Stephen Pierce lied about his sex life?"

I pushed the button and was relieved to hear their voices fade as the window went up. The nerve of these people. Who asks someone if they're having sex with someone?

Once I got into the flow of traffic, I tried to get my phone, but couldn't reach it. It had practically been ringing non-stop. I regretted not setting up the Bluetooth.

I pushed the power button for the radio. After the close of the new Drake song and a weather and traffic report, the gossip began.

"So, your boy Stephen Pierce is back in the news."

"You know I like to call him Saint Stephen. What's our video superstar up to this time?"

"Well, you know he did the worthy thing last week and proposed to his high school sweetheart, Tamar Johnson. As you know, Tamar Johnson is old girl from his nude video days."

"So, what's the rub," the other commentator asked.

"Pierce's ex, Debra McAllister, has announced she's twelve weeks pregnant and it's the superstar running back's child."

I slammed on the brakes.

"But, wait…how is that possible, I mean he's been celibate for years. Four if I'm remembering correctly."

"That's the longest gestational period on a pregnancy I've ever heard of."

"Yeah and Debra ain't no elephant."

Laughter. Laughter. Laughter.

Honk! A horn blared from my rear. I pushed the power button to silence the radio.

This wasn't happening. It couldn't be. Stephen wouldn't do this. But why would she lie? It's not like she wouldn't eventually be found out.

I was glad when it was time for me to get off the highway. I unfastened my seat belt and reached for my cell phone. Ten missed calls. Five from Stephen and twenty-four text messages. I opened the text messages first.

Babe, none of it is true. Please call.

I didn't know what Debra's game was, but something in my heart was already telling me this wasn't true. The worse thing about it was I wanted it to be true. I wanted Stephen to be a liar. That would make it so much easier for me – because I was.

Chapter 8

I couldn't stand my phone. When the text message came through, I wanted to ignore it. I picked it up, swiped the screen and read the message from Stephen:

Open the door.

I looked through the peephole and then pulled the door open. Stephen was standing there.

"I've been trying to reach you for hours," I said like he didn't know.

"I was on a plane."

I stepped back and let him in. "All the way from Giant Nation."

Stephen closed the door and turned the lock. He leaned in to kiss me, but I pulled back. "So, just like that. I don't get a kiss?"

"I've had a horrible day."

He chuckled. "You think my day's been better?"

"Debra's not my ex." I folded my hands over my chest. "I've been harassed and stalked by reporters. They came to the magazine. I had to come home, which is why I'm here. They're outside now, as you can well see. I'm tired."

"Baby, I know that, but my sugar though."

I wasn't going to let him disarm me.

He removed his jacket and fell into the sofa cushions like he was carrying the weight of a linebacker on his shoulders.

I claimed a spot on the chair across from him. "Are you thirsty, hungry? I have leftover pasta."

He waved the offer off. "Thanks, babe. I had something on the plane."

"You shouldn't have come all the way here."

"It's my day off, remember?"

I played with the buttons on my blouse. He was here. He needed to explain, so I waited.

"She's lying, Tay."

I squeezed my eyes shut against his words.

"Babe?"

I gave him my full attention.

"This is not true."

I stood and moved to the furthest location from him in the room. "What part isn't true? The pregnancy, the twelve weeks, the paternity? What part?"

"None of it is true. It's like I told you before. I never had sex with Debra. If she's pregnant, I'm not the father."

I swallowed. My heart was already pounding. The idea that I was going to have to deal with the media again was making me nauseous. "Why is she saying this?"

"I don't know."

"You don't know? You dated her for two years. How could you not know what she was capable of?"

He shrugged. "Publicity. She's a reality TV personality." He paused. "Debra likes being famous. This gets her the attention she's looking for."

"It's probably a little more than that. You dumped her."

He leaned forward and clasped his hands. "Things ended between us, but it wasn't that bad of a breakup."

I stared at him for a while. "Maybe she doesn't like the fact that you moved on so fast. The proposal probably pissed her off."

He appeared to be considering my words. "That's possible."

"Maybe she thinks we were seeing each other before you broke up."

"I doubt that."

"Have you talked to her?"

Stephen gave his head a wry shake. "Not yet."

Annoyance propelled me to my feet. "Why not?"

"Because you're the only woman I need to have a conversation with right now."

"If it's not true…"

It was Stephen who was annoyed now. "If?"

"If it's not true, how is she going to explain it when the baby is born?"

He seemed unmoved by my question. "I don't know. You want me to make sense out of something that makes no sense."

"I don't think it makes sense that you haven't called her."

"She's not going to take my call."

"What makes you say that?"

"Because I know her."

I rolled my eyes. "Which is it? Do you know her or not?"

I finally got him frustrated. He growled. "What are you asking me, Tay?"

"I'm asking you what you're afraid of!"

Stephen kept his voice even. "I'm not afraid of anything."

"Did you sleep with her? Be honest with me. I'm not your agent or your brand management people. We weren't together so it's not like you cheated on me. She says she's twelve weeks. That's long before I came back into the picture."

Stephen paused. He released a long, exhausted breath. "I haven't had sex with a woman in four years. Four, long, painful, years. This is not my baby."

"I want you to at least call her."

Stephen pulled his phone out of his pocket and put it on speaker. It began to ring. "I'm calling her." He got a "voicemail is full" message. "I bet," he murmured. "She's probably talking to every reporter and media outlet in the country."

He tossed the phone on the sofa. He flopped down onto one of the cushions next to it, again. He washed his face with a hand. "More reporters." He raised a hand to remove the hat he was wearing. "Just what I need."

"Just what you need? This isn't just happening to you."

Disappointment oozed from his pores. "Talk to me, baby."

"I think twenty reporters must have called me at work. Some of them called my personal cell. They're emailing me again. We just got over the video thing and now this. I feel like I'm living a nightmare."

Stephen shook his head. "I know, but don't focus on them. They'll eventually go away. We're strong. We can ride this out. We have to stick together and talk to each other."

"The reporters are camped outside my house and my job."

"Maybe you can take a leave of absence or something. Until it all stops."

"I don't have an off-season. I already have to help my Aunt Joe."

He sighed so heavily, it thudded against my heart. "I'm sorry. I forgot about that."

"Besides, taking time off wouldn't help. I don't know if you're used to it or what, but it doesn't seem to ever stop."

"It does, baby. I mean most of the time, I'm just playing the game. Living my life and minding my business."

I shook my head. "I didn't sign up for all this drama. You're the celebrity. I've done my time being chased by the media."

"Tamar, please stop talking about this like we can't survive a scandalous ex."

I didn't say anything. All I could think about was the fact that I wouldn't be able to go back to Yancy with Aunt Joe because I had to keep Isaiah hidden from reporters.

"You know there are days I wish I had kept my mouth shut about being Christian and being celibate. The standard people hold me to..." He shook his head. "But that never felt right. I feel like this is my ministry, but persecution has definitely come with it."

I didn't offer him the sympathy he deserved. "Well, being a public person is not my calling."

"But you love me."

I looked at him but didn't affirm his words.

Stephen stood. Walked to me, took my hands and led me to the chair where I'd been sitting. He sat and pulled me closer. "I know you don't like this, but it won't last forever."

I stared into his gorgeous, brown eyes and all I could think about was the fact that I needed to break up with him and soon. This Debra mess was a good excuse to do it.

"Babe, it's going to be okay."

"I don't know, Stephen. Maybe we should cool things."

Confusion clouded his face. "Cool what things? Things are already moving much slower than I would like."

"Stephen…"

"Tamar, no. We can't let a stupid stunt like this keep us apart."

"I'm not saying keep us apart. I'm just sayin'."

"What, babe? 'Cool it is code for breakup. I don't care how you phrase it."

I stood and stepped back a few feet. "I'm a private person."

"You're my woman."

"So, does that not make me a person? I should move to New Jersey, plan a wedding. Is this the Stephen Pierce show?"

Stephen sighed again. "Don't do that, Tay."

"Do what?"

"Start out-talking me." His frustration etched worry lines on his forehead. "Let me finish."

I shook my head. "You just said you loved me, so I need you to allow me to tell you ow I feel."

I watched his Adam's apple move up and down hard. He pressed his lips together like he was trying to keep words in his mouth.

I continued. "Like I said, I'm a private person. I

can't do twenty-eight weeks of drama with you and her. I also find it hard to believe she'd just lie about the baby being yours if there was no possible way it could be."

"So, you think I'm lying about us having sex?"

I shrugged. "I guess."

"You don't even know her."

"I feel like I don't know anything."

He shook his head. "I can't believe this is happening."

I felt terrible, but I kept it up. I had to distance myself from him. "I've been made a fool of because of you before."

"Be reasonable. We need to talk about this."

"I don't think there's anything to talk about. I've been thinking about it all day. The entire situation makes me nauseous. I had panic attacks after the video. I had to go to counseling."

Stephen tried to close the space between us, but I moved around the chair out of his reach.

"You don't understand." I was dying inside. Lying to him like this was so hard.

"This will die down. The story will go away. But that's not really the point is it?" he asked. "The real point is you don't believe me when I say I didn't have sex with her."

"She's a beautiful woman. You dated for two years. When we're together, the heat is intense. How does one sustain that for two years?"

"First of all, I didn't see Debra as much as you think. She lived in L.A. She came to the East Coast, but it wasn't like we were together all the time. And I was careful. When you want to stay celibate, you don't have a lot of extended alone time."

"It's not just Debra. It's your entire life. It's too public. I can't do it. I can't be dragged again. They're already talking about whether I'll stand by my man like a fool. How much of your sex exploits will I tolerate? It's starting again all over and I had enough of it twelve years ago. Heck, I had enough a last month when you came out publicly about the video."

Stephen stepped toward me, but I raised a hand to halt him. "I can't deal with another Stephen Pierce scandal. Not right now. If you love me, you'll understand. Let's cool it for a minute and see where this Debra thing goes."

Finally, his temper rose a bit. "I'm confused. It's either the media or I'm lying. Like, what's getting me tossed in the friend-zone?"

"Both."

"And this is not up for discussion?"

I didn't reply. I wouldn't look at him.

Stephen grabbed his jacket and marched toward the door.

"Stephen," I called his name and turned. He looked hopeful. Until he saw I had his ring in my extended palm. "You shouldn't have asked me." That much was true.

Stephen shook his head and stormed out of the

apartment.

My heart shattered into a million pieces. His face. He was so hurt. I hated to hurt him. I fell back on the chair, reached for a tissue and began to cry. This was the only way. I needed this relationship to end. I hated that Debra McAllister's lie was the foundation of my lie, but it was convenient. The timing was right. I had to let him go before he found out I was no better than Debra.

Chapter 9

"Saint Stephen," Debra's voice teased through the phone. "I was wondering when you'd climb down from the cross and call me."

"Congratulations on your pregnancy. I'm assuming you're happy about it since you've shared it with the entire world."

"Of course, I am. Babies are a blessing no matter the circumstances of their conception."

"True." I fought to keep from screaming. "Speaking of circumstances, I was pretty shocked to hear that I'm being identified as the father of your little blessing."

"I was shocked myself. I knew I was pregnant, but I didn't think I was so far along. The ultrasound…"

"Debra, stop. Do you know what you've done to me?"

"Done to you? This is my life too."

"What do you have to gain by lying about your child's paternity? One day, your child will see this. Videos last forever. You should have learned that from me."

"I'm not lying."

"Not lying? Are you crazy? Have you lost your mind since we broke up?"

"Twelve weeks ago, I was with you so that means this is your child."

"Debra, it takes sex, not wishful thinking to have a baby."

"I know you've got your head in the clouds with your little Video Virgin from the past, but don't you dare call me now and try to pretend you don't remember that night. You know, the night before you dumped me."

"I remember that night well, and I know that night didn't produce a baby."

"You must have tossed it all in the sea of forgetfulness. Being intoxicated will do that. But don't worry, I didn't. I'm also not going to stay on this phone and listen to you call me a liar. I've got to go."

"Wait, Debra…I don't. I don't want to hurt you, but if you persist with this, I'll have to sue."

"Sue for what?"

"Defamation of character. I have a brand to protect."

"I've already talked to a lawyer. There's nothing you can prove here."

"When the baby's born, there will be plenty that can be proven."

"Well, then we'll let the DNA speak for itself. In the meantime, deal with it."

I washed my hand over my head.

"That was a nice proposal last week. How's your new bae holding up?" I could practically hear the ice water running through her veins. Tamar was right. The proposal had prompted this attack.

"She's fine. She knows I wouldn't lie about this."

Debra cackled. "Naïve little thing, isn't she?"

"Loyal is more like it."

Debra grunted. "We'll see how long that lasts. Good luck in the Super Bowl."

The line went dead.

Debra had lost her mind. This didn't even sound like the woman I'd dated for two years. She'd always been a bit of a media junkie. After all, her short, reality television career was birthed out of her onscreen relationship with gospel singers Terri Mary. She'd had a few other short stints in commercials and other shows, but even this was going to too far for her. What did she, as a Christian entertainer, have to gain from publicly lying about an unwed pregnancy? She couldn't hate me this much. She hadn't loved me this much.

My cell phone rang. It was my attorney, Vince Copeland. "I found out why Debra announced the pregnancy, and why she's saying it's yours."

I closed my eyes. I could feel the bad news coming. "I'm going to hate this."

"You are," Vince confirmed. "She's signed on to do a reality television show called 'Saint Stephen's Baby'."

Blood rushed to my head. "Please tell me you're messing with me, man."

"I'm not. One of our investigators found out. The name of the show isn't in stone. The others are 'Debra's Pregnancy Vlog' and 'Pregnant NFL Baby Mamas'. They're hunting for other pregnant NFL mamas to script with her. If they don't find anyone, they'll go with Debra alone."

My stomach dropped. "This is crazy."

"I know."

"Can we stop her from doing the show?"

"We can't stop her. We can't even force her to take a DNA test right now. It's her body, her choice, but we can file a lawsuit. We can ask a judge to gag her. Keep your name out of her mouth. She wouldn't be able to mention you on the show at all or talk to the media about you if – and that's a big if – the judge rules in our favor on the motion."

I sighed. "That's better than nothing, so let's do it."

"We're already getting the brief done. We probably won't need you, but I'll let you know if I think you should join me in court."

"Yeah, man, just let me know whatever."

"Stephen, I have to ask the question."

"It's not my baby."

"I'm not asking you that. I'm asking you a much more personal question." Vince paused, "Did you have sex with Debra?"

"If I'm saying it's not my baby."

"Protection isn't foolproof. If you had sex with her, there's always a chance of a pregnancy."

"No, Vince. No sex. No sexual anything. It's not possible. It's not mine."

Confidence entered Vince's voice. "Okay, then we're good to go to court."

He shared a few more details with me and then we ended the call. I fell back on the sofa and remembered that last night Debra and I were together. The night before we broke up. I closed my eyes to the image of her naked body and shook my head. She'd tried me, hard, but we hadn't had sex.

I opened my eyes and reached for the phone. I called Tamar. I was relieved she'd answered the phone. We hadn't talked since the other day when she'd said she wanted to cool it. I was scared to know what that really meant, so I decided it meant she needed me to slow down like she'd been asking me to.

"How are you?" I asked.

"Hanging in there. What about you?"

I hesitated. I hated to tell her this, but it might come out soon and I didn't want her being blindsided. "I talked to my attorney."

Tamar was silent, obviously waiting for me to continue.

"Debra's not crazy. She's greedy."

Tamar unmuted herself. "Is she trying to get money out of you?"

"Worse. She's doing a reality television show about being pregnant with my baby." I paused again. "Vince thinks we can file a motion, or whatever you call it, to keep my name out of her mouth so she can't slander me the entire season of the show."

I heard Tamar sigh. "Okay. He thinks he can."

"We have to go to court."

There was a beat of silence before she spoke. "What kind of woman would do this? Or more importantly, who is this woman you were engaged to?"

I covered my eyes with my free hand. "Please don't ask me that. I've asked myself that 800 times today, baby. I feel like a fool. I don't need any help with it."

More silence and then. "Stephen, I need to go."

"Tay, I want to talk. We need to talk."

"It's not the time. You need to get ready for the game."

"Don't worry about the game. I've got that. I want to talk to you. We're not getting off this phone until I know where I stand with you. I feel like it's shaky ground."

Tamar was quiet and then she said, "Let's talk on Monday."

"Let's talk now." I barked. I hadn't meant to raise my voice, but I was frustrated.

"You're pushing me. I told you I need space."

"I need to know we're together. Not cooling it like high school kids. I want us to work on our thing.

We can show Debra and the media that we're strong together," I insisted. "And next week I want to go with you to South Georgia. I want to meet your aunt. Other than press, I'll be done working. I have plenty of time for the trip.

Tamar was quiet again.

"Tay," I said.

"You're forcing me to say this." She hesitated before speaking. "There's no next week for us. I want to break up."

***

There was silence on the other end of the phone. I shouldn't have said that. I should have waited. I could practically hear Stephen's heart breaking through the phone line. I closed my eyes to his pain. I hated the thought that I put it there. Especially since the truth was, I could never mean that I didn't want to be with him. But he couldn't come to South Georgia.

"This is not how people handle relationships. When you have a problem, you keep talking. You talk until you work it out." He paused. "I love you. And I believe you love me. We can't let a malicious liar like Debra break us up."

"This is not really about Debra, Stephen. It's about me not wanting to be a public person. I've already had doses of that. And I hate it. I let myself get lost for a moment being with you. But I don't want celebrity. I don't want paparazzi. I don't want any of it.

I really want to end this."

My heart broke as those words came out of my mouth. I knew they were hard. I knew they were cold. And worse than that, they were lies.

A pain-filled grunt came through the phone. "I can't make you want to be with me. I thought we had something special, but I guess it's like you said. I keep not understanding all that you went through."

I continued to be mute.

"Tay, I wish you would consider maybe talking to somebody about the experiences that you had."

"I've been to therapy. Extensively. One of the things I learned in counseling was to be okay with what I want and my choices and to not let anyone make me believe that what I want is bad."

He interrupted me. "I'm not saying—"

"Let me finish." I was firm. "One of the things that I want is a private life. I can't sacrifice that, not even for you. Not even for love."

Stephen didn't say anything for a few seconds. "You've really given this a lot of thought."

"Ever since the first reporter stuck a mic in my face at the reunion."

"Wow," he whistled. "Talk about a brother being clueless."

"You're making this about you."

"No, I think I really should have done exactly what you asked me to do and that was give you time. But now I'll do that. I'll let you go," Stephen said. "I've said all I can say right now."

Tears streamed down my face. I fought to keep the tremble out of my voice. "I'm sorry. "I mean, I hate the timing. I know you have the game."

It took Stephen a long time to respond. When he finally did, he sounded completely broken. "I'll be fine for the game. I'm a professional."

"I'll be rooting for you."

"I guess I appreciate that." The sarcasm in his voice was strong. There was a lull of silence again. Neither of us spoke. I cleared my throat. I was about to end the call when Stephen said, "This isn't the end of our story."

I squeezed my eyes tight. More tears escaped through my closed lids. I fought to keep my voice even. "Bye, Stephen."

The line went dead.

I dropped to the counter and began to sob. So many lies. Lies upon lies, every word out of my mouth. I'd hurt him, just like I said I would. But I'd made the right decision. I knew that because when I eventually told him the truth about Isaiah, he was going to hate me anyway. He might as well go ahead and start hating me now.

Chapter 10

The play wasn't supposed to go like this.

It was the fourth quarter. Eight minutes and thirty-five seconds on the clock. The Center snapped the ball. The QB received it, then he looked for open receivers. The first down pass couldn't be made. We only needed three yards. The QB ran the ball one yard before he needed to pass it.

It took a second for him to see I was open. As soon as it touched my fingers, I saw Number 54, the defensive tackle, barreling toward me – all 345 pounds of him. I cut through the middle for the run, but I was blindsided – hit high from the right. The force of the blow threw me, and then Number 54 came in low. My body twisted and I fell backwards over a body. Weight pushed me into the turf.

Pop!

Slam!

I was dying. I heard the popping sound again. It was my ankle coming apart and then there was pain in my back. Excruciating pain. I screamed inside.

Six seconds.

That was all it took to take me down.

Chapter 11

"Stephen, baby, it's Mom. Can you hear me?"

I tried to open my mouth. Where was I? I fought to open my eyes. They were heavy. They felt like they were taped down. I tried to clear my throat, but it didn't even feel like it was a part of my body. Why couldn't I see or talk?

Pain shot through me. Blinding pain.

"Stephen?"

"Give him a few minutes," a male voice over my head said. Not my father.

I fought against the blinding dark and pushed my heavy eyelids open. That was when I felt it again. The pain. Then I remembered - the game.

I was hit.

Hard.

I was down.

That was the pop. The pop that played repeatedly in my head. My ankle.

I felt my back grinding into the turf.

Slam!

More weight.

Coach's voice: Don't move, Stephen. We've got you.

"Don't try to move." It was the voice again. Not Coach. Coach was in my head, not over my head. "Be still for me."

Was I moving? I felt like a hunk of lead was weighing down my chest. Like Number 54 and his team were still on top of me. I couldn't move.

I heard people in the room. They were rushing around. There were conversations between medical staff. I tried to stay awake for it, but then I slipped back into the darkness.

My back.

My ankle.

The play wasn't supposed to go like this.

I whispered in my spirit what I couldn't say out loud.

God, please help me.

Chapter 12

I woke up to bad news. The ankle needed surgery. It had been knocked out of place. Because of the ligament damage, it was a difficult injury to rehab from. I also had an injury to my upper back at the base of my neck as well.

"He's looking good. The doctors are optimistic. Sure, we'll be in touch." At first, I could only hear him and then I could see.

Clyde slid his phone in his pocket and approached the bed. He wore stress like a weighted blanket. "How you doing, player?"

I released a frustrated breath. "You tell me."

"You did good in surgery. They got the swelling down around your neck. It's going to be fine. The injury is minor."

I swallowed. I had a sense that what was happening with my neck wasn't that serious. I mean I wasn't paralyzed, and I was grateful for that. But there was the other. "My ankle?" I whispered it like I could barely stand to know.

Clyde avoided my eyes. "The ankle is more complicated."

I gritted my teeth. "Clyde."

"It's not great, but you're young, and you're in great shape. You work hard. You'll be fine for next season."

"Is that what the doctors say?"

Clyde chuckled nervously. "The doctors talk over my head."

"But coach doesn't," I said firmly. "Has anyone else come back from what I've done?"

"From this?" Clyde raised his hand and washed it over his face. "I don't know."

"You do know."

"Stephen, I don't know. I didn't try to find out. What good would it do? This is your race. You run it the Pierce way, not the way anyone else does."

I chuckled, but I felt like crap. "It must be really bad."

Clyde frowned. "Why do you say that?"

"You just preached a sermon." I closed my eyes and pushed my fists into the bed on both sides of my body. "My career is not over." I declared through clenched teeth. "It's not over."

Clyde's hand was on my arm. "You take one day at a time. Rest your neck. Then we'll get going on the ankle."

I looked at my casted foot. I loved Clyde, but *we* were not going to rehab the ankle. I was, and if the pain in rehab was anything like the pain I was feeling right now, I was going to hate it.

"I've never been hurt," I said it like Clyde didn't know. Like he hadn't been with me from the beginning. He knew I'd never been hurt.

"Eight seasons in this sport, not including college. You've had a lifetime twice."

"It doesn't feel like it."

"Everybody gets hurt, eventually. You'll recover." Clyde raked his hand over his head.

"I know that, Clyde. I just, I don't know. A lot is messed up right now."

"I talked to Vince. He'll be in court this week. Your mother is going with him because you're here. He said he's sure the judge will gag her. He found a precedence or something. DNA don't lie. Debra will be exposed for the liar she is."

I wasn't thinking about Debra.

"I can't speak for the Tamar situation, but she was here yesterday," Clyde said.

I held my breath for a moment before responding. "Did you talk to her?"

He shook his head. "She had some words with your mother. Then she talked to your father and left."

I felt steam rise from my belly. Now she wanted to talk to me. Now that I was hurt.

"What do you want me to do?" Clyde asked. "You want me to call her?"

Tamar didn't love me. Not the way I needed her to, and I didn't need the back and forth drama with her when I was trying to get my body right. I also didn't need her pity. Not when I was like this. Neck in a brace and foot in a sling. I couldn't even relieve myself on my own. I was peeing in a bag.

"Stephen, what do you want me to do for you?"

I swallowed my frustration and my fear. "Tell the Giants, I'm coming back strong and to be ready to offer me a big contract."

Clyde nodded. His eyes filled with tears. "That's the Stephen Pierce I know." He patted my arm, and repeated the words, "That's the Stephen I know." But his voice – it didn't sound convincing.

***

My nights were horrendous. The pain was demonic. I chanted scriptures as prayers over and over.

"By your stripes I am healed. Have compassion on me, Lord. I am weak. Heal me, Lord, for my bones are in agony. God you heal all diseases, you redeem my life from the pit and crown me with love and compassion. You will restore health to me and heal my wounds. Lord, these bones can live."

I said them over and over, but the pain was excruciating. Heartbreaking.

I knocked a vase on my nightstand to the floor, and it hit with a crash. My private duty nurse rushed from the far side of the room.

"Can you take the thing off my neck? Just for a few minutes," I begged, grabbing at it.

"We can't do that, Mr. Pierce," the deep voice came back to me. I preferred a male nurse. I was glad I had one. There was kinship there that was more understanding than sympathy. The woman that worked days reeked hopelessness. I could feel her pitying the end of my career. I needed to replace her. She was no good for the atmosphere in the room.

Pain shot down my spine. Hard and sharp. I cried out. I kicked my good leg as I grabbed the sheets with both my hands.

"Mr. Pierce, please let us help you. We can give you more pain medication."

Another nurse entered the room to assist. She picked up a towel and began wiping the perspiration off my forehead.

"No!" I yelled. "They make me hallucinate. Just get me something to help me sleep."

"Right away, sir." The female nurse rushed out. She returned with a pill and raised a water jug to my lips. I swallowed the pills and sipped the water through a straw. Not much because I already needed to urinate. I hated to watch the nurses measure the contents of the Foley bag and then empty it. The entire process was humiliating.

After I calmed down, they left me alone again.

"Have compassion on me, Lord. I am weak. Have compassion on me. I am weak." I mumbled repeatedly until I fell asleep.

Chapter 13

I woke to the sound of gospel music playing and a sweet familiar scent in the room. Once my vision was clear, I saw her. Tamar was sitting on the side of my bed, next to the Foley bag, reading something on her phone. Her hair, usually a mass of curls, was blown somewhat straight. She had it pulled back into a thick ponytail.

She must have sensed my eyes on her, because she looked up at me. A slow smile crept across her face. "You're awake."

She shouldn't be here. I didn't want her here. Did I? God, she was so beautiful, but why was she sitting next to my pee bag?

Tamar stood and poured a cup of water. She offered it to me, but I declined. I heard her ask if I wanted some juice. I declined that too.

"Your breakfast is here. They said they put it in a warmer. Let me wet a cloth. You were sweating, but I didn't want to disturb your sleep."

All her sentences ran together in a blur. She went into the bathroom. My nurse stood and approached the bed. "What can I do for you?"

"I'm good," I replied.

"You want breakfast?"

"Not yet."

Dude had to feed me. I didn't want Tay seeing that.

"I can get you changed whenever you're ready," he offered.

"I just need privacy." I threw up the deuces. He grabbed the book he was reading and left the room.

Tamar came out of the bathroom with the washcloth, approached my bed and began to wipe my forehead.

"How are you feeling?"

"I feel like I look."

"That's not that bad."

I guffawed. "Really, Tay? Neck brace and foot cast?"

"You're not paralyzed. I understand neck injuries can be paralyzing."

"You're wiping my forehead. I can't feed myself. I'm paralyzed right now."

She stopped wiping and stared at me like I'd disappointed her by saying that. But she didn't chastise me. After a few seconds, she resumed dabbing my head and face. I looked up at her hand. No ring. Not that I was expecting it. She'd told me how she felt.

"You won't take my calls," Tamar whispered the words like it was a secret - like there was someone in the room who would know I was rejecting her.

"I'm not sure why you're calling."

She put a hand on a hip and sighed. "I'm calling because I care about you."

"Apparently, not enough." I coughed. I needed that water, but I didn't want her to get it for me. "Where's your ring?"

Tamar looked at her hand like she was searching for it. "It's in my box at the bank."

I closed my eyes. "At least it's safe."

She released a frustrated wind. She reached for my hand. "Stephen, you know I care about you."

I felt my body release urine. My Foley started to fill up. Heat from embarrassment swept over me. I pushed her hand away. "I'm not interested in being your friend."

"Let me be here for you."

"I don't need you to be here for me," I said. "Believe me, you've done enough, Tay."

A look of confusion came over her face. "What do you mean by that?"

I didn't respond.

"Stephen, you're not blaming me for being hurt?"

"Why not? You've been blaming me for things that aren't my fault for years. I mean who would break up with a football player before the biggest game of his life?"

My words hit her like Number 54 hit me. Her

head was spinning. I could see it.

I continued. "And for such a foul reason. You're a writer. You couldn't come up with a better story than you didn't want to deal with the media? We had been dealing with the media, so you can't tell me that's what the breakup was about."

Tamar continued to be mute. I felt like I'd spoken some truth that shook her.

"I know you're hurting. But you're being unfair," she insisted.

"No, I'm being fair. As fair as I can be to you." I sighed and then continued. "You don't owe me anything. You don't have to love me. You don't have to want to be my wife. You don't need to be here."

I thought the pain in my heart was bad, but then a pain shot up my leg from my ankle to my back. I groaned. Hard.

"Should I get the nurse?" she asked.

I spoke through grit teeth. "No. It's a spasm. It comes and goes." After a moment, my muscle relaxed.

I felt bad about the way I'd talked to her. "I don't mean to be nasty about it."

"You're right," she offered. "I should have waited to talk to you. I was wrong to say those things before the game."

"Sorry is not going to help me get better. I need to be focused on me. If you don't mind, I'd really prefer to be alone."

"You're angry, and that's not like you. Let me

pray with you."

"I've got enough prayers."

"Stephen, please. Don't shut me out."

Tamar didn't understand. If she wasn't going to say, "I love you, I want to be with you," I was going to shut her out.

The door opened and my mother entered. I sighed. Tamar's visit was definitely about to end.

My mother leaned over the bed and kissed me on the forehead. "Good morning, son."

"Morning."

My mother glared at Tamar. "Stephen's not up for visits."

Tamar put the wet cloth on the tray table next to her. "I was told he could have visitors."

My mother rolled her neck and placed a hand on her hip. "He can have the ones he wants."

"Mom," I interrupted. "Can you give us a few more minutes?"

My mother rolled her eyes again, but then dropped her handbag on the nightstand and walked out.

Once her back was through the door, Tamar and I looked at each other. She reached for my hand and I allowed her to hold it. I fought taking in her warmth. All this resistance was a lie. I was lying with every fiber in my body.

God, I need her.

But I wanted her to love me.

"I hate what you're going through."

"I'll recover."

"I know." Her voice cracked on the words.

"I don't mean to hurt you. Ever. I appreciate you coming all the way from Atlanta, but I need my head to be straight for what I have to do."

Tamar looked away from me for a moment. When her eyes returned, they were filled with tears. "I'm sorry, Stephen. I'm so sorry."

"You don't have anything to be sorry about. You've been honest with me. One could say, you've told me exactly how you've felt for months. Years really, if we think about."

"That's not fair. You know it's not."

"Why isn't it fair to say? Because I'm hurt."

"Because I've forgiven you. We forgave each other."

"I love you came out of your mouth. Before I put that ring on your finger."

"I know. But…this is not the time. It's not the place."

"It's the perfect time. It's the perfect place. Nothing gives you perspective better than an upper spinal injury, a busted ankle, and two surgeries."

Tears spilled down her cheeks. I hated to see her cry. I always had.

"I need to put my whole heart in healing. I don't

have time for distractions."

Sadness filled her eyes. Either she was wrecked from guilt, or I'd broken her. "I'll leave before your mother gets impatient."

Say you love me, and you can stay.

She leaned closer and pressed her lips against my forehead. I wanted to turn in her direction and taste her sweet mouth. But I couldn't turn. I couldn't move my neck, and she didn't want a kiss.

Tamar lingered on the side of my bed for a moment. She seemed unsure of what to do or say next and that uncertainty looked familiar. I'd seen it a few times over the months. I tried to read what was in her eyes up close, but I'd done that before. I thought I saw forever in her eyes. I was wrong.

"Okay," I released a long breath. "Take care of yourself."

"You, too. Think about what I said. I'd like to be here for you."

"The Giants will provide the best nurses in the state of New Jersey," I said. "On your way out, would you tell my mother and the nurse, I need about five minutes before they come in."

You're dismissed.

Tamar looked sad – regretful even. She'd probably had mixed feelings about having come in the first place and now she was probably unsure about what she'd done to me emotionally.

"You'll be on my mind and in my prayers," she said, picking up her bag and phone. She walked toward the door.

Don't call her back. Let her leave.

She stopped at the door for a moment, looked back at me one more time and then opened it and left.

I felt tears well in my eyes. I hadn't cried in fifteen years, not since Tamar's mother's funeral. It was one of the saddest days of my life, because Tamar and her father were utterly destroyed by her death. That day, I had shed tears of sympathy.

Today, no one was dead, but I knew what loss felt like. It was going to take a miracle for my ankle to heal enough for me to play football again. I believed in miracles, so I was up to the challenge, but getting over that woman – I didn't know if I would ever do that.

"Lord, heal my wounds, and if You're not going to bring her back to me the way I want her, I also need You to heal my heart." More tears slid down the side of my face.

We'd won the Super Bowl, but the play wasn't supposed to go like this.

Chapter 14

I was miserable. I hadn't been this miserable in years. I still hadn't forgiven myself for what I did to Stephen. It had been weeks since he put me out of his hospital room, and I was still wrecked about it.

I spent my days working, fighting not to pick up the phone and call Stephen, avoiding stories about Debra's new television show, and feeling guilty about not being with Aunt Joe.

"I think you should go to New Jersey and tell Stephen," Kim said.

We had been moving our eggs and bacon back and forth on our plates, neither of us really eating since the waitress put our meals in front of us. I was depressed, and Kim was trying to help me get it together.

"I can't. He's back in the hospital."

Annoyance flashed across Kim's face. She was sick of my excuses.

"You don't understand. He blamed me for getting hurt. If I tell him about Isaiah and he has a medical setback, he'll blame me for that too."

"Tamar, you know he was speaking out of anger.

He doesn't really blame you."

"That's what he said."

"He's had some time to think. He's not going to have a setback. He didn't have a heart attack or anything like that."

My thoughts continued to churn. "Finding out he has a son is going to be emotional. He doesn't need that kind of energy right now. He needs time for his body to heal."

"Okay, I get that, but what are you going to do about your aunt? You said she's been pretty sick from the chemo and she has more next week."

I sighed. "I've requested family medical leave."

"But you said if you go down there, the reporters might find the story about your son."

"I'm going to hope for the best."

"Isaiah looks like Stephen."

"I've thought about it. He looks like pre-teen Stephen, not really Stephen today."

Kim shook her head. "Girl, he looks like his daddy. You're worrying me. I think you're losing it."

"I'm sane. I'm just between a rock and a hard place. I don't want to hurt Stephen, but I need to take care of my aunt. I also don't want my aunt stressed out by how Stephen might respond."

Kim appeared to be thinking before she said, "Don't you think that maybe you're trying to handle too much here? This is a big problem. You need to pray and trust God with all the actions and reactions folk are going to have. He cares about both Stephen and your Auntie's health." Empathy flooded her eyes. "You can't control everything."

I groaned inwardly. "I just need a little more time. A few weeks. I'll do it right after Aunt Joe recovers from this next round of chemo and by then, Stephen will be further along in his recovery."

Kim shook her head. "I have a bad feeling."

"Don't say that."

"I can't help it. You're doing the most. It's stressful."

I picked up my coffee mug and took another sip. "How do you think I feel?" I rotated my shoulder to relieve tension. "You should have seen the look in his eyes when he all but put me out of his hospital room. I'm not used to that Stephen."

"You have to learn how to trust God with all of Stephen."

I swallowed heavy emotions. I didn't know how to trust God with this. I was trying, but I couldn't see His hand right now.

Kim interrupted my thoughts. "You say Stephen is the real deal in his faith. So, if he's the real deal, then he should forgive you."

I couldn't argue with that in theory, but I wasn't sure if Stephen could do it in practice. "Secret babies have a tendency to bring out the worst in people."

"It won't be a secret baby if you tell him before the boy is grown." Kim raised her fork to her lips. "You've got to let go and let God. This is really too much for you to do alone."

I dropped my head in my hands for a minute.

"Call him. Write him a letter. You're good on paper. But handle this. It's going to backfire on you if you don't."

We finished our breakfast in silence. I considered her words as I traveled to the office. I was overwhelmed with stress about everything. I thought about all Stephen was dealing with. The filming for Debra's show was underway. He was in a good deal of pain. I knew because his agent, Clyde, kept me updated about his health.

"I do need to tell him," I whispered. I reached into my bag for my phone and dialed his cell number. It went right to voicemail. Rather than hang up, I left a message for him to call me.

I didn't even realize how fast my heart was racing until I put my phone down. What was I doing? How had I gone from not telling him to now calling without thinking my words through?

The email icon pinged twice on my computer shaking me from my state of shock. Human resources approved my family leave. I also had an email from Eva.

I popped out of my chair and went to her office.

"I know you asked for leave, but I was wondering if you wanted to take intermittent leave instead of full leave. You could telework from your aunt's house."

I was thoughtful about that. Working part-time would give me income. I only had about three weeks of paid leave. That wouldn't last long. "What would I be doing?"

"That college intern I had on the gossip blog quit. I have to put someone on your desk, but I don't want another college kid for the blog."

I waited a beat because I knew she wasn't finished.

"I was thinking you could do the blog."

I considered the assignment. Relationship stories, mostly celebrity updates with a few unknown people with big trending stories mixed in. I had never done anything like it. I wasn't interested in it. "Is there something else? I don't follow celebrity gossip."

"I'm not going to move everyone around to accommodate you," Eva barked, spinning her chair away from me.

I rolled my eyes, before she turned back to me.

"The celebrity stuff isn't that hard. Neither are the trending stories. You stay on Twitter and grab whatever is hot and run with it."

I needed the money working part-time would net me. I had enough savings to pay my bills for a good three months, but beyond that, I would be struggling. "I'll do my best."

"Of course, you will," Eva said. "I'll email you the deets. Call if you need something."

She shooed me out of her office. I went to my desk and packed up everything I needed, which amounted to my laptop, iPad, a portable printer, printer paper, a few legal pads, and my favorite pens.

As I exited the building, relief washed over me. I was on my way to Yancy. I just hoped I wasn't going to regret not figuring out another way.

Chapter 15

I heard the door open, the alarm code being keyed, and then footsteps on the stairs.

"I'm glad you're here. I'm starving—"

My words died on my tongue when I saw my cousin, Pete. I sighed. I was feeling antisocial. My entire leg from my ankle up was hurting. I was in a mood, so he was one of the last people I wanted to see right now. "Where's mom?"

My father placed a bag of food on the kitchen island. "She saw a gray hair this morning. Her stylist had a cancellation, so she jumped on it."

I nodded, switched my weight from the wall I was leaning against to my crutches.

"You gettin' around good in that boot?" Pete pointed at my foot.

"I do what I need to do."

"How's it feeling?"

"Painful and uncomfortable," I replied, sharply.

Pete nodded.

"I thought you were in the program for four months. Don't tell me I've wasted more money." I asked referring to the drug rehab program I was paying for.

"No, I'm still in. The last thirty days I get two one-day passes. Then I go to the halfway house."

I wasn't even going to try to show enthusiasm for Pete's rehab. I'd paid for it too many times, so I nodded and said, "Yeah, I'd forgotten how it worked the other four times."

My father cleared his throat and shot me an annoyed look. He put the bag of Chinese food on the table. "Let's eat."

I'd been eating healthy, high protein meals prepared by a chef the team doctors had assigned to me. Nutrition was high on the list of conduits to healing, but today I wanted to dismiss with the green food. Not that my diet tasted bad, but nothing was as good as my favorite Asian haunt, and it was not healthy.

My father and Pete slid out of their coats. After washing their hands, they joined me at the table. I'd already taken out a set of chopsticks and said grace. We all ate with chopsticks. My father taught Pete and I how to use them when we were kids. He'd spent a few years in Japan when he was in the Marine Corp.

As always, Pete still struggled a bit with his, but he managed to get his food in. "How long are they telling you for the ankle to get better?" he asked.

"Four or five more months. I start therapy next week."

"That's fast. Do they expect you to be ready before training camp?"

"I don't know. I know I expect me to be ready," I said. "Let's change the subject. What's next for you after you go to the halfway house?"

"I have to get a job and work, or I could go to like trade school for something. I don't have any skills. Trade is kinda interesting, but I still have to work to keep a roof over my head."

"You can do anything you set your mind to," my father interjected. "And you know you're welcome to stay with us."

Pete nodded at my dad. "I'm willing to do anything honest." Pete gave my father a nervous look. It was then that I knew this visit was not just to check on me.

"What do you need, Pete?" I asked sticking a large piece of Mongolian beef into my mouth before pushing my plate away.

Pete looked from my dad to me like he wanted my father to answer the question. He swallowed his fear before saying, "A job. I was thinking since you can't get yourself around that maybe I could be your driver."

"You were?"

"I've kept my license clean. I've never gotten any kind of traffic violation or anything when I was high, so I'm good to drive."

I glanced at my father. I could see a hopeful look on his face, but I couldn't give him what he wanted. "I don't know."

"Why not?" Pete pressed. "I mean you've forgiven me. That's what you said."

"I've forgiven you." I thought about the video of Tamar and myself that Pete had uploaded to YouTube. The video that caused Tamar and I so much pain and separation. What might my life have been like if that video hadn't happened?

Tamar and I both would have gone to college, stayed a couple until graduation and then gotten married before I went to the NFL. We'd have a home and children. We'd have years of good memories instead of this mess we had right now.

I shook my head. I shouldn't have blamed her for the accident. It wasn't her fault. But our broken relationship was Pete's.

"Stephen." Pete called me from my thoughts.

"Forgiving isn't forgetting," I said coming from my fantasies about Tamar. "You being my driver is a lot of time together."

"I know, but I'd be good at it, and I'll mind my business."

I reached for my water bottle, finished it and tossed the empty container at the garbage pail. I missed. I'd been missing for weeks.

Pete walked to the trash can, picked up my bottle and threw it away before sitting back down. "How are things with you and Tamar?"

I chuckled. "You don't even have the job yet, and you're not minding your business."

"I was just asking. I don't know what's up."

"Tamar and I split before I got hurt."

Pete's eyes widened. "For real? Man, I didn't know. I saw you propose so I thought you were cool."

"It's not big news to anyone except…I guess me. The dumped fiancé."

Pete nodded. "You can fix this, though."

I stifled a groan. "I've got enough to fix without chasing after a woman who claims she doesn't want to be caught."

Pete nodded, ate for a moment and then said, "Look, I'm still being nosy here, but you got hurt in February. You didn't even see Tamar until right before Christmas. That was a quick proposal."

"I'm not like you, Pete. I'm a man who knows what he wants."

"Son," my father interrupted. He gave me a stern eye. "Enough."

I sighed. I was being nasty. I knew that. Pete had it coming. I knew that, too. I was paying for his rehab – again. Did I have to be nice to the man who had trashed my love life, too?

"You probably scared her," Pete offered. "Maybe if you slowed things down."

"Are you seriously giving me relationship advice right now?"

Pete shrugged. "I'm sorry. I know how you feel about her is all."

"I looked for Tamar because I wanted to know how she was. I wanted to apologize to her. I found that out, and I got to say I was sorry. I was obviously expecting too much."

"Give her time, man. What I saw between you two looked like love."

"It's the Debra mess," I rested a fist on my chin. "I feel like Tay should have hung in there with me. She should have given me the benefit of the doubt."

"You have to admit, the Debra mess is a mess," my father chimed in. He shook his head and frowned like he'd eaten something bad. "The TV show…"

"She said the issue was she didn't want to live a public life. She didn't want reporters and paparazzi around." I got angry all over again as I thought about it. "This stuff dies down."

"Tamar is not going to respond to this kind of thing the way most women might. Some women would love the attention, but you're talking about someone wounded. She hid for twelve years, son. Changed her name. Cut off her family."

I still didn't think it was enough to break up over. "Look, I don't want to talk about Tamar. I'm in enough pain right now."

"I promise to not bring her up again." Pete threw up his hands. "So, can I have the job or what?"

I wanted to say yes. I wanted to help him, but I wasn't going to say yes today. "I need to think about it. I can't take any more pain or disappointment right now and you and I—" I didn't want to use anymore harsh words. "Give me a minute to think about it."

Pete nodded. "You take all the minutes you need."

My father and he exchanged a look. I know my dad was rooting for his nephew, but I had to be sure before I let Pete back into my world like that. The last time he'd had access to me and my things, he'd destroyed everything and lied for years to keep his secret.

***

I made him sweat it out, but I did hire Pete. I did in-home therapy for three weeks, during which time I didn't leave my house much, so I didn't need a driver, then. But once I was in good enough shape to go to the Giant's training center, I did need someone. I lived twenty-five minutes away. Pete was more convenient than a car service, and my cousin did need a job.

We pulled in front of the Giant's Zone, officially called the Quest Diagnostics Training Center. Coming here always made my adrenaline rush. But today, it was a different kind of rush. These days, I experienced more anxiety than excitement, and I hated that. I hated the undercurrent of fear coursing through my blood. I'd never been afraid of anything in my life, but I was afraid of this injury.

What if I can't play anymore? What do I have outside of football?

I had been thinking about those questions for weeks. The answer that kept ringing in my head was nothing. Nothing that would be enough to make up for playing the game.

Pete opened my door. I pushed my cane out in

front of me. I hated this thing, too. I knew I was being immature about it, but it made me feel weak and feeble, like an old man.

"You want to come in? We have a cafeteria."

"No, I'm going to wait out here. I have a few things downloaded from Netflix."

I nodded. "I'll be at least an hour. Text me if you change your mind, and I'll call the desk to get you in."

Pete nodded and pushed my door closed.

I took the steps up to the entrance.

Pete called my name. I did a half turn in his direction. "Good luck, right?"

Luck wasn't something I was accustomed to thinking about. I wasn't lucky. I was blessed. At this minute, I didn't feel like I was either. I nodded and walked through the doors.

I already knew my therapists, Kevin and Kaci. They were the same brother-sister team that had been coming to the house. He was the expert on upper body work and she, the ankle and foot injuries. Both were there to greet me.

"Good to be back in the Zone, huh?" Kevin's energy was high. He gave me a heavy pound on the fist. "How you feeling, man?"

I took a deep breath and gave him the most upbeat answer I could come up with. "It was nice to take this drive again."

"You're doing good with the cane," Kaci added, joining us. "We'll have you off of it in no time."

Kaci and Kevin worked my upper body for forty minutes and then put me on ice therapy. As I sat there for the last twenty minutes, I visited my social media. Fans on my IG page were looking for me. I had thousands of comments asking me for an update on my last post from nearly a month ago which simply read:

Down but not out. Pray, friends. #comingback

I owed them something. I opened the camera app. Extended my arm and snapped a selfie, and then took a pic of my leg, and the machines in the training area. I uploaded all three and posted the caption:

Unbreakable #YourRunningBack

I wanted to write more. I wanted to write something inspiring and spiritual. I was a leader to so many of the young guys in the league and in college and high school. My fans always commented and liked my inspirational messages more than any others, but I didn't have it in me. Not right now.

Maybe tomorrow.

That's what I'd told myself yesterday and the day before that. Who was I without football if I couldn't even write an inspirational message? I didn't know. I hoped I didn't have to find out.

Chapter 16

I was living in constant fear of being discovered. I hated it. And because of my fear, I imagined I was being watched. Every time I left the house, I found myself looking over my shoulder. It reminded me of my time in college when I was stalked about the video and the questions:

How does it feel to be a celebrity?

Did you know you were being taped?

Who was the young man in the video?

You're a preacher's kid. Was this an act of rebellion against the church?

Can you confirm Stephen Pierce was your lover?

They never ran out of questions. Early in my first semester at Penn State, I realized I was pregnant. I thought the entire world was looking at me. I was afraid to answer unknown telephone numbers, and I hated to open emails.

Stephen had a breakout freshman year on the field, so predictions about who he was going to be after college were already happening before he even finished his first season. For that reason, the video controversy wouldn't die down.

As a result of the never-ending attention, I developed such bad anxiety that I was on my way to having a nervous breakdown. Dropping out of school was my only option. Plus, I needed to hide until I had the baby. The last thing I wanted nosy reporters to know was that I was pregnant. That would get back to my father and Stephen.

I closed my eyes against the memory. "I had no other choice," I whispered. Everything seemed so clear back then. But today, twelve years later, it did not. Was there something else I could have done? Could I have told Stephen? What would he have done?

I shook my head. "You made the best decision you could at the time."

"Ma'am, were you talking to me?"

I looked into the face of the cashier. She held my latte in her hand.

"I'm sorry. How much?" I asked, reaching into my wallet.

She repeated my total, I paid, and took a seat.

I was back in Atlanta. Eva insisted I figure out a way to attend a mandatory work conference. She was guilty of breaking all the family medical leave laws, but I couldn't be mad at her. Intermittent leave was keeping my bills paid.

Kim stopped by my apartment from time to time to water my plants. I had a lot of them. Gratefully, most were hardy, so her weekly visits kept them alive. I was looking forward to watering them myself. I was also looking forward to sleeping in my own bed for the next couple of nights.

I knew not being seen around the city was a good thing. Most of the media probably assumed I was in New Jersey with Stephen. He hadn't said anything on social media about our breakup. He hadn't said anything at all, until yesterday when he'd posted the pics from his therapy session.

It was a good picture of him. I was grateful for it, since the last time I'd seen him, he was in the hospital. I pulled out my phone and went to his Instagram page. He hadn't posted a new picture, but he had responded to a few of the comments. He had thousands of them. His fans wished him well, told him they were praying for him, asked him about me. He didn't respond to any of those.

The same way he hadn't responded to my phone call last month or the card and the note I sent him a week after the call. I'd been right and Kim was wrong. He did blame me for the accident. He couldn't even make himself return my phone call or respond to a letter.

I finished my drink and left the coffee shop. I made my way out into the freezing cold. This weather was not unheard of, but it was definitely uncharacteristic for early April in Atlanta.

A light snow had fallen last night and because it was so cold, it stuck. Snow was a nuisance in this city. Most people couldn't drive in it and once it warmed up, if the temperature dropped again, we had black ice.

Usually our rare snows made me feel nostalgic. Having grown up in Pine, I was used to snow from November to end of April, but today I couldn't shake the feeling that my past was coming back to haunt me.

The snow added to the foreboding anxiety that simmered in my emotions.

I slid my dark shades on, checked the surrounding area to make sure no one was watching me. I told myself I was being cautious, but in truth, I was getting paranoid. I promised myself I'd never let myself get that crazy again. But now that I had a job at a magazine with reporters, I knew the ins and outs of the business.

Everyone was looking for the story that would make them hot. Bylines built resumes and resumes made careers and money. As much as I wanted to be nobody, I was, technically, Stephen Pierce's fiancé. People wanted updates on his rehab. They wanted updates on our romance. Reporters wanted to be the ones to share it.

I was out of time. My paranoia was a clear sign of that. I had to tell Stephen about Isaiah and since he wasn't talking to me, I'd have to pop up on him at home.

"Tamar Johnson." My name slipped off a male tongue.

I turned.

"I'm Roy Cray with *The City Standard*. Can we talk for a few minutes?"

I hesitated. "About what?" I removed my sunglasses.

He smiled a little. It was slight, but cocky. "A story I've developed. A story about you."

My stomach dropped. I was too late.

Chapter 17

Run.

The temptation to get on a plane and fly somewhere on the other side of the world coursed through my veins. I'd run before. I'd run from school to Aunt Joe's and then back to school and then changed schools again and again and finally South Africa. I knew how to run. It had been a long time, but I had been good at it.

I closed my eyes to the temptation. I couldn't run anymore. I had people now. People who depended on me, and I was out of time. I had to answer for my past. I had to fix this mess before it exploded in my face.

I called off the work meeting and took a plane to Yancy.

"You have 24 hours," Roy Cray had said.

I sighed. At least I had that. It was enough time to tell Isaiah and then get to New Jersey to talk to Stephen. God, how I dreaded both.

I'd called ahead so Aunt Joe was expecting me. I entered the house. She was standing in the kitchen looking lost and thin. So very thin.

I'd been protecting her. I was right to protect her.

"What can I get for you, Auntie?" I asked, putting down my bag.

"I don't remember what I came in here for," she said.

I washed my hands and opened the refrigerator. "How about some Jello?"

Aunt Joe nodded and accepted the small cup from me. I handed her a spoon, too. "Where's the aide?"

"The supermarket," she said, frowning at the little cup as she stabbed the gelatin with the spoon.

"Getting what? I made sure you had everything before I left yesterday."

Aunt Joe continued to examine her snack. "I want some cornbread. I woke up with a taste for it."

And I had forgotten to add the meal to the list yesterday. I didn't think it was that big of a deal, or I would have gone back. I didn't like her being alone.

"Is Isaiah coming straight home from school today?"

She finally put a small amount of Jello on her tongue. She had sores in her mouth, so eating was hard. "He'll be here soon." She swallowed, wincing from the pain, and put the cup down. "You weren't followed, were you?"

I reached into the freezer for a pan of chicken casserole I'd made before I left. I placed it on the counter so it could begin to thaw. The home-health aide was supposed to warm up meals, but I intended to send her home as soon as she returned. "I made sure he wasn't on the plane."

We walked into the living room. I slid off my jacket and sat down. I observed her some more. She was weak.

"How are you feeling?"

"Like I have cancer," she rasped. "And that feels like the end of your life."

"I'm sorry I left."

"You hadn't been gone but a day. I know you have a job. I've got my aide and my church family. Everything here is fine."

I didn't sit. I stood behind the loveseat opposite Aunt Joe and pushed my nervous energy into a throw pillow I'd picked up.

"So, what does the reporter know?"

I was reminded of my warning. *24 hours*. "He knows I had a baby."

"You had him in this house. There aren't any hospital records."

"I don't know. I didn't ask him anything because I wasn't trying to confirm the story, but he'll find the birth record. He's probably looking for Johnsons. That will take a minute, but it won't be long before he starts looking for Fergusons. Everybody knows my pen name and Mama's maiden name isn't hard to find." I started pacing.

Aunt Joe watched me move up and down and around before losing patience. "Tamar, stop moving, you're making me dizzy." She closed her eyes.

I stopped and dropped into a chair. "I have a flight in the morning. I'm going to see Stephen first and then daddy."

"You've got your hands full." Aunt Joe grunted.

I stood again and walked to fireplace. I picked up a picture of the three of us together. Aunt Joe, my son, and I. I swallowed more disgust. Stephen Pierce wasn't the only one I had to explain myself to.

Stephen Isaiah Ferguson would want to know why his mother had pretended to be his cousin all these years. Why he'd been hidden from the rest of his family in Pennsylvania – grandparents and other relatives. I closed my eyes to the thought of my father…his only grandson. I'd robbed both of them.

"Auntie, I made the only decision I could make back then." I put down the picture and spun around to her. "Right?"

"Don't you let any of them make you feel bad about what you had to do."

"But I do feel bad."

"Hindsight is always twenty-twenty, Tamar."

"You saved me. You saved Isaiah – from me and no one knows how big of a save that was except for me." Thoughts of how depressed I was resurfaced and made my chest burn. "It's not fair for them to judge, but they're going to hate me for it."

Aunt Joe huffed. "Hate is a strong word. These are Christian people."

"What does that mean when you're talking about an unforgiveable situation?" I thought about how much my Aunt Joe disliked my father. She was a perfect example of the Christian people who hadn't risen above issues, but I dare not show her herself.

Aunt Joe raised a trembling finger to her lips and shushed me. "There are no unforgiveable situations. You didn't kill anybody."

I closed my eyes and tried to block out the angry images of their faces, but it didn't help. I opened them again and raised my hand to wipe a tear that had escaped.

"My dad will forgive me, but Stephen's parents? They're going to trip. Especially his mother. We haven't always gotten along."

Auntie cocked an eyebrow. "And why is that?"

I wiped more tears before saying, "She was afraid I was going to get pregnant and ruin his life." I hadn't thought about Stephen's mother's thoughts toward me in a long time.

A large vehicle rambled down the road outside. I walked to the windows to look out for Isaiah. It wasn't the school bus. It didn't even sound like it. My nerves were shot. I was anxious about talking to him. I moved away from the window, wringing my hands and pacing again.

"Baby, you were young and hurting and confused."

"But still, I feel like I stole something from all of them. Like I punished them because they all left me standing alone with the mess."

"Tamar, I want you to stop right now. Stop

feeling guilty."

I stopped moving. "I can't help it."

Aunt Joe shook her head. "You have something to offer Stephen. You have his son. You're not coming to him with a story about a boy who's gone. He's still here. He's still a child. He can still enjoy him."

I nodded. That was true.

"Furthermore, it's probably time for you to take him anyway. Isaiah is you and Stephen's blood. He deserves to be with you both and you deserve to be with him."

I shook my head. Where was this coming from? "No, Auntie. He's your son. You've raised him. You've been his mother."

Aunt Joe looked so tired. Chemo had taken every bit of energy she had, and I knew she felt sick – all the time. I could see it. I sat next to her. She took my hand.

"He's your son more than he is ours."

"I know that, honey. But I knew this day was coming the minute I took that baby out of your hands, so let's call it what it should have been all along. Isaiah has been with me for safe-keeping. Until you were ready for him. And now you're ready."

"Aunt Joe," I shook my head again. The sting of more tears burned my eyes.

"Take your child, fix the relationship with your man and live happily ever after." Auntie coughed, painfully. "Do that for my sister."

I fell to my knees on the floor and rested my head

on her lap. My mind went back:

"What do I do Auntie?"

"What do you want to do, Tamar?"

"I can't take care of a baby. I need to finish school. I need to..."

"Shhh...don't you cry. You give that baby to me."

I began to sob at the memory. Here I was again. Crying on her lap.

"Shhh...everything is going to be okay." She lifted my chin and looked in my eyes. "Everyone in this situation loves you. It's going to be okay."

I heard Isaiah's key in the door. I stood and wiped my eyes.

Isaiah walked in. "You're back. I thought you weren't coming until Saturday."

"I had a change," I said, turning away from him while I wiped my eyes again.

I could hear him give his mother a hug and a kiss. Then he put down his bookbag near the dining room table where he always did homework and went into the restroom. When he came out Aunt Joe asked, "How was school?"

"Good. I have a science test tomorrow."

"Change and get a snack." She told him that every day. "No TV until you finish studying."

Isaiah disappeared into his bedroom.

Aunt Joe and I locked eyes.

My insides twisted. "I can't do it tonight."

"Tamar, you can't keep putting it off."

I raised a finger to my mouth and bit down on the pad of my thumb. I wasn't ready for this. "He has a test. I'll tell him when I get back tomorrow."

Aunt Joe nodded and closed her eyes like she was relieved.

I always thought tomorrow was better, but that kind of thinking was the reason I was in trouble in the first place.

Chapter 18

Roy Cray lied. He released the story about my pregnancy with the morning news cycle. It was repeated on nearly every celebrity and gossip blog in the country.

I called Cray before I boarded my plane.

"You told me I had 24 hours."

"We decided to go to press."

"So why did you bother to call me, then?"

"Come on, Tamar, you're in the business. I'm sure you have friends who would have loved to have this story. My editor was concerned I'd tipped you off. We didn't want me getting scooped."

"Thanks for the professional courtesy."

"So, no comment? I mean, you have to tell your side to somebody? Where is the child?"

"Figure it out yourself," I yelled, ending the call.

***

My taxi stopped at the gate to Stephen's subdivision. There were a couple of reporters hanging around.

I'd texted Stephen to let him know I was here. He

texted back:

Your name is still on the guard's list.

The taxi pulled through the gate and emotional adrenaline came down heavy. I don't think I'd ever felt so tired. It was the racing of my heart. The constant, constricted pounding in my chest was wreaking havoc on every muscle in my body.

He's going to hate me.

It was all I could think. The possibility of a civil relationship between us was over. Over, again.

Stephen opened the door. He was leaning on a cane. He hadn't shaved in possibly days because he had a small beard. His curly hair was a mass of waves that wrapped around each other like plants on a vine. He reached up with his free hand and ran it through his hair like he was subconscious about it. Everything about him looked different. His looks, his physicality, and his demeanor. He didn't look bad, just different – like a recluse.

"I've been calling you for hours." His voice was sharp.

"I was on the plane. I got here as fast as I could."

"Seems like you've been getting here for twelve years." Those words were even sharper.

I hadn't even entered the house and he was jabbing at me. "Are you going to let me in?"

Stephen stepped aside.

I dropped my bag on the foyer table and shrugged out of my coat. "Let's just talk, okay?"

He nodded and took my coat. He hung it in the hall closet. He was getting around good. I was afraid to say so. I had no idea how he would take it. I didn't need him biting my head off any more than he already would be.

Once he finished with my coat, he turned to face me. "Ladies first." He'd taken the temper out of his voice. He swayed a palm in the direction of the living room. Hospitable though he was, the tight lines on his forehead and his cinched lips told me what was really in his heart right now.

I didn't waste time getting started. "I'm probably not going to be able to make this make sense to you."

Stephen raised a hand, interrupting me. "Did you have a baby eleven years ago?"

"Are you going to let me tell you what happened?"

"No, Tay." He frowned. "I'm not in the mood for your melody of words. I just want answers."

I took in a deep breath of tense air. "Here I'd prepared my speech."

Stephen said nothing.

I swallowed before saying. "I had a boy."

Stephen dropped his body onto the arm of a chair. He closed his eyes and released a long, solid, pained breath. "Is he alive?"

I cleared my throat and answered. "Yes."

He stood and took a few steps away from me, like he needed to distance himself. "Is he my son?"

I nodded. "Yes."

Stephen closed his eyes again. When he opened them, I could see the glint of tears. "Where is he?"

"He lives in South Georgia. He was adopted."

Anger flashed across his face. "By whom?"

"My mother's sister."

"Aunt Joe?" The name came out like it was stuck in his throat.

All I had were nods and yeses, so I nodded again.

Stephen didn't respond for a long minute. I could see the wheels turning in his head. He was shocked. Shocked into a temporary silence. "So, you see him?"

"Yes. I'm living with Aunt Joe right now."

He shook his head like I'd given him the wrong answer. "I mean, you've always seen him?"

"Not often. Sometimes, when I visited."

His eyes became tiny slits as he stared me down. "Does he know you're his mother?"

"No."

"Who does he think you are?"

"His cousin."

Stephen nodded. "Is he healthy? Happy?"

"He is." I tried to keep the pride out of my voice. "He's a great kid."

Stephen stood. Attempting to pace, he hobbled around on his cane before stopping and dropping down on the arm of another chair, further away from me.

"Does he have another father?"

"No, my aunt is single – you know that – but she's really active in her church, so he participates in different mentoring activities with the men."

Stephen was silent again. He raised his hand to wash over his hair and face a few times. Frustration was building and then releasing. He was like a ticking bomb. I took the moments to steel myself against whatever he would finally say when he spoke.

"Tamar, I want to understand this. I really do, but you need to tell me why you did this to me?"

I threw up my hands. "I was eighteen. I had left home. A home I didn't think I could come back to. I was pregnant. I had neither a job or the skills to get a job that would feed me, let alone a baby."

"That's because you decided to disappear. We graduated from high school and you left."

"You left first," I replied, correcting him.

Stephen frowned. "I left for two weeks. You knew I was coming home before I had to go back again—"

I interrupted him. "You're asking me what happened and I'm telling you. You left and you didn't even say goodbye to me—"

This time it was Stephen who interrupted. "Don't you dare act like I didn't try to say goodbye. I'm tired of your distorted memory of how things happened. You were locked away in the house. You wouldn't answer the door, or the phone, or an email, or a letter. Your father was like a pit bull. He wouldn't let me near you."

I closed my eyes, covered my face with both hands, and shook my head. *I did the best I could at the time.* I empowered myself with my truth before speaking again. "You asked me what happened."

Stephen sighed, calming himself. "Did you know you were pregnant when you left Pine?"

"Yes.'"

"Why didn't you think you could tell me that, Tay? We were in love."

I finally sat. The weight of my answer was like that emotional cloud that engulfed me back in the taxi. This was the hard part. "You were leaving for summer training. We weren't talking. We weren't together."

"We weren't talking because you wouldn't talk to me."

I chuckled painfully. "What difference does that make? Our relationship was over."

Stephen closed his eyes to my words. Then he opened them with his. "I loved you. You knew that."

I shook my head. "No. I knew a video was circulating. That's what I knew. I also knew you were leaving. My father hated me. I was being tortured by the entire town and the entire Internet. That's what I knew."

He shook his head. "You knew who I was, from age six. You knew I wouldn't want you dealing with a pregnancy alone."

"I hated you." My lip trembled. "I hated you back then." Tears slipped down my cheeks. "You were being celebrated, and I was being vilified. Stop acting like you don't know what was going on."

Stephen groaned. "We've hashed this out already."

"Not in the context of Isaiah."

He was propelled to his feet again. He walked in my direction, closing the gap he'd opened between us. "Isaiah?"

I reached for my bag. I removed tissues and a small photo album. "Stephen Isaiah Ferguson." I extended the album.

He accepted it and sat with it. "You named him Stephen." Wonder filled his face. It almost hinted of a smile.

"No one calls him Stephen. We call him Isaiah."

Stephen took his time going through the pictures. Occasionally, he asked me about one and I told him what I knew. Unshed tears filled his eyes. "He looks like me."

"He does."

He shook his head. "I can't believe you kept him from me."

I shrugged. "You were going to college, Stephen. We had both worked so hard. We had scholarships. You wanted to play ball. I didn't want to take that away from you."

He closed the album and placed it on the table. "I don't understand why you would let me learn about my son from a reporter. Why didn't you tell me back when you first came home?"

I spoke on an exasperated wind. "It was complicated at first, but then I knew I had to tell. That was the reason I called you. This is what I wanted to talk about."

Stephen frowned. "Called me? When?"

"A little over a month ago. I left a message, and I sent you a note in the mail with a card."

Stephen chuckled bitterly. "Are you kidding? What, is the Illuminati conspiring against us? I didn't get a message from you and sure didn't get a note. Why are you lying?"

I rolled my neck. "Lying. I've never lied to you before in my life."

"Except when you didn't tell me I had a son," he practically snarled the words.

"Don't do that."

"Do what? Let me guess a secret and a lie are two different things, right?" He raised his finger and pointed like he wanted to jab it into my face. "Tamar, they're not, so from December 22nd up until today, you lied to me every time you talked to me."

I felt heat rush to my face. I crossed my arms. "Technically you don't have a son. Like I said, he's been adopted."

"If he's my flesh and bone, I will always have a son."

I jumped back and dropped my arms. His screamed could have shattered the windows.

"You should have told me."

The door to the townhouse flew open and I heard footsteps coming from the foyer. Robert and Donna Pierce entered the room. I cringed. This was about to get worse.

Chapter 19

"I always figured you were hiding something. I never thought it would be this." Donna frowned and began pacing the room. "How could you?"

"I made the best decision I could at the time."

Donna looked at Stephen and then her husband. Both men were mute, so she redirected her attention back to me. "Were you actually planning on letting the child grow up to manhood without his knowing his father and his grandparents?"

"I gave him up for adoption."

Donna's lip trembled. "Adoption."

"It's something unwed mothers do." I turned my head, refusing to look at her. Shame came down heavy.

"You sound like you've memorized a commercial for Planned Parenthood. Something unwed mothers do." She mocked me. "You could have brought him back to Pine from wherever the heck you went."

I shook my head. "No, I couldn't."

"You could have!"

Robert stepped in and placed his hands on his wife's shoulders. He'd been invisible until this moment, but now he was trying to calm her temper. It didn't work.

Donna continued. "We could have helped you, but you didn't give us a choice. You took our options away when you ran off."

I stood. "It wasn't your choice. It wasn't your pregnancy. He wasn't your baby. It wasn't your shame, or your burden. It was mine," I said. "I considered my options. I was not going to raise a child by myself with no money and no support. I was not coming back to Pine after you all ran me out of it. My son deserved better."

"We would have helped you," Donna screeched. "Stephen would have married you."

I chuckled cheerlessly. I hadn't been prepared emotionally for Stephen's anger, but for some reason I was ready for hers. "Oh yeah, right. The son that you spent ten years grooming for the four-year full ride that he got. The son that you dreamed would go to the NFL. That son would have stayed home, got a job in the mill, and helped me raise our son – with your blessing?"

Donna's nostril's flared. I knew she resented my strength. She always had. "He still could have gone to school. We would have made it work."

"No," I shook my head. "He wouldn't have gone to Freedom University. Not with a pregnant girlfriend. And Freedom was the only school that offered Stephen a full football scholarship. The truth would have ruined him."

Donna didn't respond. I looked at Mr. Pierce. He

turned his eyes away from mine. I glanced in Stephen's direction. He still looked disappointed, but he was thoughtful, just staring like for the first time he wanted to hear what I had to say. The Pierce's were silent. I'd shut them up, so I decided to have my say.

I swallowed and worked up my courage with repetitive nods of my head. "Look at how you live. Look at this house. Your house. Stephen's house in Pine. Your cars. Everything. You're *wealthy*." I enunciated every sound in the word.

"Back then, you were living in that tiny house and struggling to make ends meet like everyone else in Pine. I refuse to let you make me feel bad when what you want now is not what you would have wanted twelve years ago."

"How could you let strangers raise him?" Donna asked.

"He isn't with strangers," Stephen interjected. His parent's attention shifted to him. "He's with Tamar's aunt."

Donna's eyes widened. "An aunt adopted him?"

"Yes," I replied.

She closed her eyes and began to cry. "This is so unfair. You got to see him whenever you wanted. You stole this from us, your father, our son."

"I didn't see him all the time. I didn't even meet him until he was almost seven years old."

"Are you kidding? He was with your aunt. How could you not?"

"Mom," Stephen interjected.

I raised a hand to halt his words. "No, Stephen, it's okay. We need to have this conversation."

I gave my attention back to Donna. "It's true. Giving him up was the hardest thing I ever had to do in my life. I was glad he was with my aunt, and I did get updates about him, but I was trying to move on with my life without him. Without a memory of Stephen and the pain." I raised a hand to wipe my tears. "I was young."

Donna shook her head rapidly. "I still don't understand."

"Of course, you don't." I shrugged. "You've never been in my position."

"You don't know what I've been through, Tamar Johnson."

"I know you weren't nude in a YouTube video with millions of views."

Donna sneered. "Black women do not give their children up for adoption."

I sneered back at her. "Black women give children up for adoption every day."

Stephen moved a few steps. His body fell between us. "Mom, it's done. She's explained herself. I won't let you beat up on her."

Donna cocked her head and put her hands on her hips. "She has not explained herself to me. If she had any kind of a conscience, we wouldn't have found out about it today. Like this."

"Mom," Stephen said firmly. "You've said enough."

Donna took a deep breath and smiled at her son. It wasn't a pleasant smile. It was a nice-nasty, I'm disappointed in you, condescending smile. "She's always had you under some kind of spell. My God, can she not do anything to open your eyes to who she is?"

Stephen looked at me, compassion in his eyes for the first time today. "My God is the one who put me and Tamar together."

Donna walked across the room and removed tissue from a holder. She wiped under her eyes. "Believe what you want. I can't stomach this talk right now." She left the room.

Stephen's father pointed toward the album. "Are those pictures?"

"Yes, sir." I walked to the table where Stephen had placed the album, picked it up, and put it in his hand.

Robert opened it and slowly went through the pictures.

"He's a good-looking young man." He smiled. "He looks like you, son."

Stephen smiled back. "He does."

"Which means he looks like me." His father chuckled. "Let me go show this to your mother."

Stephen nodded.

Robert left the room.

I released the breath I'd been holding. "I'm sorry. I need to go. I need to go talk to my father."

"Right. He didn't know he had a grandchild until

this morning, either," Stephen said. Like the years gone by, silence filled the space between us. "I wish you had told me sooner."

"I didn't want to shake up my aunt's world. She's sick and then you got hurt. There were reasons."

Stephen shook his head. "None of them good enough, Tay."

I nodded. "They were my reasons. At this point, I don't expect anyone to understand." I reached for my bag and pulled out my phone. "Are we done for now?"

Stephen looked away from me. When he looked back, he asked. "I need to know when I'm going to meet him." His jaw tightened on every word.

"Soon. I'll call you tonight."

Stephen nodded again. "How are you getting to Pine?"

"I'm not going to Pine. My dad is in Philadelphia, so I'm going to Uber back to the airport and pick up a rental."

Stephen shook his head. "You don't have to do that. Take my other truck."

I didn't have to force appreciation into my voice. "That's generous of you, but I'm flying out of Philly."

He shrugged. "You can leave the car at the airport in Philly."

"Are you sure?"

"Of course, I'm sure. The question is, are you okay to drive?"

He was concerned about me. My heart fluttered. The heaviness lifted around my soul. It threw me for a moment and then I realized what he'd asked me. "I'm fine."

"Philly is a haul. I could call Pete. He can drive you."

"Pete." I was shocked he was back in Stephen's life. "I thought he was away."

"He was, but now he's my driver."

I shook my head. "There's no need. I'd rather drive myself. ."

"Text me the parking information after you leave the car and I'll have Pete pick it up."

Stephen walked to a table in the foyer, opened the drawer and removed a set of keys."

I looked him up and down now. He'd lost a few pounds, but he was still in good physical shape. "How's the ankle?"

"Getting better every day." He handed me the key.

"Will you be ready to play next season?"

"Training camp starts in July. I expect to be."

He didn't sound certain.

"I'm sure if you keep working, you'll be ready." I walked to the closet and removed my coat.

"How's Aunt Joe? Healthwise?"

"Chemo is hard. Really hard and then she had the surgery and more radiation and chemo. It's a lot."

"I'm sure it must be." He was genuinely sympathetic. "I'm sorry if I seemed insensitive to the fact that you were trying to spare her."

I shook my head. "You don't owe me an apology."

Tears welled in his eyes again. I hadn't seen that since my mother passed.

"I'm struggling with thinking about anyone else but myself right now. I can't believe I have an eleven-year-old son."

Silence.

"All these young boys I mentor with no fathers, and I have a son I don't know about. What did I do to deserve this?"

I swallowed and let him have his words.

"I'm the guy that would have been there."

I bit my lip and sighed before speaking. "I don't know what you want me to say."

He shook his head. "There's nothing you can say until you tell me when I can meet my son."

I felt a tear fall down my own face. I reached up and wiped it. "Yeah, so I'll text you after I leave the car."

I slid my coat on, picked up my handbag, and walked to the door.

I could hear Stephen's cane on the floor behind me. Once I reached the door to the garage, he reached around and opened it for me.

"The hard part's done," Stephen said.

"I guess, but your parents will—"

"Forgive you," he offered. He was so close his breath was like a whisper on my forehead. "My parents will forgive you and so will your father."

I waited for him to say what I wanted to hear. "And you?"

"I'm in shock right now. I can't think about anything until I meet him. If I can do that…" A tear trailed down his face. Before I knew it, I'd raised my hand, and wiped it away.

Stephen caught my hand before I lowered it. He looked at it like he was searching for something. He was probably glad it no longer held the ring he'd given me. He squeezed and then released it. "Drive carefully."

I nodded because I couldn't speak. I went down to the garage. Climbed into the other SUV Stephen had, opened the garage, and started the engine. After letting it run for a few minutes, I rolled out and drove out of the subdivision. I passed through the gate and by the reporters. Getting out of Stephen's subdivision was easy. The windows were tinted. They didn't know I was in the car, so they didn't even try to bother me.

I drove a few miles down the road and stopped. I'd been waiting for the right place to park. I pulled over so I could cry my heart out. He hated me just like I thought he would. Right now, I hated myself.

Chapter 20

I was grateful for two things, one that my father wasn't in Pine and two, he'd been in meetings all day, so he'd had his phone turned off and hadn't heard any of the news. Not that my father followed such, but still, he didn't know a thing until I told him.

The conversation was the one of the hardest I'd ever had with him. The only one more difficult had been the one we'd had on the day my mother died.

My father stared at the pictures of Isaiah. "So, he's twelve."

"He's eleven. He'll turn twelve next February."

"Why do I think I know where he is?"

"Because you know me."

He shook his head. "How's Stephen?"

"Shocked, but controlled."

"And the Pierce's?"

"They came to Stephen's house when I was there."

"How was that?"

"Intense." I closed my eyes against the memory.

"Don't be angry with Aunt Joe."

"Angry with Joe?" My father merely grunted. "I've never understood that woman. She's so unlike your mother."

"That's not true, Daddy."

My father jabbed a finger on the table for emphasis. "Your mother would not do this. She wouldn't keep a secret like this."

"She was trying to help me."

"You don't know the history, Tamar. Your aunt and I have never been family, and that's not my fault." My father visibly reeled in his emotions before saying, "I wish you'd come to me."

"I wasn't going to come home and embarrass you any more than I already had."

My father and I sat there saying nothing for a long time. He was processing the news. That was easy to see.

"This would have all been done so differently if your mother was alive."

"I know," I said through tears. "I keep thinking about that. She would have helped us through."

"You would have had her to talk to. You would have had her for all of it. I feel like I failed her with you."

"Daddy, don't. You didn't fail me.

Daddy's brow wrinkled. "You got in trouble and you ran to an aunt you hardly knew and gave your son up for adoption."

"To her."

"You still felt trapped and powerless. Our house should have been home for you."

"We've talked about this before. We're not going to rehash it."

"It's not rehashing. I have to grieve this and forgive myself all over again because I didn't know all that I'd done." He banged a fist on the table.

I stood. "I won't let you beat yourself up. I'm doing that enough for everybody."

My phone rang the unique tone for Stephen. I removed it from my pocket.

"Take your call," Daddy said. "I need to cancel a counseling session for tonight. I want us to have dinner."

"Don't cancel," I said, sending the call to voicemail. "I have to get back to Yancy. My flight leaves in two hours. Aunt Joe needs me, and I need to figure out this meeting with Stephen and Isaiah."

"I can't wait to meet him myself. A grandson." Daddy's eyes shimmered with pride. He reached for my hand. "Are you sure you're okay? I don't want you going through this alone. I can come down there with you."

"I'm not alone. Aunt Joe is really good to me."

Daddy's knit brow indicated he was thinking on that, but he said, "I'm glad to hear you two are close. How is she feeling about Stephen being in Isaiah's life?"

"She says she knew the day would come when

she'd have to share him." I shrugged. "She's okay with it."

Daddy's frown deepened.

"What is it?"

"She's raised him for eleven years. No one would be okay with this kind of thing." He shook his head. "I wonder about her condition. Is your aunt sicker than you know?"

***

I could hardly breathe. My chest felt constricted for the entire ride from the hotel where my father was, to the airport parking lot.

Aunt Joe sicker than I know? I didn't even want to consider the possibility. *I know everything. Don't I?*

My father's word troubled me. I revisited the conversation with Aunt Joe over and over again. Why was she being so easy about this? Did she think she was going to die? I couldn't bear to lose her.

My cell rang in another call from Stephen.

I answered. "Hey, sorry, I was talking to my father."

"No problem. I wanted to make sure I got you before you boarded the plane."

"Why? What's up?"

"I need to know what airport I'm flying into."

I squinted. "I don't understand."

"Your aunt. Is she near Macon or Albany? I need to book a flight for tomorrow. What airport is it?"

"I said we would talk tonight."

"We'll talk right now. I want to meet my son, and I'm not willing to wait." His words were icy, but they managed to burn my heart.

"Can I at least tell him about this?"

"You can do whatever you need to do, but I want to meet him this weekend."

More coldness. I shrank. "Wow. I wasn't expecting this."

"I wasn't expecting to be a father." It was clear that Stephen had gone from shocked to angry in the hours since I'd left him. "Another thing. I talked to my attorney."

"That wasn't necessary."

"Are you kidding? I have a lawyer on retainer. Why wouldn't I talk to him?"

"I'm not your enemy, Stephen. We're not fighting here."

"I have rights."

"Of course, you do."

"I have more than you think." He was silent for a moment. So was I. "I never sighed away my paternal rights."

"One minute, you're defending me to your mother and the next, you're talking to your attorney."

"My mother was doing too much. As for the

lawyer, I'm being smart. I have a will, a trust, and a foundation. I have money. If I have a child, I need to shift things and that has to happen right away."

Stephen's bark was as bad as his bite right now. I wanted off the phone with him. "The airport is Albany. Let me know when your flight comes in and I'll pick you up."

"I'll get an Uber."

"There's no Uber service to where she lives." I sighed. "Please don't make this hostile between us."

"I'm not trying to make it hostile. I'm trying to keep the lines clear. I don't want..." he paused. "You have a way of weakening me when I need to be strong."

"I can't tell."

"That's because you've been too busy with your secrets to see." Stephen cleared his throat. "The city? Hotels nearby? I'm blind here."

"The town is Yancy. There's a Marriot about four miles from my aunt's house. There aren't many hotels, so I'd say that's going to be the closest one. I'll text you the address."

"Thanks. Have a good flight."

He ended the call. I stared at the phone.

What just happened?

Chapter 21

"He wants to meet him tomorrow." I ended my summary of the day's events with Stephen's final declaration.

Aunt Joe took in a sharp breath. "That doesn't give us much time, but I can't blame him. What's his lawyer saying?"

"I didn't ask him. He wasn't being friendly. I didn't want to get into it with him."

"They'll say you lied about the paternity. Which you did when you listed 'unknown' on the birth certificate. That was bad advice from me."

"Advice I was more than willing to take." I sighed.

"The bottom line is, Stephen never signed away his rights. That matters, even after all these years – plus he has money. People with money can get things done." Aunt Joe paused to catch her breath. "I talked to my lawyer today. He made sure I understood that."

"You called your lawyer?"

Aunt Joe cocked her head. "I called mine for the same reason Stephen called his. That's what you do in these situations."

"So, you're saying he can challenge the adoption."

"He can and he'd probably win." Aunt Joe smiled. I thought it was an odd time for that. She shook her head. "He may want to take Isaiah away from me, but he won't take him from you."

"I'm not so sure. Those lost years – he's stuck there. I can't give them back."

"That ring he put on your finger is more than enough proof that he loves you enough not to really hurt you. He's angry, Tamar. Nothing more and nothing less. That's to be expected. But anger passes. He'll come here. Meet his son. See what a great child he is, and we'll let him know he can see him all he wants. It'll be okay."

"Auntie, I can't believe you're being so easy about this."

Aunt Joe stood. I heard every bone in her body crack when she did so. "I'm exhausted. I don't have the energy to worry about a problem I don't have yet. I'm going to bed. You pray about how you want to tell Isaiah."

"Me? We're not doing it together?"

"Isaiah knows he's adopted, so at this point, this is between you and him. I'll let you handle it. Tomorrow after school. Stephen will be here by then. You can explain it all to him at one time. He'll want to know who his daddy is anyway."

"If you're sure."

"I'm sure."

I stood and gave Aunt Joe a hug. Her body was

frail. I'd been staring at her since I got home – looking for signs that she was getting healthier when in fact all I could see was failing health. Weight loss, thinning hair, her skin was pocked. She was tired. She wouldn't eat. She had those sores in her mouth.

I closed my eyes to my thoughts. Those were just side effects of the chemo. They weren't signs that it was failing. I'd let my father's words get in my head. He wasn't here. He wasn't talking to Aunt Joe. He didn't know what I knew. She was not contemplating her death. Aunt Joe fully expected to recover.

The next day, Stephen arrived a little after one. That was early enough for me to pick him up from the airport and get back to the house before Isaiah got out of school, but it was just early enough. We barely had time to talk before I heard the school bus coming down the street. I stashed Stephen in my bedroom. He agreed I could talk to Isaiah first and then he would.

I was sweating like a bull by the time Isaiah entered the house.

"Hey, Cousin Tamar," he said walking into the kitchen and opening the refrigerator for a bottle of water and an apple.

My nerves entered my voice. "How was school?"

"I got an A on my science test."

"I'm not surprised," I said.

"I gotta tell Mama," he said. "Where is she?"

"She's sleeping. She's tired today."

"I'm glad you're here then. She seems better when you're around." He walked out of the kitchen and went to his bedroom.

I followed. "What are you doing?"

"I'm going to play a video game. I can on Fridays. No homework."

I nodded. "Can I ask you to come out here for a minute? I need to talk to you."

He looked concerned. "Is it about my mama?"

"No. It's something different, but it's important though so the video game needs to wait."

Isaiah came out of his bedroom and joined me at the dining room table. I thought about Stephen standing on the other side of the door and felt the pressure of his listening. This was going to be hard enough without an audience.

"What I have to say is going to surprise you. It might even upset you, but I hope you'll let me explain and try to have an open mind."

"Okay, but you looked worried."

"I'm not worried, but it's going to be a big surprise for you." I took a deep breath. "You know how Auntie adopted you when you were a baby?"

"Yes."

"Well, she adopted you from me. I'm your birth mother."

Isaiah's eyes widened. His jaw unhinged. He processed my words for a minute and then asked, "Why didn't you tell me before?"

"Because it's complicated. I know that sounds like

an adult not wanting to tell the truth, but I was really young when I had you. I couldn't take care of you. I had no money. No job. I didn't even have a place to live. I was going through a bad time in my life."

"What kind of bad time?"

"You know I told you about how I had that experience when I was in high school when I was bullied."

Isaiah nodded. I hadn't told him about the video, but I'd told him about how I was teased. "It was then. I was sad and crying all the time. I didn't have the strength to take care of anyone. I could barely take care of myself. Aunt Joe offered to take you. I needed to know you would be safe, so I decided it was a good idea."

Isaiah looked away from me. His brow knitted like he was confused. I resisted interfering with his process. He needed time to wrap his mind around everything I was saying. He shook his head and looked at me again. "Why didn't you tell me before now?"

My mouth felt dry. It was the incessant question about why I'd waited so long. Why so many years with no real good answer for Stephen, our parents, or now Isaiah. I stammered over my answer. "I think at first to honor your mom and then I don't know. It never seemed like the right time."

"I asked her who my mother was. She said some young woman, like she didn't know."

"I'm sure she was trying to protect me."

"I don't understand. Everybody is protected but me. I'm not being protected. Why are kids the only ones that have to tell the truth?"

"Isaiah, you've never asked me who your mother was."

"But I call you Cousin Tamar."

"And I let you because technically, I am your cousin. Adoption is legal and permanent."

Isaiah got a faraway look in his eyes and then he turned back to me. "So, then if you're my mother, you know who my father is."

The door opened to my bedroom. I closed my eyes. This wasn't what we'd discussed. He was supposed to wait until I came for him, but I was glad. I was glad he was coming to take the focus off of me.

"I am," Stephen said.

Isaiah frowned. He didn't have to turn around because he was facing my door. He squinted and then snatched his head back. "You're Stephen Pierce."

With his cane clanking on the wood flooring in the corridor, Stephen approached the table where we were sitting.

Isaiah looked at me. "My father is Stephen Pierce?"

The question split my heart in two. I looked between him and Stephen. I whispered a broken, "Yes."

Stephen's eyes were on Isaiah like he was inspecting every inch of him. He was fighting tears. I could see that. I watched as his Adam's apple went up and down and up and down again. He took slow controlled breaths. I did this to him. I did this to my son.

Isaiah frowned. "Did you know you were my father?"

Stephen shook his head. "I found out yesterday."

Isaiah looked at me. His frowned turned to a scowl. "Why didn't he know?"

"Isaiah, I'm sorry," I said. "I'm sorry I—"

"Tamar." Stephen rarely called me by my name. It was odd hearing it. It was painful hearing it in the tone he was using. "Why don't you let us talk for a moment?"

I nodded, but I was afraid to leave the room. I was also anxious to escape the room. What would Stephen say about me? He didn't understand my actions. How could he explain them to Isaiah? Would he even try?

I picked up my phone and stood. "I'll go outside."

Stephen nodded and I rushed out the door. On the other side, I fell against it. I tried to stop my heart from pounding. I pushed the self-hate messages out of my head.

I did the best I could at the time.

"God, please help everyone to forgive me."

***

I couldn't believe the resemblance. My son was a cloned copy of me at that age. He was even a little chubby like I was.

"You play for the New York Giants."

"I'm a running back."

"Starting running back. You're famous."

I smiled. We were off to a good start. "I am pretty well known."

"You got hurt in the Super Bowl. Is that why you have that boot and cane?"

"Yep." I propped the cane against the table and took a seat. "I've had a few surgeries, and I'm going through rehab."

"Are you going to be able to play again?"

"Oh, for sure. I mean one injury don't stop me."

"I like the Falcons," Isaiah teased.

I smiled again. He had my sense of humor. "I bet if you go to a few Giants games, you can like us too."

Isaiah's eyes widened. "Cool, so I could go to your games?"

"Definitely, we'll make sure you go to some games," I said. "Look, Isaiah, we have plenty of time to talk about football. I want to get to know you. I was your father before I ever became a famous football player. I just didn't know it."

Isaiah nodded. "Can I ask you a question?"

"You can ask me anything."

"Why didn't you know Cousin Tamar, was having

a baby?"

"Because we broke up and she left our hometown. I went to college, and I never talked to her again until right before Christmas of last year."

"How did you talk to her at Christmas?"

"We both attended our high school reunion."

"So, she didn't tell you about me then?"

I shrugged. "She was kind of waiting for the right time."

"Are you mad at her?" Concern creased Isaiah's forehead.

Was I angry with Tamar? Of course, I was. I had to be. I wasn't even sure right now. I was still in shock. Isaiah was too young for all this grown up business, so I kept it to myself.

"I think disappointed is the right word. I'm disappointed I didn't get to know you sooner."

"I don't even know how to feel. I think I'm mad." He released a long breath. "But I don't want to be. I don't like being mad."

"You don't have to be upset with Tamar. You can feel confused or even disappointed, but you don't have to be angry."

"Grown-ups always tell us not to story and then they do."

I squinted. "Story?"

"I'm not allowed to say lie, sir."

I nodded. It must be an Aunt Joe rule. "Look,

Isaiah, the thing is that your mother is a good person. She made a young person's decision. I can't just blame her for what happened. Not really. Your mom was – is an important person to me. If I had pushed harder back then to find her and see what was up with her, I would have discovered she was pregnant. You can't hide that. So, there were mistakes all around."

Isaiah clasped his fingers together and made a fist on the table. "Do you have any other kids?"

"No."

"Do you like kids?"

"I do. I work with a lot of boys your age in my charity. I can show you some pictures if you want."

Isaiah sat. I pulled up my Instagram page and showed him pictures from my different events. "I really hate that I didn't get to know you all those years, but I'm glad that I get to know you now." My eyes filled with tears.

"My first name is Stephen."

My heart warmed. If Tamar did something right, it was his name. "I know. I'm proud of that."

"Everyone calls me Isaiah though. Do you want to call me Stephen?"

"I'll call you whatever you want to be called."

"I'm used to Isaiah. I like it."

I held up my fist for a pound. "Isaiah is a great name."

My son pounded back. Then he touched my fist. "You have big hands. I always wanted a strong dad. I always wondered if he was big like Mom says I'm going to be."

"Being big runs in our family. My dad, your grandfather is a pretty big man, too. He wants to meet you soon."

"I have a grandfather?"

"You have two."

Isaiah's eyes got big. He stared off for a moment and then when he looked back at me a half mile played on his lips. "That's cool, like I'm getting a whole new family or something."

"Cousins too," I added.

His smile was a full one now. I bit back resentment. He'd been robbed just as much as I had.

Isaiah and I continued to talk about family. I showed him family photos I had uploaded to my phone. I told him about the party I was planning for him in Pennsylvania where he would come up and meet everybody and then we talked about his life here in Yancy.

"I play baseball," Isaiah said. "I've been playing since I was five. I have trophies. You want to see them?"

"I sure do."

We both stood and went into his bedroom. He showed me his trophies and cups and toys and books. He showed me everything that had meaning to him. It was easy to see he was a well-adjusted, happy, child, just like Tamar said. But still I'd lost so much it was hard to just be grateful in this moment.

The Holy Spirit pushed a thought into my head.

You have him now.

Was that supposed to be good enough?

I glanced out Isaiah's window and spotted Tamar pacing back and forth under a tree in front of the house. I'd surprised myself when I said I'd failed her. While trying to protect her, I guess I'd been honest. But eleven years was a long time to miss out. His first words, his first steps, his first day of school, his first baseball game, first hit. I missed all the firsts. I resented it, but I couldn't rewind the hands of time. I was going to have to create more firsts.

Chapter 22

Tamar and I took Isaiah out to dinner. I didn't exactly want to include her, but she was driving, so rather than ask her to chauffer, I asked her to join us. I wanted to spend time with my son – alone. I deserved that.

But once we got to the restaurant, I was glad I'd allowed her to come along. Isaiah forgave her easily. I needed to see that. I was also glad to see how easy they interacted with each other.

But the dinner wasn't without incident. A local reporter approached out table and asked if he could have a quick interview.

"I'd appreciate it if you respected my privacy," I said.

"Just one or two," the reported insisted.

"Stephen," Tamar called my name. She slid her eyes in Isaiah's direction and whispered tightly, "Doesn't need this."

I nodded and got out of the booth. She was right. This guy wasn't going away. All I needed was for him to ask some inappropriate question.

"I just want a quote to go with the picture I

took," the reporter said. "Who would have thought your son was in Yancy? My luck."

"Look man, don't mistake this cane for a weakness." I flexed every muscle in my upper body. "Ask your questions and don't come back to my table, or you won't be what anyone would consider lucky."

Fear flashed in his eyes. He cleared his throat and said, "Sorry, Mr. Pierce, we don't get many celebrity stories down here."

"Ask your question," I repeated.

He did. He asked respectful questions and promised to publish a gentle piece. He even showed me the picture he'd taken of Isaiah and I sharing laughter and a pound across the table.

We finished our dinner in peace, but I realized this was not the time for me to take advantage of photo ops. I needed my privacy and so did my son. I might need a hat and dark glasses for my trips out with him.

"I don't know what to call you," Isaiah said to Tamar as we entered the house.

Tamar stroked his shoulder. "You can call me whatever you want."

"As long as it has a good 'Ma'am on it, it'll be fine," a voice, I presumed Aunt Joe's, called out from the kitchen. I closed the door and followed Tamar in.

Aunt Joe was a petite woman. I imagined she'd be bigger – savior size – since that was what Tamar made her out to be. She was noticeably frail. Her skin was blotchy and drawn, and she looked older than a woman in her mid-fifties. It was her eyes that aged her. She had deep, dark circles under them. She looked tired. She wore a scarf. I wondered if she'd lost her hair.

"How was dinner?" she asked, putting an arm around Isaiah's shoulder.

"It was good. We had shrimp and crabs." His eyes got as big as saucers like they had when they brought his food to the table. "Cousin Tamar brought you a salmon dinner."

Tamar raised the takeout bag, and Aunt Joe accepted it.

"Ah, the Fish House," she said. "I'm going to have to say yes the next time you all invite me to dinner."

"It would be our pleasure to have you, ma'am," I said.

Aunt Joe and I exchanged a smile. She raised a hand to Isaiah's chin. "It's late. How about you go take your shower? You can tell me more when you get out."

Isaiah nodded obediently and left to go toward his bedroom.

Aunt Joe came from around the kitchen counter and through the door. She raised her hand for a shake. "I'm Josephine Ferguson."

We shook. "Stephen Pierce."

"Nice to meet you." She smiled like she meant it. "Can I get you something?"

"No, I'm fine. We just..." Tamar made a jerky head movement that distracted me. I could tell she was trying to hide her face, but even from her profile, I could see she was fighting tears. Her bottom lip was trembling. I pushed out the desire to comfort her. God, she made me so weak. I gave Aunt Joe my attention again. "I don't need anything. We just ate, ma'am."

"I've heard a lot about you Stephen. Let's take a seat."

We all sat. Aunt Joe smiled like she was greeting some friends from church to discuss a fundraising event. "Did you get a chance to look at the photo album?"

"I did. I appreciate you putting it together."

"I've been putting it together for years," she said, pushing back into the sofa. "I figured putting it together along the way was going to be easier than pulling out a bunch of pictures and doing it at once." She prattled on nervously. "I knew this day would eventually come."

"Interesting," I said. "I didn't."

"Well, of course you didn't." Aunt Joe smiled curtly. "But we're here now."

I released a breath. I felt uncomfortable with her dismissing my loss, but I wasn't going to blame her. She wasn't the one who had my baby.

"How did the talk go?" she asked Tamar.

Tamar looked at me for a second and then gave her aunt her attention when she responded. "It went good. As well as it could go. He was surprised. He wants to meet his grandparents and cousins."

"Ice cream made it better," I offered. They weren't going to exclude me. "We went to...what was the name?"

"Topos," Tamar said.

"Oh yes, the designer burgers and milkshake that cost a fortune," Aunt Joe said. "He went once with the baseball team when they won a few years ago and had leftover money from a donation. I make hamburgers just fine and then there's the occasional trip to Wendy's."

A quiet space filled the room. I took in the modest house again. It reminded me of the house I grew up in. It was a little smaller. Small house, no fancy meals. That wouldn't have been the life my son would have had with me, but he was a nice kid. Aunt Joe obviously gave him what he needed. Still, I felt cheated.

"A reporter approached us at the restaurant," Tamar said.

Aunt Joe frowned. "Really? From the *Yancy Times*?"

"It's going to be a problem for a while," I said. "Isaiah won't be able to ride the school bus. He should be driven."

Aunt Joe and Tamar exchanged a look.

I cleared my throat. "And reporters can be pretty aggressive. The man I talked to this evening was a nice guy, but once folks roll down here from Atlanta and other places around the country, they won't be so nice."

Aunt Joe frowned again. "Around the country?"

"Yes," Tamar said. "Believe me, it'll happen. Free-lancers, in particular, will do anything to get a photo or some exclusive footage."

"With that said," I interrupted, "I've have hired a security person for Isaiah. He can also be the person to take him to school."

"Security?" Aunt Joe frowned.

I continued. "I really don't like the idea of Isaiah attending an unsecured school, but the year is almost over. I don't want to disrupt anything, but we'll have to —"

"Stephen," Tamar said. "One thing at a time."

I took a deep breath and sat back.

"My head is spinning," Aunt Joe said. "I didn't think this would be such big news."

"It shouldn't be. But it is," I said.

We all sat silent for a moment.

"Stephen, do you have anything you want to ask me?" Aunt Joe's voice pulled me from my thoughts about how this school arrangement would never do.

I cleared my throat before answering. If I had questions, they were stuck in my chest right now. I was still trying to get over the shock of having a son. Even though I'd met him, I wasn't there yet. "Not right this minute."

"Tamar says you've talked to your lawyer."

I cleared my throat. "I did. He called me when he heard the story."

Tamar frowned. "I thought you called him."

I looked at her for a long moment before speaking. "I didn't say that. I told you I talked to him."

"Anything I need to know?" Aunt Joe asked. "I mean, I'd like for us to be family."

I held back a grunt. So, we were going to be family when it was convenient for them. Bitterness froze my heart. I let out a frustrated sigh to release some of it. I shook my head. "I talked to him mostly about my will. I didn't see any need for much else at this time."

Aunt Joe nodded uncomfortably, then she stood. "Well, if you don't mind. I'm going to go and check on Isaiah. I heard the water stop. That was a quick shower for a boy going through puberty."

I stepped out of her path and watched her leave us. The cane made a clicking sound on the hard wood as she went down the hall. How odd that she and I were both on canes. I couldn't shake the symbolism – us finding each other at the lowest points in our lives.

My gaze settled on Tamar. She stuck her hands in her pocket and chuckled before saying, "That was a fast shower."

"Puberty?" I sighed. "Is he going through puberty?"

"I guess so. He's the right age."

I closed my eyes for a moment. When I opened them, I shot her an icy glare. "What do you know for sure, Tay?"

The peace that had been her countenance slipped away instantly. "I know my Aunt's been sick. I've been here, but I didn't think to ask him if he was having wet dreams."

"A father would think it."

Tamar shook her head. "I'm sorry. I'm sorry I let you down. I'm sorry you're just meeting him. I'm sorry I waited to tell you. I'm sorry about everything, Stephen." She began to cry.

I let my eyes wander around the room. I wanted to look at anything but her and those tears. I wanted to punish her, but I didn't want to see her cry.

"Where's the Range Rover?" I barked.

Tamar reached for a tissue from the box in front of her. "It's in Atlanta."

"Why aren't you driving it?"

"I don't drive it down here."

"I gave it to you," I said, like we both didn't know it.

"You gave me a $30,000 ring too. I'm not wearing that either."

I shook my head. "You think that's all your ring cost?"

Tamar bit her lip before speaking. "I wasn't counting your money."

"I never said you were."

Tamar stood. She walked around to the back of the chair she'd been in and gripped the top of it. "What are you getting at? The car? What are we talking about?"

"The least you could do is drive it. My son could be in a Range Rover."

"Is that what he needs?"

"No, that's what I've earned for him." I raised a hand to wipe my face. "At least you could enjoy the spoils of your labor."

Tamar grimaced, and her fist went to her hip. "What's that supposed to mean?"

"You made sure I went to college on my football scholarship. You helped me to be the success I am today, so I could spend a fortune on a fiancé."

Tamar rolled her neck. "What am I a witch? I knew you were going to the NFL. I knew one day we'd meet again, and I could benefit from my decision to let you go to college? Is that the fiction you've spun in your imagination?"

I sighed. "You know what, Tay. I don't know anything. All I know is I lost eleven years."

"I can't give them back. I can't even give back the last few months, but trust me, I know about losing years. I know how painful it is. So, I'm going to tell you like you told me when you didn't know how hard it was for me after the video – I'm sorry. I didn't know my choices would affect you this way."

"So, this was revenge? Is that what you were thinking when you didn't tell me you were pregnant? Was this your way of getting even with me for uploading the video I didn't actually upload?"

Tamar dropped her hand from her hip. I watched the fight go out of her. "You couldn't possibly think that."

I refused to say anything that would make her feel

better. "I don't know what to think."

"Stephen, I was just a pregnant teenager with no money and no man. It wasn't like that. It wasn't even that deep."

I didn't know how to feel right now. I needed to be away from her. "Would you take me to my hotel? I want to stretch my leg out, and I need to get out of here." I moved to the door.

Just when I put my hand on the knob I heard, "Dad?" I turned.

Isaiah was standing behind me. "Will I see you tomorrow?"

I hobbled back to him. "Yeah, I'm going to be here until Sunday."

Isaiah wrapped his arms around my waist and gave me a squeeze. "I'm glad I met you."

The ice in my heart melted a little. "I'm glad I met you too, son." I rested a hand on top of his head and put the other around his shoulders.

Tamar's red eyes looked from him to me. They held so much sorrow. Genuine pain.

I wanted to punish her, and I was succeeding. But in succeeding, I'd already forgotten Isaiah was here. I was about to leave without saying goodbye.

"I'll see you in the morning," I said. "We can have breakfast before the game."

"Cool," Isaiah said. "My team will meet you!"

I nodded.

"Come on now," Aunt Joe interjected. "Your daddy looks tired." She placed her a hand on Isaiah's shoulders and directed him toward his bedroom. She looked back to me and said, "We'll see you in the morning."

"Good night, ma'am." I force a smile I didn't feel.

They went down the hall to his bedroom.

Tamar and I stood there looking at each other for a moment. Both our pain palpable in the room, but neither of us had words to make it better.

"After you," I said.

Tamar picked up her bag, and we left the house.

The car was filled with silence on the way back to the hotel. I remembered the last time Tamar and I drove in silence. It was right before the reunion in December. I was desperate to speak to her, but she was angry with me. Was that how she was feeling now? Desperate to speak to me, but my anger was keeping her words inside?

"I appreciate tonight," I said. I was careful to make sure I wasn't snarky. I'd been nasty enough.

She took her eyes off the road for a moment to steal a peek at me. "It went well."

"I appreciate the ride and everything."

She didn't respond.

"Look, Tay, I shouldn't have –"

"Don't worry about it," she cut me off. "I didn't expect this to be easy."

"I don't have to make it harder."

She pulled into the parking space in front of my room. "You're entitled to your feelings. This isn't an easy situation."

"It's not," I said. "But I'm trying."

"Don't worry. I can take it. I'm pretty tough." She didn't look at me when she said that. She stared straight ahead like she was digging into her internal reserve for more resilience.

I was convicted. I wasn't supposed to be toughening her up. That wasn't what a man did to any woman. He certainly didn't do it to a woman he loved.

I looked at her profile. I loved her. Maybe that was a part of my frustration. She'd had my child, and she still didn't love me enough to fight for us.

"Do you need me to get you anything before I go back to the house?" Tamar half turned her head in my direction. "There's a big convenience store up the road. They have pretty much everything."

"No, I'm good." I said. "Tay—"

Tamar didn't look at me. She raised a hand to her lips and closed her eyes. "I have nothing left, Stephen. I'm emotionally spent, so let's call it a night."

I didn't know what I was going to say anyway. I pulled on the handle and got out of the car. "Breakfast tomorrow."

"I'll text you when we're on the way."

I backed away from the car. She pulled out of the space and sped as quickly as she could out of the parking lot.

Conviction came down on me. Heavy. Just months ago, I wanted her to forgive me for her years of pain and now I wouldn't forgive her for the same. I was feeling like a hypocrite.

I booked a car service online and spent the rest of the weekend being chauffeured around. Fitting into Tamar's small car was difficult with my leg. I also didn't want to spend every minute of the next two days looking into those big, brown eyes of hers.

I'd been fighting to push down my feelings for her since she broke up with me, but now being this close was making everything bubble back up to the surface. Rejection was the last thing I needed. I was already fighting my body. I didn't need to fight with her, too.

I didn't leave Yancy until the bodyguard I'd hired arrived and was in place to protect my son. I was glad I had acted quick on that, because by Sunday, there were four reporters camped out on Aunt Joe's street. The picture the reporter had taken in the restaurant was released on Saturday and had been duplicated hundreds of times all over blogs and social media. I was trending. Again.

Even triflin' Debra chimed in on Twitter with:

Pierce fertility ain't for play-play, ladies. All he needs is one shot. #potent

The following week was a three-day weekend from school for Isaiah, so I had Tamar bring him to Pennsylvania. My parents and I drove to Pine. Isaiah got to meet our parents and cousins and see where we grew up.

Tamar didn't join us for the visits. By now, the entire town knew she'd had a baby back in the day, and she was uncomfortable with the stares and questions, or at least that's what she said.

I had to be back for therapy on Monday, so my parents and I were heading back to New Jersey Sunday night. Before we left, I asked Tamar if she and I could talk.

I entered Tamar's father's house. Isaiah was in the kitchen playing checkers with her father.

Tamar and I were quiet. Neither of us knew what to say, but I asked for the time, so I broke the ice. "They enjoyed getting to know him."

She nodded. "He told me all about it. I'm sorry I didn't hang out with you all this weekend. I really felt the weight of their disappointment. I could see it in their eyes. The lost time. It was hard enough dealing with it with you."

"Is that the real reason you stayed holed up this weekend?"

"What else would it be?"

"Everybody else," I asked.

"Well, we know I'm never not going to be the subject of gossip here, but no. I feel bad. About everybody. My father. Your parents. I never thought about where this could go. I just didn't."

"Our parents will be okay."

Tamar's eyes were filled with tears that were

bursting to spill down her cheeks. "This is their grandchild they missed out on," she said. "We're both only children. What if there are no more grandchildren?"

I chuckled. "Hold up. First of all, I'm having some more children. We need to get that out in the heavenly reproductive realm right now."

Tamar cracked a hint at a smile. "And you're not talking about Debra's little saint?"

"Girl, don't play. Ain't nobody talking about that unfortunate child that crazy woman is carrying."

Tamar cleared her throat. "Well, that solves the more grandchildren issue for your parents. I can't say the same for my dad."

She sucked the air right out of my lungs. I'd thought about our children so much before the breakup. In my mind, we had a short engagement, got married, and pregnant almost immediately. That was the dream. I'd shared it with her, but she'd clearly moved on from it. I wasn't ready to let her go.

"What's second of all?" she asked.

I'd been caught up in my thoughts. She could tell I hadn't heard her, so she repeated herself.

Tamar needed me to absolve her of blame. I could feel her need, so instead of saying the silly thing I was going to say, I said, "I was thinking, I can't speak for your dad, but my parent's only child should have done better."

Tamar cocked her head. "What do you mean?"

"Tay, I owe you two dollars right now."

Tamar's mouth slid into an easy smile, so did mine. It felt good to lighten the mood. "I haven't heard that in a while," she said.

"Maybe that's part of our problem." I hesitated for a moment, nostalgia filling my heart. "Do you remember the first time I offered to pay you to talk to me?"

She pursed her lips. "Of course, I do. We were twelve and it was over gym class."

"Yeah, and I made you mad because I picked Billy Rogers to be on my team for kickball instead of you."

Tamar put a hand on her hip. "That was unforgivable. You forced me to play on Angie Smith's team. I couldn't stand her, and you knew it."

My mind went back to that. "You didn't talk to me for a week. I had to fix it. You were my best friend." I remembered how I offered her a dollar if she would talk to me, and she did. Then I was able to apologize. Every time I made her angry, I offered her money to break the ice. By the time we got to high school, I was up to two dollars because my offenses were more serious.

"So," she said breaking through my thoughts, "what have you done now?"

I released a deep breath before saying, "This situation with our parents is my fault, too. I'm the reason they don't know their grandson and so are they." I paused. Tamar's expression was unreadable. She cut her eyes away from mine and then back like she was struggling with her emotions.

"You were right. All of them would have freaked if they'd known you were pregnant. None of it would have been handled well. You knew that. Even if I struggled to admit it and even though I hate that I missed knowing my son – back then it would have been a nightmare. My parents would have tripped. Your father wouldn't have been much better."

Tamar hung her head for a moment.

I lifted her chin. "Aside from that, I'm not letting anyone disrespect you or make you feel bad. You're the mother of my child. You made sure he was safe and taken care of. You made sure he had love, even if it wasn't mine. You could have had an abortion. You could have given him up in a sealed adoption. You could have done a lot of things, but you protected him. I love you for that. Do you understand me? I love you for the choice you made."

Tamar was visibly shook. "I didn't think you would ever forgive me. I didn't expect it to happen so fast."

"That wouldn't make me a very good Christian would it?"

Her lips crooked into a half smile. "All people of faith have their limits."

"Our limits may be tested, but we don't have limits," I said. "If God can tell us to love our enemies and those that spitefully use us, how much more do we owe our family and friends? I should have at least tried to see it from your perspective. I didn't. I'm sorry."

Tamar shook her head. "I don't know what to think."

"But you knew last Christmas when you forgave me. You said, God could make the relationship between us new. He could restore what we lost."

Tamar nodded.

"He can do the same for my relationship with Isaiah and for his relationship with my parents. That's the word of God. I was a little slow to get here, but I'm standing on it and believing all of this was for a purpose."

Tamar nodded again right before the tears she'd been fighting came rushing down her face. She wept hard, like her belly was filled with her hurt. I sat next to her and held her until she cried it all out.

When she was done, she took a wad of tissues from a holder and wiped her eyes.

"I think you probably cried enough to raise the water level in every creek in Pine," I said.

She smiled a little. Her puffy, red eyes needed that smile. "Thank you for telling me all that."

"I'm sorry I didn't realize it before." I stood. "It's late. I have to report to the team meeting and PT."

Tamar stood too. "I understand. Go. I'm fine."

"Can I ask you one more thing though?"

"Sure."

"Why did you name him Isaiah?"

She released a breath and said, "I was sad the entire pregnancy. Scared and alone most of the time. Especially when I was at school. I had to hide it and then at the end of my first semester I withdrew and came to stay with Aunt Joe. I hid out there."

I nodded for her to go on.

"My mother loved the scripture, Isaiah 41:10. 'Fear not, for I *am* with you; Be not dismayed, for I *am* your God. I will strengthen you. Yes, I will help you. I will uphold you with My righteous right hand.' I read it over and over again until I memorized it.

"I was scared. I needed God to keep me strong and to help me. I needed him so much. That was my prayer. I memorized it. As you can see, I still know it." She bit her lip. "I already knew I wanted to name him Stephen. I felt like I owed both of you that, but I wanted him to have his own identity - separate from you. Isaiah felt right. He'd heard me speak those words over and over when he was in my womb."

My emotions were thick. I was reflective for a long time. "That's beautiful."

Tamar smiled again. "It wasn't all bad. I love him. I loved him so much, Stephen. I was broken and hurt and —"

I took the steps necessary to close the space between us, pulled her into my arms, and after hesitating for a moment, I kissed her. Not a peck, but a long kiss. The kind I'd been wanting since she crushed my heart.

And she let me have it. She let me have all her sweetness.

Tamar broke the kiss by pulling away from me. We stood there for a long moment staring at each other. I wanted to kiss her again – and again and again, but if I started, I would never want to leave.

I thought back to our conversation before I got injured. Tamar didn't want me and my Debra drama. She was just vulnerable right now. I released her hand and stepped away from her. "Thank you for taking care of him."

She seemed rattled. Her voice cracked when she said, "Drive safe, Stephen."

I fought the urge to tell her I loved her. It was just a kiss. There was no point in putting myself out there again. I nodded, turned, and left her father's house.

Chapter 23

Isaiah and I stopped in Atlanta before heading back to Yancy. I wanted Kim to meet him. I also wanted to show Isaiah my home. I knew Aunt Joe had help, so I didn't feel like we had to rush.

We were at Dave and Busters. They had great burgers for Kim and me, and video games for Isaiah. He enjoyed the food, but he liked the video games more. He inhaled his meal and ran off to play.

I'd filled her in on all the details of the weekend, but Kim was most excited to hear about the kiss.

She twisted her lips and rocked in her chair a little. "So, what does the kiss mean?"

I smirked. "You doin' way too much as usual."

"I'm asking, girl. I mean it seems like you two don't have anything holding you back. He knows about the child. He's forgiven you."

"I broke up with him right before the Super Bowl. Do you remember he blamed me?"

"That was anger talking. His neck was still in the brace."

"Well, he hasn't said sorry about that yet."

"Because you two people are the least talking folks I've ever seen." She cocked her head curiously. "You do, however, manage to get your lips together when you need to."

Heat rose to my face. The memory was powerful. "Stephen and I are attracted to each other. He wanted a kiss. I didn't want to fight him on the kiss. It meant nothing."

"Tamar, you're trippin' and been reading too many of those sad relationship novels. You need to start reading some romance. You might recognize love when you're in it."

I rolled my eyes.

Kim continued. "You also need to tell him that the break up wasn't about Debra. You owe him that."

"I probably do, but I can't think about Stephen right now. He's a huge distraction."

"I would think you'd want one with all the stress you're under."

"Well, I've got one. I've been writing again."

Kim's eyebrows furrowed disbelievingly. "Really? That's great. About what?"

"I've written a novel."

"I repeat, about what?"

"It's a story about a young missionary who inherits millions of dollars when her father dies and her decision about whether or not to keep the money."

A waitress approached our table, refilled our drinks, and cleared our dishes away.

Kim turned up her lip. "Sounds interesting."

"I think it is," I said. "Anyway, I know I don't talk about my experiences in South Africa that much, but I've had this story in mind since I came back."

Kim cocked an eyebrow. "What's got you feeling empowered enough to get your pen moving?"

"Aunt Joe. She's been telling me to write another book for years, but now that I'm in her house, she won't stop. Every time I open a book to read for pleasure, she reminds me I could be writing my own."

"Hmmm," Kim said. "She knows you're burying your gift. She's on you."

"Well, it worked. I started writing, and I couldn't stop."

"So, tell me what's the what? Does she keep the money or not?"

I frowned. "I'm not telling. You'll have to read it to find out."

Kim rolled her neck and slapped the table. "Well, email it on then, heifer."

I laughed. "I will. I could use a beta reader. But you have to promise to be honest with me, like brutally honest."

"I gotcha."

"I'm nervous about it. Being rejected is hard. It was hard the first time."

"If God put this project on your heart, He's going to make sure it does what it's supposed to do. You have to learn to trust in His plans. They're better than any plans you could make for yourself."

I sighed. "My father says that."

"Your father is right. So, anyway, on another subject. Have you talked to Stephen today?"

"No, why?"

"Debra's show is airing preview snippets."

"I'm not watching that trash."

"You need to. She admitted some pretty base drama on the trailer."

"What is it?"

Kim stood. She picked up her handbag. "You need to see it for yourself, so watch. It's on YouTube. I've got to get going. I loved meeting your baby."

We both looked over to the area where he was playing. He had been joined by two more boys.

"I won't disturb his little impromptu playdate," Kim said. "Tell him, I'll see him the next time he's in Atlanta."

I stood and gave my girl a hug. "Love you."

"I love you too." She walked out of the restaurant.

I sighed and picked up my phone. I swiped my screen until I opened YouTube, searched for Debra's show, and watched the trailer. My eyes bugged out my head. Stephen was going to kill her.

Chapter 24

"I'm going to kill her."

"Don't say that in public. She might die to get you locked up," Vince said. I did not hear a chuckle through the phone's speaker.

"Debra doesn't care that much. She's just trying to emasculate me." I groaned. She'd been successful.

"You should have paid her off." Clyde rose from my dining room table and went into the kitchen. He came out with a bottle of water. "I told you. Give her money and shut her up."

"I was not negotiating with that terrorist. She's messing up my reputation. She ruined my relationship with Tamar. There was no way I was going to pay her."

"She's not making a lot from the network. Paying her would have been worth it," Clyde said.

"Well, it's too late now." I could almost taste my disgust with Debra. "Look Vince, since she's admitting what she did, isn't that illegal?"

"I'm not sure," Vince replied. "I've got my research team looking for a legal precedent, but so far, we haven't found one. This is a new territory."

"A new level of ratchet," I mumbled.

"She hasn't said your name on the show. Legally she can't. She just said she did it," Clyde added. "So, the question now is…did she have an opportunity?"

"To what? Steal my sperm?" I groaned. "This is beyond embarrassing."

"We're on Team Stephen. If she did, this could be your baby," Vince added.

"She's lying." I shook my head. "There was one night. I was tired. She slept over. I woke up and she was half naked in my bed. But nothing happened. I broke up with her that morning."

"So, we aren't waiting for DNA."

"No."

They were all silent for a moment. I was annoyed that they couldn't conceive of a situation in which I had not slept with Debra. That was the thing about being celibate. No one believed you.

"How is Tamar taking the story?" Clyde asked.

"I haven't talked to her." I scratched the back of my neck and released a long sigh. "Just when I was starting to think I could have a conversation with her about a future, now this."

"The universe continues to conspire to keep you two apart," Vince said.

"The devil," I said.

"Him, too," Clyde piped in.

"I'll let you know if my team comes up with

anything. Stay strong." Vince ended the call.

Clyde walked to the coat closet and removed his jacket. "Let's go to dinner. I'm starved."

"No, man. I don't want to. I don't want to deal with any reporters. I'm staying in."

Clyde looked disappointed. "You sure?"

"Positive."

"Like Vince said, stay strong. Focus on that ankle. This will go away when you hit the field next season."

Clyde let himself out of the house. I remained seated, but now my head was in my hand.

My mind went back to that image of Debra that morning. Naked in my bed. Nothing had happened. I was glad I had been strong.

Chapter 25

"A turkey baster, baby!"

"I told you it was some base mess," Kim said. "These scandalous women do it to athletes all the time. Now you know why I told you to watch. Debra is on some stuff you had to see for yourself."

"And Stephen saw what in her?"

"Girl, you know she's gorgeous and what she's doing at the gym to keep that body, I wish they sold in a bottle. Anyway, when she first came out, she was acting like a Christian. She was sweet and anointed. I liked her. I think the heifer done fell from grace. Hold on."

I held the line while Kim gave directions to one of her employees.

"Did you hear the story about that woman who was sleeping with a bunch of pilots? She got pregnant by all of them, one after the other. That woman is collecting $100,000 a year in child support for four kids. All of the babies are turkey baster babies." Kim chuckled. "I need to get me a pilot."

"Oh yeah right, like you would steal a man's sperm."

"No, I would marry mine," Kim exclaimed. "I knew they made money, but I didn't know they were that paid enough to be coming off twenty-five bills a year in child support."

"You a mess."

Kim giggled. "Are you going to talk to Stephen about it?"

"He's already said he didn't have sex with her." I put my cup down. "I feel sorry for him."

"Then call him. Be supportive. Tell him you feel bad that his name is being dragged across the interwebs again."

Kim said something else to her employee and then came back on the line. "Support him. This is your opening."

"My opening, huh?"

"Yes."

"I guess I need to decide if I want to take it."

"You are so extra." Kim sounded genuinely disappointed. "Some of us are working today. I have to go."

"Me too," I replied, looking at the call coming through on my phone. "Saint Stephen is going to live forever. You talked him up. He's on the phone."

"Tell him I said hi," Kim said.

I accepted the incoming call from Stephen.

"Hey, Tay, how are you?"

His voice was upbeat and warm. I was instantly

soothed. "I'm good."

"Look, I was calling because I want to come down this weekend."

"Sure, when are you planning to get in?"

"I was thinking Thursday since he has a baseball game on Friday. I'll leave Sunday night. I have to get back for therapy. I want to spend as much time as I can with him before training camp."

"Training camp? So, the ankle is good?"

"It's better. I'm off the cane most days, so I'm hopeful."

For some reason, I was nervous. My armpits were starting to perspire. "I'm praying for you." Oooh, Jesus, that didn't even sound right to say that when all I could really think about was the kiss.

"I appreciate it," Stephen said. "So, is Thursday okay?"

"Thursday is great. I have to take my aunt to a specialist on Friday, so if you could get him Thursday night and keep him, that would help out."

"I'd like to keep him through the weekend if that's okay."

"He'd love that. I'll make sure he's packed."

"Just underwear and pajamas. I want to take him shopping. Spoil him a little." Stephen paused. "How is Aunt Joe?"

"She's had a really hard time with chemo. Her doctor is saying she may need more, but it makes her so sick. Anyway, there's a holistic medicine center in

Macon. They've had some success with natural solutions. I want her to talk to them and see if there's something we can do there."

"I'll be praying for her."

Neither of us said anything. Stephen broke the silence. "I'll be in around two on Thursday."

"He'll be getting home by then, so that's perfect."

"No issues with his driver?" Stephen sounded like he didn't want to end the call any more than I did.

"He's great."

"I guess that's it. I'll see you."

"Hey, Stephen," I said, thinking about the new development from Debra.

"Yes." Expectation had risen in his voice. I could hear it, even on the one little word.

I couldn't bring it up. "I uh, nothing. You travel safe."

"You sure? You sound like something is on your mind?"

"No, I was thinking about summer, but we can talk about that when I see you."

"I have time," he said. "I always have time to talk about Isaiah."

"I don't have time. I need to finish this story. It can wait."

We ended the call. Kim would be disappointed at how I failed to be supportive. I was disappointed in myself, but I shrugged it off and went back to work on the blog post I was drafting for the magazine. I hated this assignment Eva had given me for this trending stuff. I hated gossip. I didn't like spreading bad news, even the good news was fluff.

The latest story I was working on was about a politician's daughter. She'd allowed her boyfriend to take nude pictures of her, and he'd shared them all over social media. She'd taken them on her eighteenth birthday, which meant they were legal. Several hashtags were trending:

#MelissaTeasleyPhotos and #TeasleyTeases

I was mortified for her. She tried to defend herself with a few Tweets, but people were nasty.

I signed in to the anonymous Twitter account I'd created after Eva gave me this assignment to troll for stories. I stared at her profile for a minute.

Lissa Teasey *Model/Fashionista/Messenger/ I see you.* With a series of emojis behind the description.

I was surprised she hadn't deactivated her account. I tried to message her, but she had blocked that function. I'd never sent a Tweet before, but I felt compelled to share something positive on her page, so I typed one:

Sorry about your trouble. I've been through it myself. Hold your head up high. The story will die, and the trolls will go away.

I pushed *Tweet*. That was so easy. No wonder people hid behind their phones and computer screens and sent so much filth. The ability to do so took mere seconds.

My phone pinged before I could put it down. I had a message from Melissa Teasley:

Thank you. Who are you?

I messaged back:

I had a nude video when I was your age. It was horrible. I wanted to offer support.

Melissa replied:

Can I call you? I'll open my message box for your number.

I stared at the screen? Was this child kidding? She didn't know who I was. I could be one of the bad guys.

I sent her my work cell number.

She and I did a brief Facetime chat. It was the only way I could prove to her that I was, in fact, Tamar Johnson. I was relieved she had the sense to ask me to prove it.

We talked. An hour later, satisfied that I had helped her, I called Eva and told her we needed legal to reach out to her parents to make sure this young woman didn't kill herself. She kept saying she wanted to die. I wasn't sure if she meant it.

I'd never had suicidal thoughts after my situation. But there was no Facebook or Twitter or Instagram. Social media was new, so blogs and television and radio were the primary sites for publication. I'd escaped all of that. I could only imagine what it was like for someone now. Well, I didn't really have to imagine. I'd heard the tears and the pain in Melissa Teasley's voice

"I never thought something this terrible could happen. I thought he loved me," she cried.

I promised to reach out to her again. I settled back in my chair and opened my journal to add an entry about my experience with her. Then I reached under my bed for all my old journals I'd kept since I was a pre-teen. I opened the one that covered the period after the video came out and read. It was a painful journey back in time. I hadn't realized I was writing nearly every day back during that season and continued to do entries a few times a week up until my book was rejected.

I grunted. "That's when I'd stopped writing for myself."

I'd stopped writing when I was rejected.

My work cell phone pinged a text message. I looked and saw it was from Melissa. The message said:

You saved my life. Thank you for caring.

Saved her life. I thought about Aunt Joe. How much her words of encouragement and hugs meant at the time. I had been sliding into an abyss. She saved me.

Chapter 26

Isaiah helped take my mind off my problems. He was an easy kid to like. He was grateful for everything and mannerable like no child I'd ever met. I took him to a seafood restaurant on Thursday night and let him pick out his lobster. Just seeing the excitement on his face was enough to wash away some of the pain I felt about his earlier years.

Tamar's aunt had done a great job raising him, but it was time for him to come to New Jersey to live with me. They'd had him since birth. I wanted the next seven years of his childhood. Besides, he needed his father now more than ever. The teenage years were intense. There was also the issue of security and the quality of the high school. Aunt Joe was sick, so I was waiting to have this conversation, but I had rights and I was going to exercise them, one way or another.

We spent the day shopping. I'd already brought an entire suitcase full of NFL and other athletic gear for him in an extra suitcase, but now it was time to get my son the right sneakers, jeans, and everything else a preteen needed.

We grabbed dinner and rushed back to my hotel to get changed for his baseball game. Just as we were leaving, Isaiah asked, "Have you seen my glove?"

We looked around for it.

"I left it at home," he cried.

"I'm sure your coach has an extra, or you can borrow someone's."

"No, it's a special glove. It's my lucky glove that I got at ESPN at Disney. I always play with it. Hank Aaron autographed it."

"What do you want me to do? Your Mom and Tamar aren't back yet."

"I have my house key."

I nodded. "Okay, cool. We'll go get it."

We got in the car and once I turned it on, Isaiah asked, "Is the time right on there?"

I looked at the dash for the rental and checked it against my cell. I knew it was right, but I wanted to reassure him.

"Yes."

"I have to line up twenty minutes before the game, or I can't play."

I nodded again. "So, if we get the glove, you'll be late, but if we don't get the glove, you'll be feeling some kind of way about not having your glove. You call it. What am I doing?"

"I have an idea. You can drop me off at the game and then you can go get the glove."

I sighed. "I don't know if I should be in your mom's house like that."

"Please, Dad. I need my glove. She won't mind."

The way my heart ached when he whined the word "Dad" made me realize there wasn't anything I wouldn't do for my son. That was a new feeling.

I pulled out of the parking lot and headed for the recreation center where the games were played. I handed Isaiah over to the coach and explained that I was going to get the glove. The coach said it was okay for him to be left. Then I called Tamar's phone to ask if it was okay to get the glove. The call went to voicemail.

I started the car and decided to go get it. I entered the house. It was friendly and neat as always. I went to Isaiah's room and found the glove on the floor in his closet, just where he said it would be.

I exited the room and as I was walking to the door, I spotted Tamar's laptop on the dining room table. There was a stack of paper and a printer next to it. I surmised she was writing again. Curiosity got the better of me. I wanted to see what she was doing. The stack of papers was a manuscript. I flipped to the next page and read the synopsis. Another novel. I was proud of her for trying again.

There was a notebook next to the manuscript, marked "Journal." I definitely shouldn't have opened it, but once again, curiosity won out. I read an entry that had a Post-it tab sticking out on the page.

I called Stephen today to let him know to expect the letter. All I can do is pray he forgives me. I pray he understands. I don't think anyone knows where I was 12 years ago - not even Aunt Joe. I can't make anyone understand, but I know you know, God. And if Stephen really loves me, he will too.

I turned back a few pages and read more –

Stephen didn't call. He already hates me, and he doesn't even know about Isaiah. Kim thinks I should write a letter. It seems cowardly, but maybe it's the right way to go. Maybe I'm a coward. I don't have the courage to face him. Lord, help me figure out how to handle this. I love this man. I love my son. I don't know what to do.

I love this man. Warmth filled my chest. She loves me, but she thinks I hate her. Why? I was tempted to keep reading, but I didn't have the right to do this anymore than I had the right to look at her book. I made sure to leave her work as I'd found it.

Once I arrived at Isaiah's game, I searched my cell. Tamar's entry about the phone call and the letter bothered me, because I didn't get either. One missing, I could kind of understand – an unrecorded cell call happened, mail got lost from time to time, but both? That didn't feel right.

I opened my calendar to see where I was the day of Tamar's entry about the phone call. There was something in the back of my mind about the date. Once I looked at my calendar, I realized it was the day I was discharged from the hospital the second time. I tried to log in to my phone account to see if I had a missed call on that day, but my data was spotty out here. It would have to wait until we got back to the hotel.

Isaiah ran to me after the game. Another coach, one I hadn't met was behind him.

"Hey, Mr. Pierce. I'm Coach Gerald." He extended his hand and we shook. "Isaiah had a good game."

I agreed. Speaking to Isaiah, I said, "I saw the way you jumped up in the air for that last ball. That was dope."

Isaiah blushed. "I'm going to be like you." We high-fived and Isaiah said, "Our team has ice cream sandwiches. I'm going to get mine."

We both watched Isaiah run for the ice cream. "He's a good kid." Coach Gerald said. "Hey, I was wondering where Tamar was. She doesn't miss the games."

I didn't think I was hearing him correctly. Was this clown asking me about Tamar? I chuckled like he was a joke and crossed my hands over my chest. "*Tay* had something to do, so I'm here…if that's okay with you?"

"No, I mean, not that it's not good for you to be here. I was just wondering." He gave me a tight, punk smile and scooted away. I couldn't help but wonder if that was his attempt at marking his territory.

He called me Mr. Pierce, but he and Tay were on a first name basis. Once he got to where he was going, dude looked back at me. I knew that sweep he'd done. He was sizing me up – from a distance though. I smirked. "Yeah, take a good look, Gerald. You can't compete with this." But in truth, Gerald could compete. According to her journal, Tamar loved me, but I didn't a bit more have her as my woman than I had a new football contract. The only thing I had right now was the love of the eleven-year-old who was walking toward me with ice cream smeared across his mouth. I scooped Isaiah up and turned my camera around to catch the moment with a selfie.

I took Isaiah's team out for a celebratory meal at a local pizza restaurant. Coach Gerald did not join us. Once we arrived back at my hotel, Isaiah took a shower and dropped off to sleep like a two-year-old needing a mid-day nap. Between the shopping and the game, he practically crawled into bed. I, however, was wide awake and ready to get to the bottom of the missing phone message situation. It had been nagging at me since I'd left Aunt Joe's house.

I logged into my cell phone account and went back to the records. Just as she'd said, I found an incoming call from Tamar that lasted two minutes. She had to have left a message because I hadn't talked to her. The time was 11:11 a.m. That would have been a few hours before I was discharged.

I went back in my memory to recall the flow of the day. I realized during the late morning, I was getting an MRI. My orthopedic doctor had wanted to get a new set of films before I checked out. I'd left my cell phone in my room. I know it was late morning because by the time I returned, my lunch had been delivered and I celebrated the fact that it was my last meal in that place.

There was only one other person in my room that day. My mother. She'd had access to my phone when I was in radiology. But that wasn't the only thing she had access to. She'd had access to my mail all the time. She came to the house every day to check on me and every day as was her custom whenever she visited, she brought the mail inside.

I frowned. My mother had done this.

My cell rang. It was Tamar.

"How was the appointment for Aunt Joe?"

"Good. I need to do a little more research, but it looks like they're having some good results." She sounded enthusiastic.

"Well, if it's positive, you're going to go for it."

"I think it will be. I have to submit paperwork for the insurance. There's a lot of it."

"She's lucky to have you. Everyone needs to read the fine print or have someone in their circle who is willing to."

"How was the game?"

"Good." My pride came through strong. "He caught a few balls and tagged a player out."

"For real? I hate I missed it."

"Yeah, well Coach Gerald hated you missed it, too."

"Coach?"

"He asked about you. Real friendly like."

Tamar laughed.

"That's funny. I mean is that how it goes? You date your son's coaches?"

"Stephen, I'm not dating anyone. I'm definitely not thinking about dating Coach Gerald. I don't know why he asked about me."

Because why not? You're beautiful.

"I guess because he has eyes. Anyway, I'm just letting you know."

She didn't say anything for a moment and then asked, "What's Isaiah doing?"

"He crashed a while ago. I wore him out."

"I guess. He's never in bed at nine on a Friday. It's his big night to stay up late."

"I can have that sedative effect on people."

She laughed. "Careful, that could mean you're boring."

"I don't think I ever heard you complain about that."

Tamar cleared her throat. "Well, I don't want to hold you."

I frowned. "Hold me? It's 9 pm in Yancy, Georgia, and my son is snoring like a bear. What could you be keeping me from?"

She giggled. "Welcome to single-parent life."

I laughed with her. "I was thinking we'd rent or movie or something and he fell out."

"Well, I have to go. I need to read this paperwork and get some work done. Tell Isaiah to give us a call at some point tomorrow."

"I will," I agreed. I was tempted to talk to her about the Debra story, but decided not to ruin her mood with it. Then I thought I should tell her I'd discovered she'd been telling the truth about the phone call, but it would be rushed on the phone. I also wanted to talk to my mother first.

"Stephen, did you want to say something?"

"Tell Aunt Joe hello for me."

"Thanks," she replied. "Take care of our son and

please do not let him talk you into an excessive amount of junk food. He's already overweight."

"He's exactly like I was at his age. Don't worry. I'll make sure to help him with the weight." I thought about my plans to get Isaiah to New Jersey this summer. He could train with me, but now was not the time to bring it up. Serious conversations needed to be had face-to-face.

Tamar and I exchanged a few more words and then we ended the call.

I was wrong for calling her a liar the way I had. Keeping a secret and making up events were two different things. There was enough blame to pass around, but no one was getting my wrath more than my mother.

***

I'd grown to hate physical therapy. The pain was excruciating; not as bad as the pain of the actual ankle being dislocated, but it was intense. I felt like I had a vice on my muscles and a thousand tiny knives sticking into my lower thighs. And with all I was going through, no one could promise me that I would still be able to play football.

I'd never been so scared in my life. Football was everything to me. I hated to admit that, especially before God, but it was true. The threat of losing the game revealed who I truly was – a man who lived for the field and the fans. I wasn't sure how I had gotten here, but I was here. I was also bitter about it.

"Let's try some of the shockwave therapy again."

I looked at my therapist. His eyes held sympathy for me. His eyes said, "I'm doing his job, but I'm not a miracle worker." Or at least that's what they'd say, if eyes could talk.

"Are you in pain?" he asked.

I thought, "Of course. This is painful." But I replied, "I can take it."

We moved to another machine. I did more repetitions than I could stand and then he set up the shockwave treatment. I was glad for ice and a massage. Healing was as grueling as practicing.

Dr. Hogan, my orthopedic surgeon, entered my station. "How are you doing?"

I groaned one last time as I swung my leg over onto the side of the bench to stabilize it.

"I'm feeling pretty good."

"Good. It looks like you're working hard," he said touching my ankle. "The surgery outcome was great. You had the best outcome we could have hoped for."

"So, what are my chances?"

"You know this a wait-and-see situation. You have almost three months before you have to report for training."

"Give me an estimate."

"I think it's too soon for a prognosis."

"Tell me something."

"I wish I could, but I can't yet. Keep working

hard. Celebrate the fact that your neck is healed."

My neck. It seemed like a problem in my distant past. I knew a neck or spinal injury could not only end an NFL career, they could put a player in a wheelchair. I was grateful for the neck, but I hadn't stopped to celebrate it without whining and wondering about my ankle.

But the truth was, I didn't have anyone I wanted to celebrate with. Not really. Tamar passed through my mind. We should be engaged by now and moving quickly toward marital bliss, but instead, I'd been judging her harshly for a choice she made as a teenager. Granted it was a big choice – one that robbed me of something I would have wanted, but still, I was starting to wonder if I was the one who had it wrong.

I needed to spend some time in prayer. I stood and went to the spa. Praying was going to happen, right after I talked to my mother. I had a feeling I was going to have to add our relationship to my list of concerns.

I was out. Out of here to meet with my mother – to confront her about deleting my message and stealing my mail.

I loved my mother. As her only child, I was spoiled and doted on. My father was the one to bring balance and keep me grounded. So, while I appreciated her for the love and support she'd always given me, but I was the first to admit my mother could be extra. For some reason I'd never been able to figure out, probably because I chose to ignore it, she and Tamar had always had a complicated relationship. I was sick of it. It was time to get to the bottom of all my mother's hatred toward the woman I loved.

Chapter 27

I heard the front door open, the alarm silenced, and I knew my mother had arrived. My parents, Tamar, and my housekeeper were the only people who had the key and the alarm code. My parents owned a house about five miles from me in an upscale neighborhood my money gained them access to. My dad loved Pine, but my mother was more than happy to let me know she wanted out as soon as I was financially in a position to give her the new house I'd always promised.

She claimed she wanted to be close to the Giants' home stadium. I supposed that was true since she and my father never missed a game and often came to watch me practice, but I also knew it was the proximity to her sorority sisters and New York City shopping and dining that appealed to her. Even though my father was still working, she took full advantage of the stipend I gave them every month to spend as she saw fit. With a paid-for house, they did well, but what good had my generosity done me when I'd been so disrespected by her?

Her words came up the steps before she did. "Stephen, I talked to that fella from the scholarship committee at the NCAA about you—"

They stopped just as suddenly as they began when

she saw my expression. She approached the dining room table between us and put down the mail she'd retrieved. I watched her sort it – separating important mail from junk. Getting my mail was always her habit. She'd had easy access.

Concern on her face, she looked at me. "What's wrong?" She slid out of the mink jacket my dad had given her for Christmas. "Did the doctor tell you something?"

"The doctor said the same thing he said last month. It's wait-and-see."

"Why do you look like that? I know you're not letting that Debra drama bother you. There's no point –"

"Mom…" I cut her off. "I'm going to ask you a question I'm pretty sure I know the answer to." I raised a hand and cautioned her. "Please don't lie to me."

"Lie?" She cocked her head as only a black mother could and planted a fist on her hip. "What's this about?"

"Did you delete a voice mail message from Tamar from my phone on the day I was discharged from the hospital?"

She frowned. "Delete a phone message—"

I spoke over her. "And did you also take a letter she sent to me in the mail?"

My mother's lip trembled, ever so slightly. She opened her mouth and then, seeing the seriousness in my eyes, closed it.

"You were healing, Stephen. You did not need

any more Tamar Johnson drama."

I sank into the chair behind me. I hadn't wanted to believe she'd done it. I knew, but I still held out a sliver of hope that she would say no, and I would see the truth of the "no" in her eyes. I released the breath I'd been holding and washed my hand over my face. What was wrong with the women in my life?

My mother took a seat across from me. "I know you think what I did was foul."

"I do!" I yelled, slamming my fist down on the table hard enough to crack the oak in two.

Eyes widened, Mom was visibly shaken. She practically leapt back in the chair, but she recovered quickly.

"I know you aren't giving me a hard time about that girl when she kept your son from you for eleven years."

"That's not what this is about, Mom." I stood and circled my chair. "You didn't know about Isaiah when you did this. This has nothing to do with Isaiah."

"I was protecting you."

"I didn't ask for your protection."

"Well, you needed it." She rolled her neck hard enough to need physical therapy of her own. "You let Tamar break your heart and your spirit. Debra is on television spreading lies. Your taste in women leaves much to be desired."

My chest filled up with steam. I measured my words to keep my tone respectful. "I'm grown. This is my life. I wanted that phone call. I wanted the letter.

You interfered."

"I did what any mother would have done."

"Any manipulative, controlling mother. Dang, no wonder I was with Debra. She's just like you."

My mother grimaced. "Stephen, you're going too far."

"I'm not. You are going to tell me something right now. Why you have always disliked Tamar and why, even with whatever the reason is for your feelings, you think you have the right to keep her from me."

"I won't have you talking to me like this."

"Like what? Like an angry grown up who deserves answers? I'm not a child. You don't get to choose who I have a relationship or friendship with."

"She's always been bad luck, all the way back to middle school, when you lost the science fair because you picked the project she wanted to do."

I wanted to scream. "Are you serious right now?"

"The point is, you always do what she wants to do, and it's always hurt you," Mom said. "That little tramp had no business opening her legs in my house on prom night."

"Tamar and I were together because I asked her to be with me. Because she loved me, and I loved her. Why can't you understand that?"

"That little —"

I raised a hand to halt her. "Be careful." I shook my head. "She's not about to be another tramp up in here."

My mother's chest heaved in and out like she was trying to make fire. She was as hot as a dragon, but so was I. "You lost the Paul Award because of her. You earned that award. You'll never be nominated again."

"I lost the Paul because of Debra."

"Losing the Paul started with you calling Sports Center. For what? To drag your reputation through the gutter like hers."

"Telling the truth was my decision. Aside from it just being time for the truth to come out, I made that choice to prove to Tamar I loved her."

"Her love was too costly. A woman is supposed to add value to your life. Peace. What has Tamar done for you except ruin your brand?"

"You liked Debra. What's she doing for my brand?"

My mother was silent on that question.

"She was going to tell me about Isaiah. That was the point of the call. Not that this is the most relevant part of it, but since you care about my image so much, if I had known about him first, then the media wouldn't have been able to use the drama against me."

My mother stood. "You have no idea why she called you. She's telling you now that it was about Isaiah, but how do you know if that's even true?"

"I'd know if I had talked to her. If you hadn't gotten in the middle of it. You're not seeing what you've done. You never do."

My mother's lips tightened.

"And where is my letter?"

"What?" She waved me off. "I don't have it."

"Yes, you do. I want it."

"Stephen, I threw it away. Honestly, I did."

"Did you read it?"

"No. I didn't care what she wanted. I just wanted to get rid of her." My mother huffed. "For the love of God, please don't pick back up with that woman."

"For the love of God," I chuckled. "You actually said that? Tamar is a young woman who hasn't had her mother since she was fifteen years old. What have you ever done to help her, to mentor her, or to encourage her? You're supposed to be a Christian, but you made a teenager your enemy, and you've held a grudge against her ever since. What kind of love is that?"

My words seemed to enrage my mother even more. "You can say what you want. I don't think she's right for you. I never have and all I wanted to do was protect you from everything that's been happening for the past six months."

"I don't need protection." I emphasized every word.

My mother bit her lip. She was thoughtful before saying, "Even with this, you need to leave her right down there in Georgia where she belongs. You need to focus on your ankle and your son."

"You don't have the right to tell me what I need to be focused on. Not anymore. I want my key. I'm changing my code. I have nothing to say to you."

My mother snatched her head back. "What?"

"You heard me. I want you out of my house."

She stared in disbelief. She didn't move.

"I'm not going to say it again. I don't mean to be disrespectful, but I want my keys. You're not welcome here."

"Stephen Isaac Pierce. I am your mother."

"Don't remind me. I already feel sorry for myself."

My mother reached into her handbag, removed her key ring, and took my set off the clasp. She placed it on the table. "There's no need to change the code. Your father has enough trouble remembering these things."

"Bye, Mother." I turned my back.

She left the house the same way she came. The only difference was her heels hit the wooden stairs more sharply. I heard the door open and slam behind her.

I dropped back into my chair. I had never been so disappointed in her in my life. I also had no idea where she and I would go from here.

Chapter 28

I clicked the "send" icon on the email. I'd done it – pushed my fears from my mind and sent my novel to the agent Alicia had referred me to. I didn't care for Alicia when I first met her, but I had to admit, she was a great writing coach. She'd helped me with all my publishing questions and hooked me up with her contacts.

I'd queried one of them last week. I was shocked that I'd gotten a response so fast. I remembered years ago when I was shopping my novel, most of the agents never even answered me. The responses I received were all rejection letters, and they came one after another. Now, with a good contact, I'd gotten a response from one of the top agents in New York within days.

"Are you still going to the post office?" Aunt Joe's question broke through my thoughts. "I need stamps."

She'd dragged herself out of her bedroom. She was on a walker now. She fought using one for months but had no choice when she'd fallen in the bathroom a few weeks ago and bruised her hip. She was already dealing with enough pain. She didn't need to add unnecessary soft tissue injuries to the list of physical issues.

I stood and met her halfway, removing the coffee mug and magazine from her hand so she could focus on one thing – walking.

"I was about to go now, so I can pick up Isaiah on the way back. He has a dentist appointment today."

"Oh yeah. They want to put braces on his teeth, you know. My insurance doesn't cover but half."

I shook my head. "Aunt Joe. One thing we're not going to do is worry about money for anything for Isaiah."

"I don't want to start relying on Stephen. He's still my son."

"His father is a multi-millionaire. We are giving him the orthodontist bill, and that's final."

Aunt Joe let her body drop onto the sofa. "You're right. I'm being silly. I just want to be careful with him. I don't want him taking Isaiah away from me. I talked big talk about it before, but now that Stephen's really here, I'm feeling some kind of way."

I considered her thoughts. They were mine as well, but I wasn't going to let her worry. "Stephen travels too much to keep Isaiah. I'm sure that's not in his plan." I spoke confidently, but I wasn't sure.

I had no idea what Stephen was thinking. He had asked me a question about the quality of Isaiah's school. He'd also commented once about the lack of cultural activities in the town. But that had been it. He hadn't said anything else about what he thought Yancy, Georgia was missing.

"Speaking of insurance, did you call to see if they would cover the treatment from the Cancer Center?"

I cleared my throat before the lie slipped out. "No, I was busy with the book. I'll call tomorrow."

The truth was, I had called, and I found out just what I expected to find out. Many of their services were not covered at all. And it wasn't just that, although that was huge. The diet required for treatment was all organic whole foods. The cost of food was expected to run $500 to $600 a month and supplements another $300 before the medical expenses.

Aunt Joe had not opted to take long-term disability through her benefit plan. Having worked in a low paying job her entire life, her income was modest. She had a small social security check. I was only getting paid half my income from my job because I wasn't even working full-time. I was going to have to give up my apartment at the end of the lease in a few months. The money in this house was tight. I was glad I'd had the desire to write the book. I was hoping it would sell and I would get an advance that was big enough to get us back on track.

I went into the kitchen. "Do you want anything before I go?" I asked, filling a glass with water and then washing off a tangerine for her.

"Just water," she replied as I put it down in front of her.

I knew she'd be sitting there until I returned. I picked up my bag and the package I was mailing.

"Don't forget my stamps, baby."

"You have your cell phone?" I asked.

"In my pocket," she replied turning the television volume up to the loud level she liked it.

I slid on my shoes and left her with the Golden Girls.

I was almost at the post office when my phone rang. I pushed the Bluetooth speaker button. "This is Tamar," I said moving the vehicle into oncoming traffic.

"Tay, it's me." Stephen's voice filled my vehicle.

I released a plume of air. I hadn't even realized I'd been holding my breath. I'd probably been doing it since I'd lied to Aunt Joe.

"Hey," I said, my heartbeat speeding up.

"Do you have a minute to talk?"

"I'm in the car so I can."

"How's Aunt Joe?" he asked. I appreciated that he never forgot to ask about her.

"She's tired today. She's supposed to start another round of chemo next week, but she's too weak to begin. I'm not sure what I can do to get her to eat."

"Well, what about the new place you're taking her, what was it?"

"Cancer Center of Georgia. I still have to work out the insurance stuff."

"But you want her to go there, right?"

"Yes, of course."

"Let me help you out."

"Uh, no. My Aunt Joe is not going to accept

charity. She and I just had a conversation about Isaiah needing braces, and I had to talk her into allowing you to pay for them," I said. "By the way, you're paying for braces."

Stephen chuckled. "That would be my pleasure." He paused. "There are ways around pride. When people think they've earned something, they take money. We could tell her it's back child support. I think we need to talk about it anyway."

"She's not going to take it." *Even though she needs it*, I thought. "Legally, Isaiah is her child. He was her responsibility. That's how she feels."

"But I'm his father, and I can afford it."

"You don't have to tell me that. Let's let her get healthy. I can't put any more stress on her."

Stephen was silent again before he spoke. "Tay, the reason I was calling is that I need to talk to you about something important. When can we chat?"

"I'm on the way to the post office to mail some paperwork for my aunt and then I have to take Isaiah for his dentist appointment, so it's going to have to be later. After Isaiah goes to bed is best."

"Okay, that's cool. I'll call then."

"Do I need to prepare myself?"

"No, it's cool. I just need to say a few things. I don't want you to be distracted."

"Now I'm more curious."

"It's all good. I'll talk to you later."

I released a long sigh. He didn't sound agitated, so

maybe there weren't going to be angry words or drama. Hopefully, it wouldn't be a new scandal or some mess with Debra. Isaiah was already getting told in school that he had a baby brother or sister on the way.

I pulled into the post office and got out of the car. I was sending some medical record information off for my aunt. I was also mailing a copy of my manuscript to Kim. She was dying to read it and I was hungry for her feedback. She wouldn't read a digital copy. I rushed in and before I could get in line, I heard my name. I turned to find Isaiah's coach, Gerald.

"I'm sorry, I was out of order calling you Tamar. I meant, Ms. Johnson," he said.

I shook my head. "Tamar is fine. How are you?"

"I'm good. We missed you Friday night."

"I had to take my aunt out of town."

Concern showed on his face. "How is she?"

"She's..." I paused thinking about the right answer to the question. "She's hanging in there. Getting treatment and trusting God."

"I'll continue to pray for her."

"We appreciate it. This disease is hard."

His eyebrows went up. "I know, my dad had lung cancer. It was a tough time for our family."

"Is he in remission?"

He frowned. "No, he passed a few years ago."

I raised a hand to cover my mouth. "I'm sorry to hear that."

"He actually died from a heart attack, but it was the disease. It was too much for him."

I nodded understanding.

"I don't want to hold you up. I know the kids are getting out of school soon. But I did want to say that, if you ever need someone to talk to, I'm willing to be a shoulder to cry on or a sounding board, or even if you need a good dinner - I'd love to be there for you."

I thought about Stephen's comment from the other night. This was awkward.

I opened my mouth, but it locked into a fake smile. I was glad he reached for his wallet and lowered his eyes to search it, because it gave me a few seconds to fix my face.

"Here's my card. My office and personal cell are both on there. Please feel free to call me any time."

"Thanks, Gerald. I appreciate the offer."

"Because you're not with Isaiah's father, right? He's still with that reality television woman."

My eyes widened. "I can't say. You know legal stuff." I shrugged. "I can't keep up."

Gerald nodded. "Smart. Who needs that drama? Everyone knows those football players have a harem of women."

I fought rolling my eyes at his attempt to discredit Stephen.

He smiled, gave me a sloppy, lusty, greedy once over and walked toward the post office boxes. "I hope to hear from you."

"Not in a million years," I whispered under my breath as I walked to the counter. I took care of my business and was back in the car in less than ten minutes.

I sent Kim a text letting her know the package would be arriving in a few days.

My phone rang in a call from a strange number. I took it.

"Ms. Johnson, this is the financial officer from the Cancer Center of Georgia."

"Oh, yes."

"You were sending some paperwork to us?"

"Yes, I don't have access to a fax or scanner, so I put it all in the mail. I'm leaving the post office right now."

"Okay, I could have saved you some postage. I was hoping we could schedule an appointment for your aunt this Thursday so we can complete our tests and develop a treatment plan."

I hesitated. "I, uh, we're still looking at our options. I haven't really talked to her doctors."

"Well, Dr. Mowry referred you."

"She did, but we hadn't followed up with her."

"I see. I assumed you'd decided. We just received a donation for your aunt's care."

"Donation? My aunt doesn't have anyone who would —" I paused. I realized my aunt did have someone who would donate money.

Stephen.

"Are you sure the money was for Josephine Ferguson?"

"Of course. We received a commitment to the funds a little while ago. My understanding is the balance of any monies needed will be coming through a charity, the S.I. Pierce Foundation."

I twisted my lips in an effort to hold back my tears, but it wasn't working. "I wasn't aware that things would move so quickly."

I couldn't believe he had done that. There was no point arguing with him about the money. Auntie needed it, besides, he'd already done it. She didn't need to know that insurance wasn't covering everything. I had no idea what Stephen wanted to say to me tonight but "thank you" and "God bless you" were definitely coming off my lips.

"Ms. Johnson?"

"Yes, I apologize for being distracted." I wiped a tear from my face. "I'd like to set up the appointment."

***

Isaiah and Aunt Joe were in bed. Auntie was alternating between watching television and playing Candy Crush on her cell phone. She was in a good mood. She'd had a brief visit from Dr. Butler tonight, and it wasn't a medical house call. I knew the two of them still talked on the phone from time to time because he was the only person in the world that made her blush. I looked in on her. She didn't need anything, so I decided to get in the tub.

I knew Stephen would be calling soon. I planned to talk to him on speaker while I soaked. I stripped down and went into the bathroom to start the water. Just as I put my hand on the knob, my phone rang. It was him.

"Hey, Tay. I'm at the front door."

I stared at the phone in disbelief, put on my robe, went to the door and pulled it open.

Stephen was standing there. He was wearing a Freedom University hoodie, jeans and sneakers. He'd gotten a fresh haircut. It was the lowest it had been in a long time. His goatee was trimmed neat and the scent that was coming off him was warm and woodsy. It prickled my nose and made my head swim for a moment.

He was smiling. "You look, clean."

"I haven't taken the bath yet, so I'm actually dirty." I opened the door wider to let him in.

"You're dirty." Stephen's smile widened. I think I saw all thirty-two of his teeth. "A wordsmith should be more careful."

"Don't put that on me. You're the one with the less than clean mind."

"That may be true, so let's move the topic on over." He chuckled. "I don't want to disturb anyone. Get dressed and come out."

I bit my lip. "Give me a minute."

He walked down the steps and went back to the SUV he was driving. I closed the door.

What was up?

I looked in at my aunt. She'd fallen asleep. I went into my room and slid on some clothes.

Stephen was leaning against the truck when I approached it. He was on his cell phone.

I threw up my hands. "So, what made you get on a plane?"

He frowned. "Let me finish this."

I looked over his shoulder. I could see he was on IG.

He groaned. "I'm getting a lot of comments about Debra's show." He closed the app and stuck the phone in his pocket.

"I heard it premiered with pretty high ratings. I guess the trailer accomplished what she needed it to do." I bit my lip, waiting for him to finally talk about it.

Stephen waved that off. "Yeah, I've been avoiding that conversation with you."

"You've done a good job." I chuckled. "I don't mean to laugh. I know it's got to be hard."

Stephen nodded.

"So, is Debra's new story more lies, or is there something for you to be concerned about?"

"Let me ask you a question." His deep, velvety voice got deeper. "Why are you so curious?"

"Because I try to be prepared for Isaiah on this

stuff. One of his schoolmates already told him he was having a little brother or sister."

Stephen poked out his lip. "Too bad. I was hoping it was something else." He smiled again. At the angle he stood, the moonlight bounced off his teeth. "I'll talk to Isaiah, but just in case you're curious for another reason, I am an innocent man."

I nodded. "If you're going to talk to Isaiah, you don't owe me an explanation."

Stephen sighed. He reached for my hand and pulled me a little closer to him. The same way he used to do when we were a couple.

"Tay, I'm here because I felt like I owed you this in person."

I frowned. "Just say it. You're scaring me."

"No need to be scared. I'm here to apologize."

"Apologize?"

"For calling you a liar. For not believing you called me. You know the call about Isaiah and the note."

I stepped back, crossed my arms and cocked my head to the side a little. "Okay, but I don't understand. You didn't believe me then. Why do you believe me now?"

"I got curious, so I went back to the date in my phone records. I found a missed call from you. My mother deleted it. She took your letter too."

The hairs on the back of my neck stood up. I fought to hide my disgust. "How could she?"

"How could she indeed," he said.

"Why?" I shook my head, but I knew the answer. There was no point in making him explain.

"You know why. But I'm not letting her get away with it. I'm not dismissing it." He dropped his head back for a moment. "But you know what?" he asked looking in my eyes. "My mother is the least of my concerns right now. I'm going to let her sit in her mess for a minute. She needs to do that."

I didn't like what his mother did to me, but I didn't want him having any additional stress, so I decided to stay out of it. "I understand."

Stephen cleared his throat. He pushed his body off the SUV. He took a few steps back and forth – a mini-pace and then stopped closer to me than he'd been. "I've been trying to play it cool, but my head has been messed up for a minute. This thing with my ankle has got me like crazy. I haven't been myself, Tay. I feel like a different Stephen sometimes."

I placed a hand on his forearm. "You're not a different Stephen. You're human. This is hard. You're entitled to your emotions and your feelings," I said. "But what is the main issue? Is it physical, mental, or spiritual?"

"Probably all three." He raised his free hand to the back of his neck like he always did when he was stressed.

I reached up and pulled his arm down. I slipped my hands into both his hands and squeezed. "Stephen, you're rehabbing as hard as you can. You have no control over the physical, but you can work on the other two."

"Tay," he shook his head. He looked lost. "I need a friend. I miss you. I keep coming down here and seeing Isaiah, but I feel alone." He groaned so hard it came out like a growl. It was painful to hear him express himself that way.

I waited for him to continue.

"I'm usually crazy busy this time of year, you know, with my foundation, but all I do is go to PT and come home and I can't stop thinking about what if. What if I can't play ball?"

"You can't worry about something you can't control."

"I know that, but I also can't stop myself."

"What about therapy, not physical? I know they have to recommend it for stuff like this."

"I'm seeing someone – kind of."

"Kind of?" I didn't know what that meant, so I pushed for an answer.

"He's the team psychologist, but I'm not feeling him. I don't know. I might need to try someone else."

"What about the chaplain?"

"He's not around right now. He got married and he's on an extended trip or something."

I wasn't giving up. I could see he needed help. "What about your pastor? I know he's not a sports specialist, but surely he can help you or refer you."

Stephen raised a hand and swiped my chin. His

eyes burrowed into mine with an intensity that stole my breath. "My pastor is your dad, Tay."

"You don't have a church in New Jersey?"

"No. I have games on Sundays. When I'm not playing football, I'm in Pine, so I repeat, your father is still my pastor."

"Then call my dad, Stephen."

He raised my hand and stared at it in the full light of the moon.

"I'll think about," he said. "I guess I could have apologized over the phone." We were quiet for a moment.

"The truth is, I wanted to see you. I don't care what you do or what we go through, you're still my peace."

I pulled my hand out of his.

"You were wearing my ring. I know it was a promise ring." I could see the glint of wetness in his eyes. He raised his hands and pinched his fingers together. "But I was this close to having everything I wanted in life. How did it all go so bad?"

I stepped back. I stuck my hands in my pockets.

"I was sure about you," he said. "From the time I was a kid...but I'm not sure about anything right now."

He sounded defeated. He looked defeated. I didn't know what to say. His ankle was clearly giving him more pain than a drug or therapy could fix.

"We're at least friends, right?" he asked. "I know I rejected that in the hospital, but I didn't mean it." He was so pitiful. So, unlike himself.

I sighed. "Of course, we are. Do you want to come in for some coffee or tea or something?"

"No, believe it or not, I have a flight back in an hour. I have PT tomorrow. I have PT every day. I can't miss."

"Stephen."

"But I'm not supposed to complain, right? I have to be grateful that I didn't break my neck. It doesn't matter that I tore my ankle up because my neck is okay."

He raised his hands and gripped his head. "This is a season. This too shall pass." The words came out of his mouth, but they lacked conviction.

I got closer to him. I pulled his arms down from his head and held onto his hands. "It will pass. You know that better than I do."

"It doesn't look like it's going to pass," he said, shaking his head.

Our eyes locked and silence filled time.

Stephen spoke first. "You are so beautiful. Seeing you was worth the flight down. It always is." Sadness oozed from him. "I'm really sorry for talking to you like that. You didn't deserve it. You've never deserved any of the crap I've put on you."

Stephen slid his hands out of mine and turned back toward the car.

"Thank you for the money." I'd almost forgotten it. "The woman called from Cancer Center of GA. She told me there was a donation."

Stephen did a half turn. "That was supposed to be a secret."

"Well, she missed the memo. I appreciate it. It was kind of you, and it took a huge weight off my shoulders."

"I'd do anything for you," he whispered. "Anything. All you have to do is call. I'm here for you – forever."

I took a few steps toward him and wrapped my arms around his neck. We hugged, longer than we should have, because Stephen's hands found their way to my waist. He pulled me back and our faces were inches from each other. We were frozen there, under the moon like twin owls on a branch. Both our hearts were pounding. I felt mine and nearly heard his.

"You should go." I stepped back.

He smiled like that hug did something for him. "Enjoy your soak." He climbed into the truck and started it.

"Travel safe."

I stood there while he backed the truck out of the driveway and pulled out onto the road and drove away. Other than the time I visited him in the hospital, I don't think I've ever seen Stephen Pierce this broken.

Chapter 29

This weekend was my first official Mother's Day, but I didn't feel like a mother. I still felt like Cousin Tamar. Isaiah was still calling me Cousin Tamar. Aunt Joe said she didn't know if she would be alive in a year, so she wanted to spend this Mother's Day with Isaiah. I hated she was thinking that way, but I understood, and I wanted to give them their time without my biological motherhood hovering over the celebration.

I hired a home health aide to check in on her and keep things tidy while I was gone. I didn't have to worry about meals. One of the referrals from the Cancer Center was an organic meal service. They delivered chef prepared meals once a week. I'd put spaghetti and a few other kid friendly meals in the fridge for Isaiah.

They'd do fine without me for a few days, so I was spending the weekend in Pine with my father. It was his fifty-fifth birthday. His congregation was hosting a dinner for him. I would also get a chance to visit my own mother's grave. I hadn't done that on Mother's Day in years.

I stopped in at Dell's Diner to pick up breakfast and was told Dell had taken the day off. I smiled to myself. I'm sure she was in a beauty salon getting all fixed up for my dad's party. I ordered the lunch special to go and stopped at the florist to pick up a bouquet of white roses for my mother's grave. My mother loved all things white, including the snow. She believed white was pure and honest. She told me you couldn't hide anything on a white surface. I hated that as a kid because it meant extra cleaning in areas of the house that had white furniture and rugs, but now as an adult, I was drawn to the color that wasn't even technically a color. I wore something white almost every day.

I entered my father's house, kicked off my shoes and put my flowers in the extra refrigerator in the mudroom out back. After unpacking, I took a hot shower, came downstairs, lit a fire and settled in the family room with my meal and a book. Quiet and no responsibilities - when had I last had this?

I knew my father was hunting. He rarely hunted when I was a child, but he told me he usually went most Fridays and Saturday mornings when something was in season to hunt and he didn't have an obligation at the church. I was glad he had a hobby to take his mind off his deceased wife and prior to my reappearance, his missing daughter.

The doorbell rang, stealing my peace instantly.

I pulled it open to a teenager who was holding a large vase with a beautiful floral arrangement.

"He's got a bunch of flowers at the church too," the young man said.

"Fifty-five is a big birthday." I put the vase on the foyer table. "Give me a minute."

"I already got a big tip," he said, having read my

mind.

I nodded and he walked back down the steps to his van.

I pushed the vase back further to ensure it didn't tip over. Then I returned to my comfy chair.

My cell phone rang in a call from Kim.

"Hey girl, what are you doing having time to call on the day before Mother's Day? Aren't you jammed with press and curls and weaves?"

"Honey, I am, but I'm sitting out here taking a break. My plantar fasciitis is acting up. I had to get off my feet for a minute," Kim said. "And I had to call. I'm so proud of you I don't know what to say."

I stuck my spoon in the chili and placed it on the table next to me. "Proud of me for what?"

"The Melissa Teasley thing."

I frowned. "Melissa Teasley? How do you know about her? What thing?"

"Her mother just made a public statement. She said you saved her daughter's life."

I sat up straighter. "Kim, what are you talking about?"

"Go to her Twitter or something. It came on television a little while ago. She said this would have been the worse Mother's Day ever if it wasn't for Tamar Johnson reaching out to her daughter. Eva hasn't called you?"

"Eva is in Cancun. She told us she was turning off her phone," I replied. "Let me look this up and call you back."

I signed onto Twitter and went to Congresswoman Teasley's page. Sure enough, she had posted a video of a statement she'd made. With a trembling voice, the congresswoman said:

"Prior to talking to Tamar Johnson, my daughter, Melissa was locked in her bedroom with a bottle full of sleeping pills. She'd intended to kill herself that night, but Ms. Johnson took the time to encourage her to survive this nightmare. I thank Ms. Johnson from the bottom of my heart. I will be reaching out to her personally."

Then she went on a rant about cyberbullying and revenge porn and shared the different agencies that were available to help women.

"Wow!" I knew she was in a bad way, but I didn't know she was really planning to kill herself. She'd mentioned wanting to die, but she actually had pills. I couldn't believe I had played a part in someone's life this way. My heart started pounding. Now I was emotional, as emotional as her mother had been when she'd made the statement. I took a few deep breaths to calm my racing pulse before I called Kim. "I'm shocked."

"You're shocked? I'm shocked. You didn't tell me you called that girl."

"I don't tell you everything."

"Obviously you don't, Anne Ferguson, mother of Isaiah Ferguson, former Video Virgin. But I'm saying, this was nothing to hide."

"I didn't think about it. I mean, I was reposting the story about her and I decided to send her a message to encourage her. Lord knows if she was reading the stuff on her Twitter feed, she probably needed one."

"Well, God used you to do a work," Kim said.

The shock hadn't left me yet, but hearing Kim say God had used me made me feel even more emotional.

"So, how's your dad?" Kim's voice broke through my thoughts.

"I haven't seen him yet. He's hunting. I have the house to myself. I'm going to relax until it's time for the party.

"I'm glad to hear that. You need to. You've been stressed."

"Things are getting better. Auntie has been feeling a little better. I think she's getting her strength up with all these green meals and supplements she's taking."

"That's good. She'll need it. Chemo begins again in a few weeks, right?"

"Yes, which is why I have no guilt about getting away this weekend."

"You shouldn't have guilt about anything. You've really been there for her."

"She's my family. I look at her and even though she looks nothing like my mother, I see similar mannerisms. They say the same kind of things. I've enjoyed her. I know my mother would be proud that I'm caring for her."

"She would. But look, I have to tell you something else. I finished your book last night. I started to text you, but I didn't want to wake you up. The book is so cute. You're a really great writer."

"But you used the word cute. That's not what I was hoping for."

"It's young adult fiction. It's for kids."

"Not really. It's New Adult so that's like age 17-22."

"Well, maybe cute isn't the right word. It's good. I liked it."

"Really, Kim? You're not being nice?"

"I enjoyed it. I couldn't believe that girl didn't take the money though."

That was disappointing. She should have understood why the girl didn't take the money. Now I wished I had waited to talk to her before sending it to the agent.

Kim was quiet and I knew that meant she had something else on her mind. "Okay, say it."

"I like that you're writing, and maybe I'm too close to you, but I was wondering if you ever thought about a memoir?"

I frowned. Alicia's words about my story skittered through my mind. "No. I would never."

"But why not? You kinda did a little with this book. This girl was living down in the jungle because her parents were running from an old scandal. She didn't want the money because she didn't want the fame. I felt a little bit of you up in there. I think it's obvious you want to talk about the topic. And now that you've reached out to Melissa, it's even more obvious.

Why not tell your story?"

"Because my story is private. This is completely made up."

"Tamar, you went through a lot. You've got a testimony that would help young women. I think that's obvious."

I thought about my journals. My story was embedded in them, but they were private and painful. I couldn't share that with the world.

"I feel like you think your story has no value because it was so ugly, but as you can see, what you went through is not unique to you. It's a problem for young women. They need to know what not to do, but even if they get in a bad situation, they need to know they can survive it." Kim paused and then continued. "I've never told you this, but when I pray for you, I see you speaking. I see high schools and college auditoriums full of young women."

I frowned. "Kim."

"It's true. I haven't said anything to you about it because I know you had to be ready to hear it." Kim sighed. "The novel is the first step. You're putting yourself back out into the world as a voice, but I really think you should ask God what He wants you to use your voice and your words to do. Your real life is more powerful than fiction, boo."

I was stunned into silence. My heart was racing. I'd had this thought that God wanted more from me, but I pushed it out of my head every time it entered.

"Hey, did I freak you out?"

"There's nothing to freak out about." I laughed, uncomfortably. "I'm not that person. I don't speak and even if I did, I don't think schools would want my past nude video being a conversation starter with their students."

"These schools need what you've got. The devil is not playing with our young people. Administrators are dealing with some real issues with these kids, and you have a real issue. When God comes for you, you're going. He'll use you any way He sees fit, Tamar Johnson, so you might as well go ahead and get ready."

"I hear what you're saying, friend. I appreciate your confidence in me."

"Auditoriums full. I'm telling you," Kim said. "I need to go. Let me step myself back in this shop and finish these folks' heads so I can get home and get off my feet."

"I love you, girl."

"I love you," Kim said. "Enjoy your dad's party."

We ended the call.

The doorbell rang again. It was possible my father would be getting gifts all day. So much for rest. I groaned and went to answer it.

I peeked out to find my former tenth grade gym teacher standing on the porch. I opened the door.

"Tamar, I'm so glad you're here." She pulled me into a hug, and I invited her in.

"Mrs. Hatcher, this is a surprise."

"It's wonderful to see you, Tamar. You look

fantastic."

"Thank you, ma'am. What can I do for you?"

"My son told me he saw you at Dell's earlier. I was hoping you were here, so please excuse my coming like this."

"No, it's fine."

"I'm in a bit of a jam. I'm going to ask a huge favor."

I waited.

"I'm the troop leader for the Girl Scouts. We have a meeting in an hour. I had a speaker scheduled. She was coming from Bethel, but she's gotten into a car wreck, and she's had to go to the emergency room. She won't make it."

I continued to wait. Mrs. Hatcher seemed to be waiting with me, because she didn't continue and then I realized, she was looking for.

"Mrs. Hatcher, my father isn't here."

"I'm not looking for your father, dear. I was hoping you could speak to my girls."

I was shocked, but I managed. "Me. Speak about what?"

"I was thinking bullying. Your experiences. I just heard how you helped Melissa Teasley."

I wasn't sure I was hearing her right. I had to make sure she'd said what I'd thought. "Speak?"

"I'm sure you'd be great."

"Mrs. Hatcher, I've never done any speaking."

"Tamar, they are girls between the ages of ten and fifteen. They don't need anything fancy. Just some advice on how to protect themselves from what you experienced."

"I've never talked about what I've experienced."

Shaking her head, Mrs. Hatcher released a solid wind. "Well, don't you think it's about time? There are young people who need to learn from you. Young people like Teasley. Sweetheart, your being in town and my speaker wrecking her car is no coincidence. Your father would tell you that."

I thought about the conversation I'd just had with Kim. The timing of this was too close to be coincidental.

Really God? You're doing this now?

I took a deep breath and said, "Please have a seat and excuse me for a moment."

I left her standing there and went into the powder room. I stood in front of the mirror for a long time, staring at myself. I was seeing that eighteen-year-old girl who was taunted and teased and harassed by everyone in her entire high school and college. That Tamar was so afraid. I closed my eyes and pushed her out of my mind.

"I'm not eighteen anymore." When I opened my eyes, I saw who I was today and for a brief second, I made myself reflect on a memory of my mother. She would stand behind me in my bedroom vanity. She'd braid my hair and we'd talk, exchanging glances in the mirror.

My mother had worked tirelessly with young girls

in our church and the community. Aside from her family, it was her one true passion. I was here to honor her this weekend. God sure knew how to give me a nudge.

I rejoined Mrs. Hatcher. She stood when I entered the room.

"My suggestion didn't make you sick, did it?"

I smiled. "No, ma'am. I just needed a minute to think about it." I paused for a moment, and then I forced the words I was still fighting from my throat. "I'll do it. Tell me the details."

She hugged me and told me to be at the community center in an hour. It was less than a ten-minute drive. Everything in Pine was less than a ten-minute drive. I let her out and rushed up the stairs to change out of my sweats and make a few notes. I was going to do this.

Chapter 30

The church fellowship hall was decorated in gold and black for my father's birthday party. I arrived just in time, having spent much more than time speaking and answering questions than I had anticipated.

Mrs. Hatcher had not told me it was not just the local troop in attendance, but a group of girls from two of the other neighboring towns. I spoke to a total of eighty young women.

They were completely captivated by my story and horrified at the aftermath. I had to cut back on the details because so many of them were too young to understand the whole "losing your virginity" thing, but it went well. Talking about it felt good. They learned a lot, and I felt empowered by their new knowledge.

Kim was right. God was up to something and He had moved fast. Would He do what my mother always said He would do? "Take evil and turn it into good." I never thought I'd see the day when my heartache could have some value.

My mother's words slipped into my memory. "All pain has a purpose, baby, and it's rarely about us. You have to go through it and wait for God to reveal His plan."

It was happening. God was fulfilling His word.

"Tamar, did you hear me?"

I shook off my deep thought and addressed the church member in front of me. "Sister Thomas, how are you?"

"I'm good, honey. I was telling you that you have a seat up front with your dad. I want to show you to it."

I nodded and followed her through the room. All eyes were on me as typical of a small church and a latecomer. Stephen stepped out from a group of men and approached me.

I wasn't expecting to see him, and I said so. "I'm surprised to see you here."

"It's my church, and it's a big birthday for your dad." For a moment he looked insulted, but then he quickly moved on. "You look beautiful."

Heat rose to my face. "Thank you."

"Are you just getting in from Georgia?"

"No, I got in early this morning."

"Just tardy," he took a sip of his punch. "Girl, you know you and that colored people disease."

I smirked. I was in the habit of being a little on the dot for events like this, but today I had an excuse.

"For your information, I had a speaking engagement at lunchtime and the event ran over."

Stephen frowned. "Speaking, in Pine? What were you speaking about?"

I cleared my throat. I realized I'd said more than I

meant. This was still private for me.

He pressed. "Tay, what kind of speaking?"

"My life experiences. Being bullied. I spoke to a group of girl scouts"

Stephen was thoughtful for a moment and then he smiled. "Wow, that's pretty amazing. First Melissa Teasley and now this." He gave me a thumbs up. "God is working."

We were interrupted. "Tamar, we're ready to get started."

I turned. I'd forgotten Sister Thomas was waiting for me.

Stephen's gaze was warm and affectionate. He said, "I'll talk to you later."

Another rush of heat came to my face. I nodded and joined my father at the head table. My heart was pounding. There was something about Stephen's statement that God was working that shook me. I realized God was, in fact, working. But now what was He going to require of me? And would I be up for the challenge?

***

The dinner was nice. The planning committee brought in some pastors from neighboring churches and they roasted my dad. Members stood up and made small speeches about him, he was presented with gifts, and those who hadn't spoken took the time to wish him well.

I hung around until the end, choosing to talk to a few of the women I'd spent my life attending church with and getting caught up on their stories. I could feel Stephen's eyes on me. Every time I glanced in his direction, he was looking at me, which was causing me to perspire in the warm room.

I kissed my father and hugged Dell. They were leaving with the bulk of the crowd, but a few minutes later, my father came back into the hall.

"We've got car trouble. I came with Dell because I couldn't get the dead animal smell out of my truck and now her car won't start."

"Does she know what's wrong with it?"

"I think it's the starter. She had some trouble with it yesterday. She was planning to take it to the mechanic on Monday. You know these newer cars don't warn you like the older ones did."

"Well, I'm ready," I said.

"She's got to go to the diner and close up, so I was wondering if you could maybe catch a ride and let me borrow your rental."

Stephen stepped in the midst of us. "I can take you home when you're ready, Tamar."

"I don't want to put you out. I'm going in the opposite direction of your house," I said. He already had my arm pits sweating. I didn't need to be in the car with him.

He chuckled. "Put me out? It's Pine, not Atlanta."

I reached into my clutch and handed my father the keys. Kissed him again and watched him leave.

"Should I go warm up my truck?" Stephen asked.

"No need. I can handle a little chill."

I told the women I'd been chatting with good night. They'd begun cleaning up, a duty they refused to let me share in, so I went to the front coat rack and retrieved my jacket.

Stephen and I stepped out into the chilly, night air. There was a full moon in the sky and a million stars sparkled in the background.

"They did your dad right," Stephen said, opening the door for me. "I want Isaiah to spend some time up here this summer. I was hoping once school got out that he could stay for a while."

"Sure," I replied knowing what he would ask. "He'd love your house and the animals. He'd get to spend some time with my dad."

"I don't know that I'll be here in Pine. I have to be in New Jersey for therapy."

I nodded. "Oh yeah, I forgot about that, but it's closer to my dad anyway, so I'm sure you could get him over here a few times."

Stephen's nod was agreeable.

"I was expecting you to ask, in fact, Aunt Joe and I already talked about it. Maybe he could stay until you go to training camp."

Stephen looked down. When he looked back up, worry filled his eyes. "I'm glad to see we're on the same page."

He started the car. I didn't know what that look was about, but I let it go. Suddenly I was craving the comfort of my own ride.

"You look nice, Tay."

"You told me that."

"I noticed again." He chuckled. "I keep noticing."

He was making me blush. I couldn't stand the fact that a few words from his lips had this effect on me.

"So," he clapped his hands together. "Back to your speech today. I'm proud of you for talking to those girls. I know it couldn't have been easy."

"Actually, it was easy. I wasn't even prepared for it. It was a last-minute thing and the words just – spilled right out of me." I paused remembering the event. "I'm starting to wonder if I'm a better speaker than I am a writer."

"I'm sure you're a great writer."

"We'll see. Speaking of writing, I've been doing some."

"Yeah, good for you."

"I finished a book and I got an agent."

"Really?"

"She's sent it to a few publishers. I haven't heard anything yet."

"So, is it a memoir or something?"

I frowned. "A memoir? Why would you ask me

that? Have you been talking to Kim?"

Stephen shook his head. "Kim? No, why would I talk to Kim?"

"Because she told me to write a memoir."

"I assure you, I'm not in collusion with your best friend that I hardly know," he said. "I just thought with what you said about the speaking that maybe it had crossed your mind to do it."

"First of all, I'm private. You know that. And second of all, it's not like it's just my story. It's yours, too."

"Some of it is mine," he said. "But why should I care. I mean people know anyway. Besides, if I can survive "Making Saint Stephen"…"

We both laughed.

"I can survive anything." Stephen paused. "Seriously, Tay, if you can do something to help a young woman like you did with Melissa Teasley, maybe what you went through would be worth it."

"Stephen," I said firmly. "I don't have the courage to write a memoir, okay? I wrote a novel. Fiction. Let's drop it."

"Okay, okay," he said. "Tell me what the fiction is about."

My nerves were shot. I couldn't believe he'd mentioned a memoir. Kim's saying it earlier was easy to dismiss, but now his saying it felt too much like déjà vu. I was trapped in this conversation about a topic I didn't want to discuss. I knew God wasn't trying to tell me to write a memoir. I chuckled. That was ridiculous.

"So, it's a comedy," Stephen asked. "I see you're laughing."

"No," I shook my head. "It's a story about a missionary and an inheritance. She's conflicted about whether to keep the money."

"Sounds interesting." Stephen grunted. "What inspired it?"

"A bunch of things. I was reading something one day and just kind of went down that 'what if' rabbit hole we writers go down. The missionary character was inspired by someone I knew when I was in Cape Town." I shrugged. "Now, I'm just waiting to see if anyone else thinks it's interesting."

We came to a traffic stop and he looked in my direction.

His expression relaxed me. "Doesn't it take time to hear back?"

"I have a celebrity agent, so I think I thought I'd get pushed to the top of the pile, or at least I was hoping I would."

"I look forward to reading it. Let me know when I can."

I smiled. He smiled back. The light changed and he moved the car through the intersection.

"Sorry about the memoir thing. I don't know why it even popped in my head."

Heat rose in my belly to my chest. "I'm just uncomfortable with it. But it's not the first time it's been mentioned."

"I'm surprised the agent didn't suggest it."

"She didn't. I'm praying something happens with what she has."

We pulled into the driveway of my father's house. He turned off the vehicle.

"How's the ankle?"

He gripped the steering wheel and let out a long breath. "I feel great."

"Good."

"Yeah."

I hesitated for a moment and then said, "Well, I better get inside."

Stephen reached for my hand. "Wait. Can we talk?"

I cleared my throat. "About?"

"You know what." He looked away and out the window before turning back to face me. "I can't be the only one that feels this," he squeezed my hand. "I want to talk about us."

Heat rushed to my face. "We're doing a good job co-parenting Isaiah. After everything that's happened, we're civil. That's a miracle. Let's leave things the way they are."

"Let's not." He turned his body in my direction. "I miss you."

I laughed. "You miss me."

"What's hard to believe about that?"

I sighed. "You miss me because what, I look

beautiful tonight?"

"No, it's not like that."

"It seems to be an out of sight, out of mind thing for you. For twelve years you didn't care and for the past few months—"

"Tay, I've been dealing with this injury. I've been in pain and honestly, fighting wanting to feel this way about you and then I was angry about Isaiah, but now, I'm not angry anymore and I'm not in pain anymore. I miss you."

I didn't even know what to say.

"You're always on my mind." Stephen continued. "I can't go a day without thinking about you. Wanting you. Why do you think I'm here?"

"It's Mother's Day weekend. I saw your mom's car parked at your uncle's house on the way in."

"I'm not here for my mother." He frowned. "I'm not even talking to my mother."

It was my turn to frown. "Not talking to her?"

He looked away. "I told you. I'm not letting her get away with what she did. I'm here for you. I knew about your father's party. I came because I'm doing the same thing I've done for twelve years. Wait for you. Watch for you. Hope you show up so I can..." He growled. It was a frustrated, angry sound that did not inspire confidence in his feelings.

I opened the door. "I can't. I don't want to do it again." I stepped out.

Stephen was behind me before I could reach the

door. He grabbed my elbow and pulled me into his arms. He held me in a tight embrace, pressing my head into his chest and clutching me like he couldn't make it without me. "Tay, I –"

"Don't say it." I pulled back. "Please. I'm just getting my head together and feeling good about me. I spoke today. In front of a crowd."

"What am I, bad karma? Why can't we feel good about ourselves together?"

I shook my head. "Because we can't. You're all over the place Stephen. Angry at me, not angry with me. And now you're mad at your mother."

Stephen took a deep breath and shook his head. "My mother and I will eventually work it out."

"Of course, you will," I said. "But you need to get back to football and get to know Isaiah. That's what you need to do, and I need to take care of my aunt and figure out who I want to be."

Stephen's jaw clenched. "None of those are things we need to do alone."

"I liked my life better when I was alone."

Stephen shook his head. "No, you didn't." He took a few steps down and onto the walkway. "You didn't." He cleared his throat. "Just to be sure, this isn't about Debra is it?"

"No."

"I know it's not about living public anymore. You spoke today. You reached out to Melissa."

I swallowed. He was right.

Stephen nodded. "I know you better than you think. I said I'd wait for you. I mean that, so think about it."

I removed my key and inserted it in the door.

"Don't be afraid of happiness, Tamar. Your mother would want you to be happy. I could make you happy. We could make each other happy."

I stared at him for a minute. I didn't say anything and neither did he. Then I turned and stepped inside.

I got on the other side of the door. A vision of my mother's reflection in the mirror came to me again.

"Stephen's a nice young man. I think you've already found your love."

The tears fell. I turned on the foyer light and listened for the engine to Stephen's truck. He'd started it, but he had not moved. We were both frozen in place. Me inside and him out. I didn't know how to be happy. I released a heavy sigh with the revelation. I was too afraid to be happy.

I looked up and the flowers my father had received this morning caught my eyes. The blooms had opened. It was an incredible arrangement and clearly expensive. Curious about who had spent so much money, I picked up the card. I was surprised to see my name and not my dad's. I read the note:

"Tamar, Thank you for my son. He's an amazing young man. I appreciate you bringing him into the world and adding to my legacy – Love, Stephen."

Love Stephen. I thought about love. God had shown me the true meaning of 1 Corinthians 13 last year when Stephen and I rekindled our love. Love bears all things, believes all things, hopes all things, endures all things. Love never fails.

Think about it.

I could make you happy.

We could make each other happy.

I turned back to the door and peeked through the curtain. I could see the taillights of his truck moving away from the house.

I wait for you. I watch for you.

I wasn't ready. I hadn't been ready in December, and I wasn't ready now.

I turned on the porch light for my dad and climbed the stairs.

Chapter 31

"You're at eighty percent, Stephen. Unfortunately, that's not good enough."

I felt like I'd had the wind knocked out of me. Six weeks from training camp and I wasn't cleared to play?

"My PT has gone great. My therapist told me so. And I feel like myself." I protested.

"I know all of this, but you don't have enough function," Dr. Hogan said.

"You've said that a player's capacity can only really be realized on the field." I replied, quoting him from a pep talk he'd given me last month.

"I meant that a player who was testing in the range of ninety percent or better. Stephen, you know we're not talking about every day usage. We're not even talking about playing in a game. We're talking about training and conditioning. Running stairs, squats and everything else you have to do to be strong on the field," Doctor Hogan said. "And not being strong on the field puts you at risk for reinjury or even another injury. You could get hurt again, possibly worse."

I groaned. This was painful, but I knew he was right. I wasn't ready.

"I think you have the potential, but you're just not as far along as I'd hoped. You're less than two months out from camp—"

"So, you're talking about the season?"

"I'm not going to speculate," Dr. Hogan said. "You need more time to heal. This is not an easy injury to recover from."

"Thanks, Doc."

"Continue the therapy. Maybe take a week or so off with light exercises. You could use a break. It might do you good to not be focused on it." He offered a few other suggestions and left the room.

I sighed. "No football." I never anticipated I'd hear that. In my mind, I was going to go out like one of the greats – Tiki Barber, Emmitt Smith, and the Pro Football Hall of Fame. I wanted to be like Michael Strahan, fifteen years with the Giants organization and retire on a career high. Michael had called me, and I hadn't called him back. Maybe I should.

Call me.

I closed my eyes to the sound of the voice of the Holy Spirit. I'd been calling on God my entire life and still, I was here dealing with the worst news of my career. I stood and left the examination room. I exited the center with a legion of pats on the back from my teammates. I didn't stop to see the coaches. No doubt they already knew what was happening. They were probably busy figuring out the strategy for a season without me.

I pushed the exit door open and made a quick trip to my SUV. I didn't want to see another soul. I didn't want any more sympathy, or pity, or whatever people were feeling toward me. My cell phone rang. Clyde. I silenced the call, climbed inside my truck and cried. I cried like a baby.

Hours later, I was lying in my bed when my cell phone woke me. I had taken a muscle relaxer, not because I needed it, but because they always put me to sleep. I didn't want to be awake anymore today. It was Tamar's number on the screen. I sighed and let it go to voicemail.

I went to Instagram. Read some of the comments fans had left for me and realized there was a story about me on ESPN, so I went to their page. It was an interview with Coach Nye.

"From the time we finish, until the time we start in Rutherford, is between five and six weeks. That's plenty of time,"

"I'm completely comfortable with him running when he's ready and the doctors say he's almost ready. He's totally engaged in every aspect of what we're doing mentally. The physical part for a guy like him, I think you've got to work at it. But I'm not worried about it. I'm comfortable with the process that is in place. We expect him to make it camp and start like he has since his rookie season.

"I'm not worried at all."

I grunted and put down the phone. Coach wasn't worried. Yeah, right.

I stood and headed toward the bathroom. In the sliver of moonlight that swept the room, a picture of

Isaiah that I kept on my dresser caught my eye.

That's when it hit me, I couldn't ignore Tamar's calls. My son lived with her. I rushed back to the phone and listened to the message. It was Isaiah. I returned the call.

Tamar answered.

"Hey, Isaiah called me."

"Hey, yourself," she said it with enough snark to let me know I was being rude.

"I'm sorry. I've had a rough day."

"You a rough day? Lord, is the eastern sky going to split?"

I was slow to respond, because it had split, at least for me anyway and I'd been left behind. "Maybe you can just put him on for me."

"I'm sorry, it was just a little humor." She paused. "Are you sure you want to talk to him like this? He's way too excited for a grumpy dad."

My heart was a crushing weight in my chest. "What's he excited about?" I asked, trying to keep my voice even.

"Something about the baseball finals. I'll let him tell you, but is there something I can help with? I'm a good listener."

I couldn't even answer her. The realization that I might not be playing hadn't fully sunk in yet. Right now, I didn't want a sounding board. I wanted to disappear. I wanted her and not for a pep talk.

Hearing her voice reminded me of what I'd been

thinking about prior to going to sleep. I'd been thinking about the only thing I thought would distract me – disappearing in a woman. I'd had to knock myself out to stop the urge from sending me out to some club to look for one. I was twenty minutes from NYC. There was always a club, always a party, always somewhere a pro-athlete could find a woman.

"Stephen," she called. "Is it…" Hesitation on the other end. "…your ankle?"

I dropped my head. Pushed bass into my struggling voice. "Yeah, it's my ankle."

"I'm so sorry."

"Don't tell him I called," I said. I felt like I was going to lose it again. "I'll call back later when I'm better, okay?"

"Okay," she said. "Stephen?"

I waited.

"It's going to be okay."

"It's not, Tay. I don't think it ever will be."

"You can't think like that. You have to remain optimistic."

I was silent for a long time. Optimism wasn't what I was thinking about.

"Would you?" I started. The next words out of my mouth were going to be to ask her to come up here. I wanted to ask her to drop everything and just come be with me. Hug me, kiss me, lie with me, love me, but we weren't those people anymore. I wasn't her husband. I wasn't even her man.

If I was completely honest, I still blamed her a little. Any time I got bad news about my ankle, I thought about how distracted I was by our breakup. That was crazy. This wasn't Tamar's fault, but I kept revisiting the thought. *The devil.*

"Would I what?"

"Would you pray for me, Tay? I really need prayer." I didn't wait for her response. It would include a what and a why, so I ended the call and turned off my cell phone.

Chapter 32

I hated cancer so much. It was ugly, evil, and vile. I couldn't stop the tears. I didn't like for people to see me cry. I'd gotten good at keeping my tears under control. My public life toughed me up, but this was not me. This was not upset over a video. This was my aunt's life, the lack of quality of life she had, and all the pain. I was wrecked.

A text message came in from Isaiah.

How is mama?

A loud sob erupted from my belly. I raised my hand to wipe my face. I needed tissues. I needed to clean up. I couldn't let the hospital staff or, God forbid, Aunt Joe see me like this. I escaped into the restroom.

My phone rang. It was Aunt Joe's pastor, Reverend Kelly. I answered.

"I've been told Sister Josephine is in the hospital."

"We're at the ER, pastor. She had a bad reaction after the chemo. She's being seen right now."

"I'm on my way back from Alabama, so I'm sending one of the members of the prayer board to join you. I heard your pain, Tamar. Stay strong in God. This weeping will only endure for the night. We know that God is a healer and joy will come in the morning when Sister Josephine is healed. I want you to speak words in the Spirit over her. Do it as you care for her. Not out loud, but in your heart."

"Words?"

"Aunt Joe will live and not die. The sickness is not unto death. Things like that. Use scriptures. Cancer can be just as much a spiritual battle as it is a physical one. Stand in the gap for her, Sister Tamar."

I nodded. "I understand."

"I know you know. I just want to remind you. I know in the moment it can be hard to remember what to do. I'm praying for her. We are all praying without ceasing."

"Thank you, pastor."

He assured me he would visit tomorrow, and we ended the call.

Aunt Joe was so sick that I thought she might die. Chemo is worse than the disease. It's said so often it sounds like a cliché, but once you see it up close, watch it tear its way through a person's body, you understood. You understood why people say it.

I didn't want Isaiah seeing how sick she was. I didn't want him to remember her this way.

I texted him back:

The doctors are helping her. I'll call as soon as I can.

I took a deep breath, washed my face, and pulled

myself together. I left the restroom and went back across the hall to Aunt Joe's room.

Aunt Joe turned her head in my direction. I went to the bed and took her hand.

"I feel better," she said.

She didn't look better. Her voice was a little stronger, but I knew that might be her sheer will to get out of the ER. She hated hospitals.

The ER doc that had been taking care of her entered the room. "I talked to Doctor Mowry, and she wants to admit you at least overnight. Get some fluids in you, okay?"

Aunt Joe groaned. "I guess if I don't have a choice."

"No choice right now," he said. "We'll get you a room and take good care of you."

Aunt Joe nodded and he left.

I was so relieved. If they sent her home tonight, I would have died myself.

"I'm tired of this place," Aunt Joe said.

"Auntie, it's a good thing. Like they said, it's just overnight. You vomited so much. You need the fluids."

"Hospitals are full of germs. I could catch something worse overnight in this place," Aunt Joe said. "You know people get sick in the hospital, especially people who've had chemo."

"They'll take care of you."

Aunt Joe groaned. She turned her back to me and

closed her eyes. Within a few minutes, she had fallen asleep again.

I closed my eyes and whispered, "You will live and not die. By His stripes you are healed and made whole." I said it over and over again until I felt the burden of my sorrow lift from my heart. *This is a season. It's a hard one, but it will pass.*

My thoughts were interrupted by a transport team. I followed as they moved her to the Intensive Care Unit.

I waited until she got settled in and comfortable and then once she fell asleep, I left. The nurses and doctor insisted. I could only visit her for short periods of time. They'd given her something to help her sleep, so she wouldn't even know I was there.

They didn't have to do much convincing. I had been up all of the night before and then hovering over her all day. I was tired.

I climbed into my car and my cell phone rang. It was my father.

"Hey, Daddy."

"Hey, baby, how are you?"

"Stressed. Aunt Joe is sick. She's having a bad reaction to the chemo."

"I'm sorry to hear that. I've been praying for her and you. I know this is hard on you, and you don't have any help."

"I'm leaving the hospital now. They admitted her, so I'm going home to get some sleep."

"That's good. Where's Isaiah?"

"He's staying with a friend overnight."

"Good, good, good. He doesn't have to be around, and you don't have to worry about him. I know it's got to be hard for him, too."

"So, what did you need, Daddy?"

"Nothing. I was checking on you all. I hadn't heard anything from you in a few days."

"I'm sorry. I've been busy. Isaiah had a project to do for a social studies fair and then with Aunt Joe, I've been doing stuff non-stop."

"I understand, Baby Girl. I just want you to know I'm here."

"I'm glad you called. I was wondering if you could do something."

"Sure."

"It's Stephen. He found out some bad news about his ankle yesterday. He called me. He doesn't sound good. He asked me to pray for him. I think he needs you."

I could hear the concern in my father's voice when he said, "He's been on my mind lately. I'm glad you told me."

"I've never heard him sound so down. I mean, well, he was down when he first got injured, but he hasn't been like this since."

"Do you know if he's home?"

"I think so. I didn't ask, but I got the sense that

he was."

"Maybe I'll drive over to New Jersey and see him in person. Dell might be able to come with me. She's been wanting to get out of town for some shopping."

I smiled. "When are you and Dell going to get married, Daddy?"

"That's a good question. I think I put off proposing to Dell because I didn't want you to come back into my life and I'd taken a new wife. But now that you're back, I don't know, I guess it is time."

"She's a good woman. She seems to make you happy and I want you to be happy."

"Her birthday is in a few weeks. I was thinking maybe then."

"Just do it, Daddy. Propose. Don't let more time go by. Taking care of Aunt Joe has taught me that tomorrow isn't promised. Sometimes I forget that lesson."

"Well, you might want to consider taking that advice yourself."

"Daddy…"

"I saw the size of those flowers Stephen sent here for Mother's Day and he hasn't come to any of my birthday dinners in the past."

It was just like my father to lobby for him. "Always Team Stephen."

"Team love," he said. "You two have overcome too much to not have your destinies tied together. You've found a way to not hate each over Isaiah. That young man is still in love with you, Tamar. I told him he could have your hand in marriage. I haven't taken that permission back."

I was frustrated and I didn't try to hide it. "Don't I matter in the equation?"

"Of course, you do. That's not what I mean."

"Well, he's in no condition to marry anyone right now. Let me know how he is, okay?"

"Will do. Give your aunt my love and hug my grandson for me."

"I will."

"And Tamar. Pray on John 11. The sickness will not end in death. I'll talk to you later, baby."

Chapter 33

I had to clean up in the Aunt Joe's bedroom. She had vomited several times in the pail she kept by her bed. Even though I'd emptied it, the room still smelled foul. I opened the window, turned on the fan, and sprinkled baking soda on the carpet. I wiped all the wood down, changed the bedding, and vacuumed. The last thing I did was turn on a diffuser and add lemon essential oil to the water to clear and purify the air.

I spent the evening taking care of myself. I took a hot bath, and then sat the table to eat the salad I had picked up on the way home. Aunt Joe's reading glasses and magazine were at the setting across from me. I needed to remember to take her glasses just in case she wanted them tomorrow. I picked up the magazine. The story it was open to was, "What Does Cancer Smell Like?" I frowned and began reading. It was about how dogs were being trained to recognize cancer.

I read, "Increased cell proliferation and raised polyamine levels are typical in cancer. What's more, polyamines actually smell bad. Dogs have been successful in find cancer."

I closed the magazine. Interesting, but obviously still in the early stages. Decades of research and still no cure. I shook my head. This evil disease destroyed so many lives.

Once I was finished eating, I closed Aunt Joe's windows and then went to my bedroom and climbed into bed, read a little and fell asleep.

At 2 a.m. I woke up. I tried to get back to sleep, but I couldn't. I reached for my Bible. I wanted to read Lazarus because both Pastor Kelly and my father had talked about the sickness not ending in death. I turned to the 11th chapter in the Gospel of John and read the entire thing through. I focused on verse 4, When Jesus heard *that,* He said, *"This sickness is not unto death, but for the glory of God, that the Son of God may be glorified through it."*

I prayed, "Aunt Joe's sickness is not unto death. Jesus, you will be glorified. People will see her healed. She will be well and whole again. People will know that you delivered her from death. In your name, Lord Jesus, I pray, amen."

I put the Bible on my nightstand and tried to go back to sleep, but I couldn't. Something in the story was calling me to take another look. I picked up the Bible again and read the chapter again. Once I was finished, my eyes fell again on verse 38 –

Then Jesus, again groaning in Himself, came to the tomb. It was a cave, and a stone lay against it. Jesus said, "Take away the stone."

Martha, the sister of him who was dead, said to Him, "Lord, by this time there is a stench, for he has been dead four days."

Jesus said to her, "Did I not say to you that if you would believe you would see the glory of God?" Then they took away the stone from the place where the dead man was lying. And Jesus lifted up His eyes and said, "Father, I thank You that You have heard Me. And I know that You always hear Me, but because of the people who are standing by I said this, that they may believe that You sent Me." Now when He had said these things, He cried with a loud voice, "Lazarus, come forth!" And he who had died came out bound hand and foot with graveclothes, and his face was wrapped with a cloth. Jesus said to them, "Loose him, and let him go."

By this time there is a stench. This verse stuck with me. I thought about the article I read earlier about the smell of cancer. I went back to the verse: *Lord, by this time there is a stench.*

I was reminded of that smell in Aunt Joe's room before I cleaned it. Is that what death smelled liked? A human rotting from the inside out? That's what the vomit smelled like. It smelled like she was dying inside.

But Jesus brought him back from death. The word said:

And he who had died came out bound hand and foot with graveclothes, and his face was wrapped with a cloth. Jesus said to them, "Loose him, and let him go."

What did this mean for Aunt Joe?

That I'd have to continue to care for her after she came back from the brink of death?

It's not about her.

"Then what's it about, Lord?" I sighed. I had no idea, nor the brain cells left to figure it out. God would have to reveal it. As my father always said, in His time, God would reveal all.

Chapter 34

Early the next morning, the house phone rang. Aunt Joe still had one, claiming she needed a wired phone in case of a natural disaster. I considered two phone bills on a tight budget to be a natural disaster, but it wasn't for me to say. I just answered it when it rang.

"Hello, my name is LaDonna Abrams. I am the principal at North Christian High School and I'm looking for Tamar Johnson."

"This is Tamar Johnson."

"Ms. Johnson, I'm so glad I have the right contact information for you. I heard you were residing in town with your aunt. She worked for us during the summer a few years ago. We are all praying for her here at North Christian."

"Thank you. I'll let her know."

"The reason I was calling is I was hoping you would accept invitation from us."

"An invitation to do what?"

"We need a speaker for our annual life skills program for young women."

I frowned. "Really?"

"Yes, I'm familiar with your story and then I saw what you did for Melissa Teasley. I thought you'd be the perfect person to speak at our event."

"Ms. Abrams, I'm not a speaker."

"None of us are until we open our mouths and as far as I can see, when you open your mouth, it's quite powerful. Talking a stranger out of suicide is not easy task." She paused. "Ms. Johnson, let me be completely frank. I'm concerned. We have good girls here, but they are so caught up in social media and some of them have begun to post pictures and share things that they should not and may regret. Perhaps hearing you—"

"I'll do it," I said it before I lost the nerve.

Ms. Abrams chuckled. "Wonderful. Oh my. I'm so excited." I could hear it in her voice. "Let me get your email address. I'll send you the particulars. I'll include the honorarium we can offer."

I hadn't even considered that I'd be paid. I gave her my email address and then with my hand trembling out of control, I hung up the phone.

I walked over to the desk where I kept my laptop and sat down in front of it. I opened it, pulled up some of my recent writings. I wouldn't let myself call it a manuscript because I wasn't going to write my story. But I had begun something, and it had practically leapt out of me onto the page.

"I grew up hearing and chanting the old adage: Sticks and stones may break my bones, but words will never hurt me. We

were taught to believe that, but it's not true. It's a false narrative, spun by someone who had no understanding of the frailty of human emotions. Maybe a bully made it up himself. The thing I realize about words is that they have the power to reach into places that sticks and stones never could. Words touch our hearts and minds and spirits. Words can be like a cancer that eats up all the good words about ourselves that we had stored up. Mean words are parasitic. They plant themselves inside their host and grow and grow until there's no more space for the truth. Sticks and stones bruise. Words burn. Have you ever been burned? It's a pain that stings. It won't relent.

Overnight, I went from being a shy teenager, to a publicly humiliated Internet phenomenon because someone clicked a mouse on an icon that said "Upload." That one click made me, the daughter of a preacher in a small rural church in Pennsylvania, an overnight scandalous figure. My life was destroyed.

I wasn't just embarrassed. I was ashamed. I wasn't ashamed a little. I was ashamed deep down in my soul. There was nowhere to run and nowhere to hide from my shame. The video had 2 million hits. That's nothing you may think today, but 12 years ago, YouTube was a new platform and 2 million hits was about the largest number they had had to date. Nothing had been more viral. The video of me losing my virginity on prom night broke records.

I'll share all the details about exactly what happened to me, but I want to stop and say, right here and now, I've written this book for you. I don't know you. I will probably never know you. But you are a human being and because words can hurt you, because they can destroy you, I am telling my story.

I released a plume of air. Six months ago, I was living my life as Anne Ferguson, a nonessential features writer at a small magazine. I'd been hiding for twelve years. I thought I'd always be hiding. I lived my life day by day, not even trying to figure out if it was time for me to step out of hiding. Could I have continued that way for the rest of my life?

I think I could have and if I had, I wouldn't be out of the closet as Isaiah's mother. I would not be talking to my father. I would not have written this book. I would not be speaking to young women. I would just be a victim, roadkill that no one cared about or even buried. Now, I was becoming someone who had something to say. Someone who might change the course of a young woman's life.

My phone chirped, and I was reminded that I needed to login to Isaiah's lunch account and add money. I had bells and whistles dinging on my phone all day that reminded me of the tasks I needed to take care of. Six months ago, I had only been responsible for myself. The only obligation I had in life was to show up at my job.

I tapped the return button to remove the screensaver, logged into the school account and put money on Isaiah's lunch card. Then I checked my email and found I had two. One from the principal at North Christian and one from my agent. I opened the one from my agent first.

Dear Tamar,

Just wanted to inform you I received a rejection letter from Machette House Publishers. They said they'd just acquired something similar. No worries, I have it out to 4 more editors.

Rejection. That was familiar. The novel I'd written five years ago was rejected by nearly forty publishers. Not a single one gave me a reason. At least with this one, I knew why. I opened the North Christian email. The date for the speech was August 10th. The same date I'd packed my bags and run away from home at eighteen. The name of the program was *Becoming: Lessons from Mary and Martha.*

I frowned as I thought about the scripture from the other night. I went to my bedroom. My Bible was still open. I remembered how the Holy Spirit had told me the reading wasn't about Aunt Joe. I didn't understand. I'd have to pray about it later. No matter what, I knew God was on the job. If it wasn't about Aunt Joe, I needed to figure out who it was for and what it meant.

Chapter 35

My eyes were locked with Pastor Johnson's. I wanted to keep my thoughts to myself, but he'd come all this way, so it was time for me to man up and have this conversation with someone other than myself.

"I've read scriptures about persecution and sickness. I thought when things got tough, I would come through the refiner's fire like pure silver, but now I realize the heat is killing me. I'm melting. I ain't no Job." Shame seeped from my pores, but I continued.

"And I also realize that some of the problem is that I think I thought those experiences were for someone else. Someone would be sick, someone else would go through. Like I was exempt because I've always been good. Like I was the Golden Boy." I paused. "I thought I was better than all the other guys in the NFL. I got angry because I do what's right and some of these guys – they sleep with a different woman every night. They've got baby mamas in five cities. They do whatever they think they're big and bad enough to do."

I was silent for a moment. Heartbroken and mouth dry, I waited to see if Pastor Johnson had a comment. He crossed his hands in front of him on the table and nodded for me to go on.

"I work with kids." I jabbed my thumb backward at my chest. "I've immersed myself in community service my whole career and not for show, but because I love it. I love those kids. I love my life. I love what I stand for. And I couldn't be protected from this. I might be done playing ball. I have a son that I meet at eleven. I haven't had sex in four years. Football is the only thing that keeps me sane. Why do you think I run so fast and hit so hard? That's not about money. That's about passion. That's what I do. That's all I have and now I don't even have that anymore."

Pastor Johnson continued to be mute. "And then there's your daughter. I've loved her my whole life, and she doesn't want me. I'm not enough for her. I don't even have a woman to love me. I'm starting to think I've got a warped sense of who I am. There's something wrong with me."

Tamar's father raised an eyebrow for a moment. He'd asked me what was on my mind and now he had it. All of it.

"Stephen, you know that trials don't come to kill us. Even Jesus endured trials."

"Yeah, he did, pastor, but there's a difference between Him and me." I began to talk with my hands. "I'm not God. I'm a man, living better than most of the men I know, so why did this happen to me? Why me? Why couldn't I be protected? Where is God in this? Where is he for me?"

"Stephen, have you ever considered that God may be trying to use you?" Pastor Johnson's tone held no nonsense.

"Son, it's easy to praise Him and talk about His

goodness when you're up. It's easy to act like the Golden Boy when it's all good. People aren't impressed by that. Nobody close to you – and I'm talking your team here – none of them are impressed by the fact that you pray at games and talk about God in your interviews or even that you've chosen to be celibate. But I bet you they're looking at you now. Now that your life is in the valley - your teammates are circling, waiting to see what Stephen Pierce is going to do. Is he going to bless his God or curse him? Can Stephen Pierce still walk through this locker room and around all this equipment with his busted leg and say, 'God is good. Though he slay me, yet will I trust him'."

He slapped a palm on the table. "Will you say that? Will you say it with a smile?"

My lip trembled. I was so convicted by his words, I wanted them to stop.

"God is trying to use you to witness, and you're missing the opportunity for the greatest witness of your life because you're angry. He needs your praises and your testimony right now. This is a defining hour for you."

Pastor Johnson paused and let me process his words for a minute, then he crossed his arms over his chest. "And with respect to my daughter. She loves you. She's dealing with a lot. Coming out of her hiding place has presented new challenges. She's used to dealing with everything alone. Tamar had become a runner. She knows how to hide. You have to chase her and if you're not willing to do that, then..."

"I love Tamar. I do, I just."

"Just what, Stephen?"

I shook my head. "She rejected me. She told me she didn't want to be a part of my world. The football world."

Pastor shook his head. "I don't know. I don't get a sense of that being the issue. I don't pretend to know what is in the mind of you young people sometimes, but when you came to me and asked me for my daughter's hand, I said yes, because I thought you had what she needed."

"I thought I did too," I offered weakly.

"Son, you've got to be sure. I thought you were sure." Pastor Johnson paused. He took a deep breath and continued. "Tamar has struggled with her faith, ever since her mother died. You've always been stronger than her in that respect. I wanted my daughter to marry a man who would pray for her. She needs a man to spiritually take the lead in a relationship until she can confidently lead herself. If you're not that man, I don't want her to marry you, because I want better for her. Do you understand that?"

I felt the first hot tear leave my eye and slide down my face. "Yes, sir."

"Can I pray with you, son?"

I nodded.

Pastor Johnson stood and came around to my side of the table. He placed a hand on my shoulder. We bowed our heads and he began to pray.

"Father, we come before you as humbly as we know how. We come before you as men, imperfect in every way, needing to be fashioned like clay by You, the Master Potter. Lord, I pray for Stephen. I thank You for his honesty. I thank You that You have revealed to him where he is weak. Now Lord, I pray for You to make him strong.

"Take away feelings of anger, contempt, entitlement, and self-righteousness. None of them are like You. None of them display Your character. None of them display Your glory. Remove his pride. Peel back the layers of it, so he can understand his purpose in this season in his life. Remind him of Your word in 2 Chronicles 14. Let him cry out, 'Help me, O Lord my God, for I rely on You.' Let him remember, weeping endures for the night, but joy comes in the morning. In Exodus 15:26, You say, 'For I am the Lord who heals you.' For You, Lord are Jehovah Rapha, the God who heals him. You will do as Your word says in Psalm 147:2. Heal his broken heart and bandage his wound. Grow him in this season. He will soar on wings like an eagle. He will run and not grow weary. He will walk and not faint. In the precious name of our Lord and Savior Jesus Christ, I pray. Amen."

I stood and wrapped my arms around his neck and squeezed as more tears erupted. "Thank you, Pastor. I needed that. I needed to see you." I released him.

His eyes were on me. All I saw was love and compassion.

"You will come through the refiner's fire as pure silver, because pure silver is what you are." He reached into his pocket. "I wrote down some scriptures on these cards. Keep them with you. Read them several times a day, over and over, and be strengthened in the Word. The Word of God is what's going to get you through this."

I accepted the stack from his hand.

"And, son, be grateful. Find something to be grateful about every day. Gratitude takes the focus off what we don't have."

Pastor looked around the room and said, "I know money isn't everything, but you're the 15-million-dollar man. That shouldn't be too hard." He smiled and patted me on the shoulder before leaving me with my thoughts, and tears, and gratitude that he had come to bless me.

Chapter 36

The next day I was on a flight to Georgia. Tamar didn't want to leave Aunt Joe, so we decided to have dinner together at the house. I'd brought Isaiah a new video game. As soon as he scarfed down his meal, he asked to be excused so he could go put it in.

"You're not allowed to play video games on weeknights," Tamar said before he could jump up from the table.

"Please," Isaiah begged. "Just a few minutes of it." He looked to me. "Dad, you'll play with me? You can make sure I don't play that long."

I smiled. "You set it up while I talk to your mom."

Isaiah flew from the table.

Tamar pinned me with a look. "We have rules here, Mr. Pierce. You can't let him play us against each other."

I accepted my lashes. "I know, but he's done with his homework. I need him to be occupied while I talk to you."

"He could read to be occupied or clean his room or a number of other things I can think of." She wasn't letting it go.

I threw up my hands. "That's fair. I'll defer to you next time because this is y'alls house."

Tamar smiled. "I'm messin' with you. I just wanted to see what you would say, Dad."

She stood and went to the stove to put the kettle on. I could see a little hint of a smile on her face as she worked. She had indeed been messin' with me. "So," she crossed her arms over her chest. "What's going on with the ankle?"

I gave her an update and shared some of what her father told me. Thanks to him, I was able to keep the fear and fret out of my voice as I spoke.

"I'm glad my dad was able to help."

"I appreciate you calling him."

She blessed me with a full smile and a nod. "You asked me to pray. I did. I felt like that was the right thing to do."

"You definitely heard from the Holy Spirit," I said. "He was right on time."

Tamar dropped her arms and her eyes for a moment. "I don't know about all that. I think any friend would have thought to call your pastor."

I grimaced. Friend. There was that word again. I stood and joined her in the kitchen.

Tamar frowned against the intrusion. I stepped closer, like I was playing a game of red light-green light. She looked trapped, but she didn't move away. She cleared her throat and said, "Go ahead and say what you want to say before Isaiah comes out of that room."

"Maybe do what I want to do." I paused, my eyes dropping to her lips and then rising again.

Tamar's eyes bulged a little. She was not giving me permission to get closer.

Mission aborted, I looked in the direction of Isaiah's bedroom. "The fact that there is an Isaiah still seems surreal on some days."

The small galley kitchen was narrow. Tamar was able to place one hand on the counter and the other on the stove on the opposite side. She did so briefly and then something in her eyes shifted. She crossed her arms and leaned her hip against the counter like she'd closed herself up.

"I birthed him and some days it's surreal to me," she whispered. "But I can't keep going around about this, Stephen. I know you're hurt, but I want this to be our last hard talk about Isaiah," she insisted. "I can't—"

"Tay." I raised a hand to stop her emotional breakdown. "It's okay. Let me say what I need to say."

She released a sigh on a long wind of frustration, shifted her weight from one foot to the other and waited for me.

"Initially, I thought you must really have hated me to keep my son a secret, but I realize, you were just trying to survive back then. This was not all your fault." I shook my head. "I told you before, I played a part and I own that."

Tamar bit her lip. Her eyes misted over with tears.

"I had to get hurt to understand pain. The mind

can convince you of some things when you're in survival mode."

Tamar nodded. "Survival mode is hard, and it's ugly. When you're in it, it feels like it's never going to end."

I reached for one of her hands. "I understand now. I didn't before because I never had to."

"You've lived a charmed life, Stephen." Tamar looked down at our hands, then raised her eyes to mine. "That's not a crime. It just doesn't always help when a person needs empathy."

The words were tight in my throat, but I said, "I agree."

Tamar pulled her hand out of mine. "Speaking of hate," she began, "I know I should have told you back in December, but I was terrified. I thought you were going to hate me."

I shook my head. "I could never hate you."

"Then what about your ankle?"

I frowned. She'd changed the subject so quickly. "What about it?"

"You blamed me for your accident."

I shook my head. "I shouldn't have said that. I didn't mean it."

She raised an eyebrow. "Are you sure?"

I dropped my head back and sighed. "I wanted you out of that hospital room. I was in pain. I was embarrassed. I felt weak and I didn't think you loved me, so I used whatever I could to get you to leave, babe. That's all that was."

She was in my arms in seconds. I squeezed her tight and kissed the top of her head.

"All this time," she cried. "I thought you blamed me."

I raised my hands and placed them on either side of her face. "The game happened to me. I'm so sorry you believed that."

Tamar took a deep breath. I could see she really needed to hear that. Her eyes spoke before she did. "I'm glad you came."

She took a step away from me, opened the cupboard, and removed a box of tea bags. She held the box up to me, and I shook my head. Then she removed a mug from the counter and dropped a bag in it. She finished what she was doing and turned toward me. She folded her hands over her chest again. "Something else is on your mind."

I almost smiled. I was glad she knew me, but I couldn't smile about what I had to say.

Tamar's eyebrows bunched together. "What is it?"

I looked down at my feet and then up again. "I'm not sure I'm going to be able to play."

Now she was shocked. My own heart was pounding.

Tamar dropped her arms. "Don't say that. You can't give up because it looks bad."

"I know that in my head, but my heart is like

frozen in my chest. I'm not ready to be finished, but I'm not better. I have pain in this ankle every day."

Tamar stepped closer again. She placed a hand on my arm and tugged at it a little. "Listen to me. You're not finished. You have to be optimistic. That's a part of the healing process."

I looked down at her hand on my arm and then back into her eyes. "You've always been my peace. Do you know that? Even when you were gone all those years, I would remember the things you said to me before my games. 'Stephen, no one is faster than you. You have the best record in the state. No one can beat you. You're a winner.' Those words played in my head like a tape."

Tamar looked away. I raised a hand to her chin and turned her face back to mine. "You forgot about all that didn't you?" I chuckled. "I never did, but I didn't come here to talk about football. I came here to say what you wouldn't let me say before."

Heat darkened her eyes. Her mouth dropped open. "Stephen, please."

"Please?" I know I looked puzzled because I was. "Are you begging me not to tell the truth? I've got zero interest in secrets, Tay. I love you, and I'm not going to let you or me or anyone keep me from telling you the truth."

Tamar stared at me like she was processing what I was saying. I leaned closer and kissed her. One quick kiss on the cheek and then the lips.

She shoved me away. "No. You can't just come here and say I'm sorry, I love you, and kiss me."

"If you don't want a kiss that's fine. I mean, I don't understand it. Who wouldn't want this kiss," I teased, "but you can't stop me from saying how I feel."

She wouldn't look at me now. I know she was fighting to keep her heart closed.

"Tamar, you're not the only person in this relationship. You can call us friends and co-parents until Jesus comes back, but we're more than that."

She rolled her eyes but didn't speak in the break I gave her to do so.

"I gave you a ring. You asked me for time. I think you've had enough time. You're making excuses, and I'm not going to let you do that."

Her defenses were activated. "I'm not making excuses."

I stepped back, giving her the space I suspected she needed. "Last year, you told me that you believed God could make the relationship between you and me new again. That He could restore our love."

She nodded. "I remember that."

"Do you still believe that God has the power to make something new?"

"If it's His will." Her tone hinted of exasperation.

"I've told you this before. I've always known you were supposed to be my wife. The first time I heard your father preach about the woman being the man's rib, I knew. I was like ten years old and you popped into my mind. There was never any doubt that my life would include you." I paused.

"I still believe that. Even after everything we've been through. Even after my lost time with Isaiah. I could never hate you. But I'm not going to lie. I wanted to be angry with you. I wanted to move on, but I couldn't because it's not God's will that I leave my rib by the side of the road like it came from another man."

Tamar took backward steps. She picked up the kettle and filled it with water and turned on the stove. Her hand trembled the entire time. She obviously felt the same way, but she was fighting it. When she looked at me, her eyes searched mine like she was looking for a lie.

"I'll work at us," I promised. "I know that if I want something, I have to put in work. I've been living clean for a long time, so work is all I know how to do. That's why I'm here asking for a second chance."

Tamar scrunched up her nose. "Second?"

I chuckled. "Maybe it's a third chance."

She shook her head. I peeped that she was attempting to hide a smile.

"Do you love me, Tamar?" I asked. "I mean, not as a friend, but when you look at me. Do you still have romantic feelings?"

She threw up her hands. "I don't know. I don't know how I feel about you. You're overwhelming me."

I stepped closer. I put my hand over her heart. "I don't believe that racing of your heart when I get close is overwhelm. I'm going to prove to you that I'm worthy of that love you're trying to keep to yourself."

I stepped back and Tamar noticeably began to

breathe again.

"I want this to be the last go 'round and to make it official and proper, I'll do it the right way. Tamar Johnson, if you'll let me, I'd like to court you?"

She frowned. "Court? Do people still do that?"

"Yes."

Isaiah's voice came from the bedroom at the same time the kettle whistled. "Dad, it's downloaded. Come on!"

"My time is up." I raised a hand and stroked her cheek. "Saved by the kid."

Tamar moved the kettle from the hot burner. "I don't need the kid to save me."

"Oh, but you do. I'm coming for you hard this time." I leaned toward her and kissed her cheek. "You were right about me. I am a winner."

I winked, left the kitchen, and joined Isaiah in his bedroom.

Chapter 37

Draining the pulp from the bottom of my smoothie cup, I checked my watch. Again. My father was late. I was about to put the food in the warming oven when I heard the doorbell and then the alarm being disabled.

"Sorry," my father said, rushing into the room. "I had to go through fifty questions with your mother about where I was going."

He was baiting me and I wasn't going to talk about my mother. "No problem. Everything is ready."

I slid a plate of bacon, eggs, and toast across the breakfast bar toward him. Then I removed juice from the refrigerator, poured two glasses and took a seat. I said grace and began to eat.

My father went to the restroom. He slid into his chair. "So, you said you wanted to talk about Tamar."

I nodded and updated him on the last talk I'd had with Tamar. "So, now that I've opened my mouth and inserted my foot, I'm trying to come up with a way to impress her. I don't have any ideas about how to court her. It's not like we can sit on her father's porch on Sunday after church," I said through chews. "I know Tamar, but I don't. I don't know what she would consider a date that would prove my worth."

My father raised his glass and took a thoughtful sip. "Grand gestures go far with women. I know they did with your mother."

"I've done a lot of that. The ring. The car. She didn't care about either. She's not wearing the ring and the car is sitting in Atlanta. Something grand would just be more of the same. I want her to feel my effort, not my money."

"Well, do something like this." My father extended his hands over the table.

I didn't know what he was talking about and I said so, "Like what?"

"Cook for her. Do things that don't cost any money. Be creative. Be the Stephen she fell in love with in high school. The one who was broke."

I knit my brows together. "You mean dates that don't cost money. That's a novel idea, Dad." I chuckled.

"Not so novel for about fifty percent of the male population, son. I didn't have anything when I met your mother. I made a picnic lunch. Took her for walks. We fed the ducks. She fell in love with me, not my money, because I didn't have any."

"Okay, that's it. That's what's up. I'll come up with a list of romantic dates that don't cost money."

My dad and I pounded and continued to eat.

"So," my father hesitated. "Your mother is wondering how long you intend to ignore her."

I shrugged. "I'm not ignoring her. I haven't heard from her."

My father cleared his throat. "She feels like you owe her an apology."

"For what?" I scowled. "Oh, let me guess, I disrespected her by expecting more from her."

"She feels you disrespected her by asking for your key and then putting her out."

I pushed my plate away from me. Thinking about my mother put a knot in my gut. "I asked her to leave. It was for the best."

"Son, I know your mother did a terrible thing. Believe me, I have made sure she knows I agree with you, but she is your mother."

"I know that, dad, but I just need a minute to figure out how to bridge this gap between us. I just have to —"

"Forgive her," My father said. "The forgiveness you've wanted from Tamar and from God is no different from what you need to give your mother."

I avoided my father's eyes on that point. "What's going on with Mom? It seems like she's changed."

"She has a little." He shook his head. "Your money has brought out the worst in her, but she's always been a little more focused on the – let's see how I can say it – worldly things."

"When you were dating?"

"Sure. But I loved her anyway. I still do." My father threw up his hands. He grunted. "Do you know why my father gave his church to Johnson?"

I sat back in my chair now. I was ready for the story I'd never had the courage to ask for.

"It was a big deal that I didn't get the church. I was heavily involved in ministry. But I married a woman your grandfather didn't deem fit to be a First Lady."

I snatched back my head. "Really?"

"Your mother doesn't know. I never told her. She wanted to be the First Lady of Pine Christian Church, but my father wouldn't budge. He bypassed me and gave it to Johnson. He had a wife that was good First Lady material and she was, a wonderful woman who served in a way your mother never would have."

"Dad, do you think she resented Tamar's mother and Pastor Johnson for that?"

"Oh sure. She's said things over the years."

"Do you think that could be the reason she resents Tamar?"

My father shook his head. "No, I can't," he paused. "I don't think so, son. I just think she's controlling. She didn't like Debra either."

I stood and put our dishes in the sink. "I thought she did."

"Not really, but she liked Debra's screen presence, so she gave her some grace."

I clenched my teeth and shook my head against thoughts of Debra. "Everybody saw who Debra was except me."

My father wiped his mouth and put his napkin down. "You were lonely. It happens. For the record, I never thought you'd marry her."

I shook my head. "Making Saint Stephen's Baby. That's who I was engaged to."

My father laughed. "That too shall pass." He stood. "Look, I have to go. Your mother thinks I'm at the bookstore. If she finds out I'm here, she'll kill me or die from jealousy."

I sighed. "I'm sorry, Dad."

"Nope. Deal with it your way. Just remember, none of us are perfect. In relationships, you have to love someone through their imperfections. Mothers are not exempt from grace."

I leaned back against the counter and crossed my arms over my chest. "I understand. I guess right now, I'm trying to figure out how to trust her. I need some time."

"I'm praying for both of you."

My father left the house.

I cleared the rest of the dishes and went into my office. I picked up my iPad and pulled up a search window and typed in: "Inexpensive dates" because I hadn't had one those since college. I didn't even know what might be good. I found a list. A long one. I smiled.

"Okay, Tamar Johnson, be prepared to be swept off your feet."

I sat down began to scroll.

Chapter 38

Going to the supermarket was a form of self-care. It was a way for me to get alone time. I exited my bedroom with my bag and keys. I was on my way again.

"Where are you going?" Aunt Joe eyes widened like I'd come out of my bedroom with two heads.

Maybe I'd startled her. "To the store. We need a few things."

She frowned. "You have to go now?"

I frowned back. "Is there a reason I shouldn't go now. You're good and Isaiah's not even here."

"No…I mean, I need some things too. I haven't gotten my list together. You shoulda asked me earlier."

I hadn't asked her, but she'd been doing so well sticking to her meal plan, I didn't think she needed anything different other than the few things I always made sure to stock. "I'll have a seat. You tell me what you want." I dropped next to her.

Aunt Joe rolled her eyes. "I have to think about it." She picked up her cell phone and opened to the Candy Crush app.

I glared at her curiously. "Can you go ahead and

do that?"

She received a phone call. I waited as she chatted with her church sister.

When she got off the phone, she picked up the remote control like I wasn't waiting for her to give me her grocery list. Was she getting senile? She was too young for that.

"Auntie," I pressed. "You do know I'm waiting for you."

A text message pinged in on her phone, and she picked it up.

"Aunt Joe!" I exclaimed.

She looked at her phone and then turned to me. "I don't want anything, honey. You go ahead."

"Really?" I stood. I was annoyed but kept it out of my voice.

I went to the door and pulled it open. Stephen was standing there with a slick grin on his face.

"Surprise!" He handed me a bouquet of barely alive wildflowers I suspected he'd picked off the side of the highway. I knew the honeysuckles in the arrangement had come off Aunt Joe's tree. I scrunched up my face. "No time for a real florist?"

Stephen smiled. "I made sure to get some purple ones in there. I know it's your favorite color."

"Stephen!" Aunt Joe's greeting was a little more enthusiastic than usual. Now I knew why she was delaying my exit. She was in cahoots with him.

He walked into the house and gave her a hug.

"How are you feeling today?"

She slapped him on the forearm. "Fair to middling. How 'bout you? How's the ankle?"

Stephen raised his leg and twisted his ankle around. "Middling to better."

Aunt Joe shook her head. "Northerners. That's not a thing. But praise the Lord anyway."

We laughed.

"I almost forgot." Stephen reached into his pocket and removed a small box. "I have something for you."

Aunt Joe's eyes gleamed. "Is this my oil?"

"Best in the country." Stephen clapped his hands together and threw a thumb up.

I went into the kitchen for a mason jar. I filled it with water for my sorry, weepy flowers that I was certain would not reach the height of a vase. Curious about the exchange in the other room, I asked, "What kind of oil?"

"CBD," Aunt Joe replied.

I frowned. "Is that like cannabis oil?" I asked walking back into the living room.

"Yes, it's for the inflammation and sleep, but you have to have the good stuff." Aunt Joe twisted the top of the lid and took a whiff. "My doctor told me it was okay to try."

I looked at him. "You're not getting my aunt high are you?"

Stephen laughed. "Do I look like a weed man? Come on. It's hemp CBD. Perfectly legit and legal in all fifty states."

I nodded. "Okay, I just want to make sure you didn't let her talk you into some shenanigans."

"Like tricking you into staying in the house." Aunt Joe cackled. "Y'all git on. The Golden Girls have a marathon today. Sister Williams is on her way over here to watch some of it with me."

I picked up my bag and exited the house with Stephen. "Surprise, ha?"

"I told you I'd be back soon," Stephen said, hitting the key fob to open the doors of his rental.

I looked down at my worn jeans and tee-shirt. "I'm not exactly date ready. What are we doing?"

"We are going to the movies and having dinner," Stephen replied. "You look fine as is."

Stephen opened my car door and I got inside the SUV. "What movie are we going to see?"

"I'm not sure. I'll let you pick when we get there."

He joined me in the car, and we got on the road. After a few miles, I noticed he was going in the wrong way and I told him so. "You just missed the turn for the mall."

"I'm not going to the mall."

He kept driving, until he came to the side of town where the old broke down mall was that I never went to. He got a hat from the back seat and put it on. Then he put on a dark pair of sunglasses. "My disguise."

I chuckled. "No one would recognize you in a Falcon's hat."

"Absolutely not," he replied.

I looked up and saw the sign for Dollar Theater and realized this was it.

"Why are we at the dollar movie theater?"

Stephen placed a hand on my knee. "Do you remember our first date?"

I tried to recall, but I was drawing a blank.

"We went to Philadelphia for the debate competition thing. You and I snuck out of the hotel and went to see *Halloween*. The theater was showing the old version."

"The one we'd never been allowed to see because it was evil," I confirmed.

Stephen laughed. "Yes. What year was that?"

I shrugged. "I don't know…circa early 2000's. That wasn't a date. I couldn't date until I was sixteen."

Stephen cocked an eyebrow. "I know, but we were rebelling. We snuck out for it."

I frowned at his distorted memory of the event. "Yeah, we snuck out, but it wasn't a date."

Stephen smirked. "You ain't have no dollar, girl, so that was a date. You just didn't know it."

Stephen hopped out of the car. He came around and opened my door. "I thought this would be nostalgic. I wanted you to know that I remember everything about you and everything about us."

I took his hand. "Okay, but I hope our butts don't stick to the cheap, soiled seats up in this spot."

"That's why I told you that you were dressed fine. We can always burn these clothes."

I laughed and walked to the entrance. The ticket line was filled with teenagers and the movies were old. Some were probably already available for rent.

"Let's see," Stephen said. "We have a choice between the new Viola Davis film and this D.C. comic flick."

"Sir, there ain't nothing new about that Viola Davis movie," I replied smartly.

Stephen ignored me. "Oh, and Brat Pitt, you had a crush on him in high school, right?"

I squinted at the poster. "I guess Brad will work. I've seen Viola, and I prefer Marvel to D.C."

"Cool." Stephen removed $2 and some change from his wallet and went to the box office to pay.

Once inside, we chose popcorn and drinks from the concession stand. The theatre was nearly empty, most of the kids opting to see the D.C. Comic movie and a horror movie Stephen hadn't even suggested.

We enjoyed the film, with Stephen chatting all the way through like he always did. When it was over, we found we weren't sticking to the cushions. We laughed and exited the theater.

"You were as bad as those kids with all that talking."

He chuckled. "I didn't know there was going to

be so much suspense." He opened my car door and we were back on the highway in minutes.

"What next? McDonalds?" I asked.

"No, I wouldn't take you to McDonald's. It's unhealthy."

We drove away from the mall area. Stephen stopped the car at a park in Aunt Joe's neighborhood.

"I thought we were eating." My stomach confirmed I was ready with a rolling growl.

"We are. One minute." Stephen popped the trunk and climbed out the vehicle. He opened my door and helped me out and then went to the trunk and removed a picnic basket and a blanket. "Your dinner, Madame."

I twisted my lips to keep from smiling. "This is different."

Stephen took my hands and pulled me to a shady tree under which he put down the blanket. He got busy setting out paper plates, bottles of water and other juices. Then he removed bags of chips, a loaf of bread and two disposable containers, mayo and mustard.

I dropped to my knees. "What in the world?"

He opened the containers. "I got you all the cheddar cheese and fried baloney, you can handle, girl."

I squealed when I looked at the boloney. "It's burnt on the edges."

"Of course, what other way is there to eat fried baloney?"

I threw my head back and laughed. "You're silly, you know that?"

Getting more comfortable, he shifted his position on the blanket. "I got you hooked up."

I looked at the cheese. "Hooked up with constipation. This looks like some old school government cheese right here."

Stephen laughed. "I went to a supermarket in a really questionable part of town for this cheese. Risked my entire life."

I slapped him on the arm but welcomed the opportunity to try the hood meal. We laughed and ate sandwiches and then lay on the blanket. Our bodies were in opposite directions, but our heads were next to each other.

"I'm surprisingly very full," I said.

"You ate three sandwiches. That's like a half a loaf of bread." Stephen chuckled.

I laughed. "It is not."

"You gonna have to spend some time in the gym this week or something," he teased.

"Not before I hit the toilet. I haven't had a cheese sandwich in forever. God, it's funny how you stop doing stuff, right?"

I could see Stephen nod in my peripheral vision. "It is."

I was sated. "That was nice. It took me back to my childhood."

"A simpler time," he added propping himself up and looking down into my eyes.

I agreed. "A much simpler time."

"The movie wasn't bad."

"I wasn't sure if we were going to be able to get out of those seats. I thought my feet were stuck to the floor."

Stephen smiled. "Yeah, that was a train wreck."

"But the company was good."

Stephen smiled again. "So, if you had to give a score on this here date, where would I be?" he asked. "I know I have competition, Gerald and all."

I sat up and propped myself on one elbow. "Stop it with Gerald. I am not interested in that man."

"He's gonna be trying to holler soon."

I pressed my lips together before telling the truth. "You're late. He gave me his number a few weeks ago."

Stephen nodded. "I knew it. I knew that dude was gonna shoot his shot."

I waved my free hand. "Anyway, I would give this date a solid B."

Stephen frowned. "B, huh? What could I have done to improve my score?"

I shrugged. "Dessert."

"Oh, well, then get ready to make an adjustment in my grade." He sat up, reached into the basket, and pulled out two packs of cookies. The kind we ate in the cafeteria in high school.

"No way," I shrieked. "I didn't even know they still made these."

He handed me a pack. I squealed like an excited

five-year-old and opened them. The first bite was like heaven.

Stephen chewed and swallowed. "These bad boys taste exactly the same."

"They do."

We ate our cookies and then Stephen asked, "So, you know I'm an overachiever. Am I working with an A today?"

I made him wait while I pretended to be thinking about my answer. "Definitely, an A."

He met me halfway across the blanket for a kiss. Stephen whispered, "You might have to go to the gym twice. This courtship is not supposed to end with you fat."

"Shut up!" Just like a blushing high school girl, I playfully slapped him on the arm.

***

Over the course of the next few weeks, Stephen continued his romantic gestures. He cooked for me, cut Aunt Joe's grass, he planted my favorite flowers in the front yard – dug up the dirt himself and everything. He wrote me a poem, brought me ice cream, and we went for long walks. He had a picture of Isaiah and me blown up to a poster size. He even highjacked my grocery list and went to the supermarket for me. I was enjoying our time together. It was nice to get to know him again and to realize he hadn't changed. Sometimes that was hard to see in fancy restaurants.

Now he was standing at the door dressed in old jeans and a t-shirt insisting he was going to change the oil in my car. His effort to impress me had gone too far.

"But you probably shouldn't get down on your ankle like that," I said, attempting to steer this courting thing in a different direction.

"My ankle is cool. I have one of those roller things to wheel myself around."

Isaiah came flying out of his bedroom, dressed to assist with the job.

Stephen winked at me. "Just go back inside. We've got this."

I made one final plea. "It's my car."

Stephen opened the car door and popped the hood. "Babe, I got it."

Hesitantly, I went back inside and climbed onto my bed with my e-reader.

I woke to the sound of banging and looked at my cell phone. I'd been sleeping for more than an hour. I had a text message from my agent that said:

Three publishers are interested in you. Call me, so we can discuss.

I called her immediately.

"Tamar, I didn't want to turn you off by sending the real message in the text."

I frowned. "What do you mean?"

"They aren't interested in the novel," she said. "They all like your writing, but they want a series that connects to your brand. Maybe a novel about cyberbullying or revenge porn."

My heart sank. "Are you serious? I don't even want that to be my brand."

"But honey, it is. It's what you're known for and quite frankly, it's not a terrible thing."

I rolled my eyes. Disappointment crept into my heart. Rejection again.

"Tamar?"

I sighed heavily. I wanted her to hear my disappointment. "I'm here."

"This is good."

"It feels horrible. My brand is not a cool thing. Only people who haven't been through what I've been through think so."

"These people are serious about wanting a book. They can market fiction around the issues you've dealt with. The recent Melissa Teasley intervention probably helped put it on their minds. But a memoir, Tamar, a memoir would be gold."

I sighed. "I wasn't expecting this."

"I know but think about it. Think about a bigger contribution to society, our culture. The same web that tore you apart can be used to restore others, if you'll let yourself open up and share."

I had that feeling again. Like my stomach was rising into my chest. Fear.

"Give it some thought. Make some notes and give me a call when you're done. No commitment.

We'll just have a conversation about your notes."

I hung up, reached for my laptop, opened it and went to the manuscript I'd been working on. It read:

The first time I saw Stephen Pierce was in church. I was six and I remember him because afterward, he offered me a piece of candy. It was an apple Jolly Rancher. My favorite. I hadn't even asked for it. Getting that candy on the backsteps of my father's church was one I never forgot. I think I fell in love with him then. At six. I don't know when he fell in love with me, but he eventually did. And that love was the worst victim of the video.

When I was done, she'd said. I was done. I had written a first draft of my memoir. Between the journal entries and my thoughts, it had written itself, but I couldn't actually send it, could I?

Take off the grave clothes, Tamar. Set yourself free, dropped into my spirit.

I shook my head. "God, I'm scared."

I waited for anxiety to rise, for that sick feeling to come back, but it didn't. My heart was beating fast, but the Holy Spirit's voice had given me confidence. My hand trembled as I reached for my Bible. I went to the story of Lazarus and read it again. The man came back to life, but he needed someone to unwrap the cloth that bound him to truly be free.

I opened my journal. I began to write a letter to God and then I prayed. I prayed about my fear and my shame. In prayer, I was assured that my suffering had a purpose. God had a plan for my life. I was out of the tomb, but I had to let this book be the thing that unraveled my grave clothes and set me free. I had to give power and purpose to my past and let those things overtake the fear and the shame. When I was finished, I had two pages of words and tear stains.

"God, have I just thought of the introduction?" It was the only part of this book that wasn't written.

I turned more pages in my journal. I cried harder as I read the scriptures I'd been meditating on for the past few months.

Jeremiah 29:11 *For I know the plans I have for you," declares the Lord, "plans to prosper you and not to harm you, plans to give you hope and a future."*

1 John 2:20 *But you have been anointed by the Holy One, and you all have knowledge.*

James 1:2-3 *Consider it pure joy, my brothers and sisters, whenever you face trials of many kinds, because you know that the testing of your faith produces perseverance.*

Romans 8:28 *And we know that for those who love God all things work together for good, for those who are called according to his purpose.*

Romans 8:37 *In all these things we are more than conquerors through him who loved us.*

Habakkuk 2:3 *For still the vision awaits its appointed time; it hastens to the end – it will not lie. If it seems slow, wait for it, it will surely come; it will not delay.*

And then finally the words He gave me just last Christmas when I was praying about Stephen:

Joel 2:25-26. I turned the pages until I found it.

And I will restore to you the years that the locust hath eaten, the cankerworm, and the caterpillar, and the palmerworm, my great army which I sent among you. And ye shall eat in plenty, and be satisfied, and praise the name of the Lord your God, that hath dealt wondrously with you: and my people shall never be ashamed.

But what if I can't handle the pressure?

The Holy Spirit whispered to my heart. "I am perfecting everything that concerns you." Psalm 138. I knew it well.

"I trust you, Lord." I wiped a tear away. "I trust you."

My phone pinged. I had a text message from Kim. It was a simple message to say she was thinking about me. I texted her back:

I've written my memoir. I know God wants me to publish it.

She returned three smiley emojis and **Give me a minute.**

I put my phone down and went into the restroom to wash my face. When I came back, I had a message from Kim.

God is within her, she will not fail. Psalm 46:5

And then she texted:

I'm your girl. Send me that book!

I laughed, but the word of the Lord was confirmed in my spirit. I was not going to be afraid. Not anymore.

I jumped up and went outside. Stephen and Isaiah were leaning against my car like they were trying to figure something out.

"She looks happy," Stephen said, elbowing Isaiah.

"She is," I said. "My agent just told me none of the publishers want my novel."

Stephen frowned, and then looked at Isaiah who shrugged. He raised a hand to scratch his chin. "So, that's something to be happy about?"

I nodded and stuck my hands in my pockets. "It is, because they like my writing, and they are interested in me. They want my story."

Stephen's face took on a curious expression. "I hate to say the dirty 'm' word, but is that what you're talking about?"

I shrugged. "It's no longer dirty."

Stephen smiled and then wrapped his arms around me and squeezed. "Baby, that's great news."

"What's the 'm' word?" Isaiah asked.

"Memoir," I said.

"Oh, a book about yourself," Isaiah said. "So, you have to write another book?"

I put a finger under his chin. "Actually, I've already written most of it. I've been kind of writing it for years."

I was answering Isaiah, but I was looking in Stephen's eyes for approval. I know he'd told me he didn't care about the memoir, but I had to be sure. I wanted to see the truth. I found what I was looking for. Unabashed support.

"I still journal. I have all my old ones. I've read them over the past few months. I couldn't stop myself from organizing my thoughts. Once I started typing, it just flowed."

Stephen released a satisfied sigh. "I'm proud of you."

My heart smiled. "God has been doing a work. You just don't know."

"I think I've recently become familiar with how hard he can go." Stephen chuckled.

"So, you're going to be rich," Isaiah exclaimed. 'I'm going to have two rich parents."

Hearing him call me his parent pushed even more emotions into my heart. He'd never said that before. Stephen noticed the misty condition of my eyes. He smiled warmly and nodded. "Two rich parents."

Then I noticed what I'd missed in my excitement – both of them were covered in oil. It was all over their hands and arms and faces and clothes. They looked like two grease monkeys.

"Is the oil change complete, or are you two wearing the oil?"

"It was fun," Isaiah said. "But can I take a shower and go play videos games with Dante?"

"Please make sure to use a lot of soap and wash your hair. Go straight to the laundry room and put those shoes and clothes into the washing machine."

Isaiah agreed and we watched as he left us to enter the house.

Certain they were wearing more oil than could possibly be in my car, I crossed my arms. "So, is my oil actually changed?"

"Yeah, I'm pretty much going to have to break this DIY date thing and either get the Range Rover down here or buy you another car. I can't do nothing with my hands to fix the mess we made." Stephen was amused.

I gasped. "Are you serious? You ruined my car?"

He shrugged. "It's kind of an old car anyway."

"Dude, my car is not old."

"Well, it might not be old, but it durn sure won't start. I don' tore this up, babe."

I was fighting to put my lips back together. "I can't believe you broke my car."

"The word says money answereth all things. Aren't you glad you're going to be rich?"

I chuckled. "You got jokes." I stepped right up to him. My face was inches from his. "I was going to kiss you, but you're covered in grease."

He pulled me to him. I squealed, and he got grease all over me. I tried to escape him, but Stephen fell backward and pulled me to the ground with him. He began to tickle me.

"Tell me this courtin' thing is over. Tell me I've earned your love."

"No!" I screamed.

He tickled me until I couldn't take it anymore. "Okay!" I relented. "We're done courting. You're worthy. I'm lucky to have you."

Stephen's expression became serious. He stroked the side of my face. "That's what I've been waiting to hear."

My heart melted.

"Tell me you love me." His eyes beamed with anticipation.

I teasingly hesitated and then when I knew he couldn't take the delay anymore, I said "I love you, Stephen Pierce."

He closed his eyes for a moment, savoring my words. When he opened his eyes he said, "You a mess now, so you might as well give me a kiss."

I smiled. "I think you've earned it." I gave him a quick peck on the lips.

"So, can I be done with this dating on a shoestring? I'm about tapped out of ideas."

I shrugged. "I guess if I must settle for being in love with someone as scandalous as you, you might as well be spending money."

Stephen laughed. "You got jokes."

"I'm a writer."

"I think being with me will save you from Gerald."

I laughed. "You a step up from Gerald, but I'm the one really doing something for the culture. I'm saving you from the Debra's of the world."

Stephen laughed again. It was a deep roar from his belly. "Tamar Johnson, baby, you win."

Chapter 39

A bead of sweat the size of a football traveled down my back. Perspiration formed little beads all over my body. I caught a glimpse of myself in the mirrored wall. My face, neck, and arms were glistening. I banged my leg back against the exam room table. Clyde looked up from his cell, cocked an eyebrow, and gave me the eye, like my father would when I was a kid getting into mischief.

"What?" I asked, raising my arms.

Clyde nodded in the direction of my bobbing legs.

"I'm fine. If it can't take a bang against a table, it won't be able to take it on the field."

I looked through the glass wall that separated Clyde and I from Dr. Hogan and his associate. They been staring at films and other papers for five minutes. Five that felt like an eternity. They re-entered the room with Coach Nye dead on their heels. He and I had talked earlier, so he just gave me a nod and grabbed a spot against the wall next to Clyde.

Dr. Hogan's face revealed nothing. He had that stoic physician routine down in Oscar worthy fashion. I figured they must take a class in medical school on how to not show before telling.

"Stephen, my colleague and I are in agreement." My heart skittered wildly as his words traveled from his mouth in slow motion. "You are not ready for training camp."

The rest of what he was saying was like the *womp, womp, womp* of an adult Charlie Brown character.

Coach Nye dropped his head. The burn of disappointment was on his face when he raised it. He responded to Dr. Hogan, but it was more *womp, womp* in my ear. I did however hear him say IR.

Injured reserve. An involuntary shudder racked me from head to toe. I knew I'd been injured. I knew athletes got hurt and couldn't play. But I never expected to come here today to be told I couldn't. I released a long breath. I saw my career flash in images through my memory.

Clyde stepped closer. "It's going to be okay." He patted me on the shoulder. "A few more months and you'll be on the field."

Clyde continued his conversation with Coach Nye, but my thoughts drowned out his incessant chatter. My heart felt like it was caving in. I needed to think clearly. I needed a solitary moment. I slid off the table and backed to the door. "I need a minute." I left the room, closing the door behind me.

Once outside, a mixture of pain and sorrow fueled the energy I pushed into my hand. Flex-clench-release, flex-clench-release on repeat. I threw my head back against the wall and groaned the words, "This is happening," on a long breath and then I spun into the wall.

Lord, I wasn't expecting this. You know I want to play football.

Silence.

I hope this is a delay and not a no, but I'll do whatever You want me to do. I'm ready for whatever I have to deal with.

More silence. I was lying. I didn't mean what I said, but I was trying to mean it.

I want to play football.

I turned away from the wall, looked through the glass partition that separated me from one of the workout areas, into the faces of my teammates. The area was almost full. Players were here for mini-camp, but no one was working out. They were watching me. Watching the air deflate my soul. Wondering if they would have their starting running back to lead them to wins. I was sure they knew they would not.

I thought about what Pastor Johnson told me.

Have you ever considered that God may be trying to use you? It's easy to praise Him and talk about His goodness when you're up. None of them are impressed by the fact that you pray at games and talk about God. - Your teammates are circling, waiting to see what Stephen Pierce is going to do.

I washed a hand over my face, opened and closed my fists for the last time, and went back into the room.

Dr. Hogan, Coach Nye, and Clyde stood straighter.

I pushed as much confidence as I could into my voice, and asked, "What's the plan?" I hopped up on the exam table.

Dr. Hogan tapped on an iPad. Using a stylus, he projected notes and images onto a big screen against the wall. We went over the treatment plan he'd put together. It was simple. It included light PT, work on my core, and rest.

I was listening, trying, but I had to talk to God. I had to tap into His power. I wasn't strong enough for this.

I want to play again. But help me glorify You before these people. Help me keep it together, God. I have to make it out of this building.

I repeated the prayer a few times before I felt peace. When I did, I whispered, "*Amen.*" No one heard me.

"Okay, Stephen." Coach Nye placed a hand on my shoulder. "We've got some paperwork for you in the office. We'll talk." He left the room.

I gave the doctor my attention again. "You have an estimate for me?"

"I think you'll be ready early in the season. Remember the rest part. We don't want a stress injury. There is such a thing as too much. Listen to your trainers." He, too, gave me the man-I'm-sorry pat and left the room.

It was just Clyde and I, and Clyde looked like he'd eaten a pound of sour grapes. He was rarely without words, but the taut twist of his lips conveyed he was struggling with them. "Look," he began, "they're going to hurt without you. We're in the fourth year of this contract. Next year we were going to be negotiating anyway. It might not be terrible that they'll miss you."

"Clyde."

"I'm trying to find the upside," Clyde said. "I'm sorry. You're not just a client. You're my friend."

"I'm going to be okay."

"I know you're going to be okay. You're going to be great. This thing is a minor setback."

"Clyde," I said firmly. "I'm okay. I'm good."

Clyde raised his hand to his chin. "You're sure?"

"I'm not going to trip. I trust God."

Clyde nodded. "Okay, that's good. God is your answer here. We need God right now."

I chuckled. "We need God all the time. In good and bad times."

"I knew that," Clyde said. "I've heard it before."

"Well, let me finish your speech," I said. "Injured reserve is not the end of the world. I'm still on the team. I'm still getting paid. I have more time to heal and come back strong."

Clyde nodded. "That's right. That's exactly what I was going to say. More time to heal is better. You'll be back on the field before we eat turkey."

We pounded and left the room.

As we walked through the training area, I approached a few huddled teammates.

"What's up? What's good? You ready for camp?" They asked.

I shook my head. "I won't make it to camp, but we're optimistic that I'll be back mid-season."

A round of "Cool, good, and a'ight," filled the quiet.

"I'm still coming to watch you clowns."

"No doubt, and we expect you," they said in unison.

I smiled and turned to join Clyde at the area that led to the exit.

"Stephen," one of the players called to me. I looked back. "Keep your head up."

"I keep it down," I said, raising my hands and clasping them in an expression of prayer. "You know Who I trust."

They all nodded, and I felt good that I'd left that energy in the room.

Clyde pushed the door open, and we walked through. "So, how are things with Isaiah and Tamar?"

I smiled. "Excellent."

"Soon the Debra mess will be resolved. She's big as a house. That baby is coming any second."

I shrugged. "We don't even talk about Debra."

"You mean you and Tamar don't watch the show?"

I laughed. "I've watched a few minutes here and there. I needed to make sure she was keeping my name out of her mouth."

Clyde waved. "Don't worry. Legal is on that. She utters your name one time and she loses all her money."

"I don't think Tamar has watched much of it."

"Good. She trusts you. Trust is important," Clyde said and then he chuckled. "Not that any of my relationships require it."

We walked out the front door.

"One day you're going to meet a woman who is going to change all that."

"No one woman is going to change that. I'm not like you Saint Stephen. Women are like slow raindrops. There's one falling from the sky every few seconds."

I shook my head. "Not the right woman, man. The right woman does not fall from the sky. Believe me when I tell you, after I let Tamar go, I experienced a drought."

Clyde smirked.

"I mean an emotional drought, Clyde. Sex and a real connection aren't the same thing. Someone having your back, sharing your dreams, supporting you, and really loving you is not easy to find. But when you have it, it's like gold, man."

"I am too old for lover's fairy tales."

"You're not much older than me."

"Well, the five years I have on you have been hard. I like to keep my dalliances light, unlike my meals. I'm starved. You want to have lunch?" Clyde asked.

"No, I need to take care of some things. I'm going to Georgia tomorrow."

"Okay. Well, keep your hands together." Clyde pressed his palms together in a praying posture. "A little help from the Man upstairs is welcome."

I didn't care for references to God as the Man upstairs, but I knew Clyde's heart. He was acknowledging God's power the best way he knew how. "He's on it. Trust me. I don't keep it together without Him."

Clyde's lip turned up. "I was proud of you in there. You did good."

I could see that he really was. I nodded. "I'll talk to you later."

We went in opposite directions to our vehicles.

I climbed in and started my truck. I had a twenty-minute drive. Twenty minutes until I was in the privacy of my home. I pulled out of the parking lot and willed myself to make the drive without breaking down. Ten minutes later, I was on the side of the road, sobbing my heart out.

God, I want to play football. Please heal me.

Chapter 40

It was a good week. I heard back from my agent about the book proposal. All three publishers wanted it. We had meetings with offers and then my agent wrapped up the negotiations. I had a book deal and a quarter of a million-dollar advance.

If that wasn't enough to celebrate, there was the news about Debra McAllister's secret wedding. Photos were posted all over social media. Fans were surprised and some disappointed she'd announced her new husband – some big money business man – was the father of her child.

Debra posted the following under a picture of them frolicking in the waters on a Fiji beach:

We had an in utero paternity test. #HeDaDaddy

Questions about her original claim regarding Stephen Pierce were met with Debra's response that she would prefer not to share anymore statements because the Internet was forever.

"Twenty years from now my son will have access to the comments. We can't take words back, so let's just move forward with who his father is," she said in a ten second IG story.

I couldn't deny her claim. What we put on the Internet never went away, but I still slid her the side-eye. This slick chick didn't seem to have any issues with television being forever.

And just like that, the mess was over.

I sent a text to Stephen:

So, you not da daddy!

Stephen replied:

Was there any doubt? Smiley emojis. My lawyer requested and received proof of the DNA test. I'm with my trainer. I'll call later.

I smiled. But I still resented her. "What a manipulative little…"

"Tamar, did you get more yogurt from the store?"

I looked up from my cell phone and placed it on the table. "I did. What flavor do you want?"

Aunt Joe pushed herself up from the sofa. "I'll get it. I just wanted to make sure I didn't get my mouth ready for something we didn't have." She took a few steps without her cane, got her footing and went into the kitchen.

Aunt Joe was done with treatment. She was eating more and working harder to get things for herself. She was stronger, which meant she was better. I closed my eyes and prayed. "Lord, please continue to heal her."

I opened my eyes just as Aunt Joe came out of the kitchen and took a seat on the sofa where she'd been.

"I hope you learned a valuable lesson from this,"

Aunt Joe said.

I cocked an eyebrow. "I've learned a lot of lessons. Which one are you referring to?"

"That you have to stop letting the world come between you and Stephen." Aunt Joe pointed at my phone. "I know it looks like I don't know anything about social media, but I saw that Debra woman's videos on the Instagram site."

"I wasn't stressed about that."

"That may be true this time, but you can't let people's words come between you. Baby, Stephen Pierce is still a celebrity. This Debra situation won't be the last mess he'll be in. He'll be in mess as long as he's playing ball and as long as he's living a life to honor God."

I released a breath. I wished what she was saying was false, but I knew it wasn't.

She continued. "He has a public side to his life. You have to be strong enough to deal with it."

I joined my aunt on the sofa. I wrapped my arm around her. "Have I ever told you you are the best substitute mother a woman could ever have?"

Aunt Joe fought smiling. She patted my arm. "You are better than any daughter I could have ever prayed for." She looked me squarely in the eyes. "Your mother would be so proud of you."

Her words made my heart melt. "I wish she was here with me now. I wish she could know my son. She would love Stephen. She did love Stephen, but she'd be so proud of who he is today."

Aunt Joe raised a hand to sweep a loose curl off my face. "You've got to learn how to take praise, baby. I'm talking about you right now."

I lowered my eyes. She put a finger under my chin and lifted my head. "Your mother's heart would be full of joy over the beautiful, talented, kind daughter she raised. I'm sorry she can only see you from heaven, but I sure am glad that I get to enjoy who you are."

I hugged her again.

"Thank you for being here for me. Thank you for taking such good care of me."

Tears filled my eyes. "I wouldn't have it any other way."

"I know. You're a good girl, but now I need you to get back to your life. I'm starting to feel like my old self, and I have help. I'm not alone here."

I frowned. "Maybe just a few more weeks."

Aunt Joe shook her head. "No. I want you to leave soon, and I want you to take Isaiah with you."

My frown deepened. "Auntie, I can't do that to you."

"Tamar, Isaiah is your child. He's Stephen's child. I love him. God knows I do, but Stephen has a right to his son. And I'm not just talking legally because I know he has that too. He's been patient, but all that traveling back and forth is going to get old."

"Aunt Joe, he and I haven't even talked about this at all."

Aunt Joe pressed her lips together. "He's being

patient. But he's been patient enough. I have prepared myself for the day when Isaiah would find out who his father was. I knew this was coming and I have not made this decision lightly."

My heart sank. I felt like I was betraying her. "I'm so shocked."

"The world doesn't need another black boy growing up without a daddy in the house. If things had not come to a head like they did, I was going to talk to you about it. I had plans to do it before Isaiah turned thirteen. Thirteen was the age I promised myself I wouldn't let it get beyond. It's obvious that was God's plan too, so I'm ready."

I squeezed Aunt Joe's hand again.

"I want you to pack up your stuff – you and Isaiah's – and after my doctor's appointment on Thursday, you know the one where the doctor gives me the all clear, I want you to leave."

I released a long breath. "I do miss home."

Aunt Joe rolled her neck. "Atlanta is not where Stephen Pierce is. You can just stay on the plane and keep heading north."

I chuckled. "I have to talk to Stephen about that."

"I said Isaiah needs to be around his father. I'm sure Stephen will be more than willing to rent you a place near him. He's ready to take care of his family. You all could use the time before he starts the new season."

My heart sank a little. "If he starts."

"He's playing. I had a dream about him the other

night. I saw him playing ball. And Isaiah is too excited to see his daddy on that field. God is handing out miracles." Aunt Joe raised her hands in praise. "Look at me." She did a little dance and shoved her spoon into the yogurt cup.

I smiled with her. "Yeah, look at you," I whispered.

Then I whispered in my soul. *Lord, thank You.*

Chapter 41

"I've got good news," I shrieked. Before Stephen could ask what, I told him about Aunt Joe's medical report."

My joy was contagious. I could hear it in Stephen's voice. "So, she's good. That's great."

"The doctors don't quite say it that way, but she's done with treatment. Things look clear, so I say she's healed," I exclaimed. "She's stronger, and she's been getting around really good. I can see her health is coming back."

"God is good."

I slowed my words. "So, since she's better. I thought, there's really no reason for me to be here anymore. I was planning to head back to Atlanta with Isaiah, but—"

Stephen was quick to interrupt. "Atlanta?"

"Let me finish," I teased. "I was going to say that is, unless you want us to come to New Jersey."

Stephen was silent for a moment. A long moment. When he spoke, his voice cracked like he was fighting to keep from crying. "You know there's nothing I want more. When?"

His excitement brought a smile to my face. "I'm packing now. We're going to drive to Atlanta after lunch. I want to leave my car with Kim. She has an old clunker and since this one is really in good shape now that you've put a ton of money into it—"

"Thanks to the failed oil change," Stephen interjected.

"Yes, I want her to have it. I have my beloved, abandoned Range Rover." I pulled the box that held my journals from under my bed.

"I can have a moving service bring it up," Stephen offered.

"I don't think there's any need yet. You have two SUVs, and I'll need to get around when I come back here for work.

"Whatever you want. I'll book flights for you out of Atlanta for tomorrow afternoon."

I laughed. "Give me until Saturday. I want to stop by the office tomorrow and talk to my boss. I need to get permission to continue teleworking now that Aunt Joe is better. I'm no longer going to be using Family Medical Leave."

"Okay, but early on Saturday. I miss you. I miss him."

This time it was my heart that smiled. "We miss you too," I said. "Although, Isaiah may eventually miss his friends. You know this is his home."

"I know, babe. We'll deal with that when the time comes. Right now, I want you guys with me. We need to spend as much time together as we can before the season starts."

I blinked and paused sure that meant something. "You mean before camp." There was a stillness on the other end that told me I didn't know everything. "Stephen?"

"I'm on the injured reserve list, babe."

The gasp slipped out before I could stop it. "But...when did you find out?"

"The other day."

I fought to keep the groan in my spirit from passing through my lips. I know he was heartbroken. "Why didn't you tell me?"

I could feel him shrug through the phone. "I was waiting until I saw you, but I just saw a story about my status on ESPN, so I was thinking I was going to tell you like now. That's why I was calling."

The phone had been lying on the bed. I sat, picked it up and took it off speaker like that was going to bring us closer. "Are you okay?"

"I'm strong in God. He knows what I want. And if I can't play football anymore, I'll find something else to do."

My heart sank. "I'm so sorry."

"I'm good. Really. I feel what I'm saying most of the time. It's a minute-by-minute thing. I'm scared, but I'm trying not to worry, you know."

"Being anxious is normal."

"Maybe, but God tells me do not be anxious, so I'm trying to keep my mind occupied. You guys being up here will completely solve that." I heard a smile slip back into his voice. "I was planning to head down there. Now I don't have to. I'd be lying to both of us if I didn't tell you I need you right now."

I felt his words. I felt them in my own heart as well. I missed him. Missed his hugs and his kisses. His warmth. I missed being with him period.

I was proud of him. "I'm so glad to hear the real Stephen Pierce again."

Stephen chuckled. "He's back, and he's never leaving again."

It was relief that filled my heart this time. "I'm going to get off this phone and do some more packing."

"Don't try to bring it all. We can get the rest later. I want us to pop back down so we can take Aunt Joe out to celebrate. I mean, really do it up."

"About that. I have an idea." I stood and went back to putting things in the suitcase. "I was thinking about having a party at the church."

"That's cool. Invite everybody in town if you want. It's on me."

"Ooh, on you. I'm 'bout to spend some money," I teased. "Let me pack, so I can get on the road early. I love you, Stephen."

"I love you too, babe."

We lingered on the phone for a moment and then ended the call. I danced to the closet for the rest of my clothes.

Chapter 42

A Federal Express van stopped in front of the house. The timing couldn't have been better. I'd been listening for the sound of a delivery truck all morning. It was the contract for my book.

After the driver gave it to me, I squealed and pulled it to my chest.

With my second mug of coffee in hand, I sat at the kitchen table and opened the envelope. The contract was lengthy. My agent was an attorney, but I still took the time to read every word.

It was all good until the end. The requirements for marketing were included. Most of the information was expected. I was required to do book signings and interviews and such, but there was one other clearly defined responsibility. I had to promote my book using social media. It basically said I was required to have Instagram, Twitter, Facebook accounts, and any other media deemed an appropriate promotion funnel.

I pushed the offending document away and took the last sip of my cold coffee.

I hated social media.

Social media was the reason I had the book in the

first place. I picked up my phone and called my agent.

"Tamar, social media is the main way that people sell merchandise. It's an absolute must for books and speaking," she said.

I sighed. Did I really expect her to tell me I didn't have to do it? I didn't. I just wanted someone to know that I didn't want to.

"I realize you're gun-shy, but you don't have to share your life. I'd like you to work with a brand specialist. I have a few people I can recommend. I'll email their names."

I was stuck. Social media was a part of our culture; therefore, social media was happening. I took a deep breath. It was just something I was going to have to get over.

Or did I?

I wasn't the kind of woman who wanted to rely solely on her man, but my man was worth a fortune. Stephen came out his rookie year at $6 million and had been playing for seven years with his current contract being a guaranteed $45 million. I didn't have to worry about the $250,000. I could walk away from it and leave social media to the rest of the world.

But I was sure this was my calling. God had confirmed it in too many ways and on too many days. Although I had only done two speaking engagements, they were important to me. And then there were the Melissa Teasley's of the world. The young women who needed my book.

I called Kim. She would talk some sense into me and push out any lingering doubt. Before I could say anything, she spoke.

"I finished your book last night. I started to text you, but I didn't want to wake you up. Girl, this book is so powerful. You are a great writer, but I didn't know you had this in you."

I sat up straighter. "Really? It's a rough draft."

"It's fire, Tamar. I know we've talked about your journey some, but you laid it bare in a way that made me think about how vulnerable we all are. I cried several times."

My heart leapt. "Wow! Really?"

"I prayed while I was reading. I prayed for victims out there right now dealing with this. Girl, you're going to help so many young people. You're going to save lives with your testimony. Just like you did with Melissa."

"I just let the words flow."

"They were smart to give you a book deal. That's for sure. You need to get yourself ready for the speaking engagements. Like I told you, I see high schools and college auditoriums in your future."

"You really believe that? I hope so. I don't want to be out in these streets baring my soul for nothing."

"No worries about that. It's a powerhouse. You need to also start a YouTube channel or something. I know you don't want to, but young people are on YouTube and Instagram trolling for videos and sound bites."

"Funny you should suggest it. That's kind of why I was calling. I have to do social media. It's in my contract. You know how much I hate it."

Kim's voice rose an octave. "Listen, the same way you had to gather up your little courage to go and speak at those events, you can gather it up to post on IG. It ain't even that serious."

"I know. I just needed to vent about it."

"And you can hire somebody. They'll schedule your content for you. I have a client who does that. She picks the things that make your brand work. You can be hands off."

I went to Stephen's IG page. He posted a pair of sneakers he'd purchased for himself and Isaiah. He'd hashtagged: **#timewithmyson #shoppingisfun #ilovemylife**

Early this morning he'd posted a graphic of the scripture John 14:23 with the message: Faith is what you do. Do the necessary. **#besalt #belight**

"Stephen manages his own social media."

"Because he likes it," Kim said. "You don't have to if you don't want to. Spend some of the money on an assistant. You're going to be rich."

I chuckled. "Sometimes you sound happier about that than I am."

"Because I am happier about that than you. You can be kinda cray-cray." I heard a hair dryer come on. Kim was practically screaming in the phone to speak over it. "Being the bestie of a rich person is like rich by association. Birthdays, Christmas, just-because gifts, and our quarterly girl trips are going to be bomb. I don't have to pay for anything," Kim cackled.

This girl was hilarious. "Did you say quarterly trips?"

"Yeah, why not?"

"You ever think I might be busy? I'll be a famous author, a sought-after speaker, and a wife and mother."

Kim grunted. "I suppose. And there will be the new baby."

"New baby." I cut my eyes at the phone. "Now you doin' too much. We haven't even talked about that. I mean I know he wants kids, but I have no idea how many. I don't even know what I want."

"This is what's wrong with the two of you. The next time I talk to you, I want you to tell me you've had this conversation. Y'all need to talk about everything. Children, his money, and a whole bunch of other stuff. Let's get this communication thang going before you find a reason to break up again, and I lose my benefits."

I shook my head. "You're a nut. I need to get out of here." I paused again. "Thanks for the feedback on the book. I want it to be good. I know how honest you are, so I know you're telling me how you really feel."

"Oh yes, you know if you needed to put some more anointing on this baby, I would tell you. No half stepping in the kingdom."

I ended the call with a smile on my face and in my heart. I went to Instagram and Twitter and scrolled through the content. It was a bit overwhelming, but it wouldn't be so bad. This is what I needed to do to move forward. I wasn't going to let my past keep me from my future.

Chapter 43

Aunt Joe, Isaiah, and I had a celebratory lunch. We celebrated Aunt Joe's health, my contract, and Isaiah and my moving to New Jersey.

I had been fighting tears all morning. The thought of taking Isaiah and leaving Aunt Joe was overwhelming. It felt like I was betraying her and abandoning her at the same time. I was struggling until I found out she had dinner plans with none other than Dr. Butler. She was glad to be getting some space to herself, but I could see she was having a hard time letting go of Isaiah.

I stood in the doorway of her bedroom watching her sift through dresses in search of something appropriate for dinner. "Too churchy, too workplace, too short, too long, too ugly, too big..." in succession as she pushed everything down the closet bar. There was a lot of too churchy.

I stepped further into the room and sat on a chair. "Let's go to Belk's and get you a new dress. New season. New dress."

"Girlie, I am not an old wineskin. I got something in here that'll work. Besides you and Isaiah need to get on the road."

That's what I'd been avoiding doing. "We don't have to leave now, Auntie. We're not in a rush."

"Yes, you are." Her tone was firm. "And I don't care if you leave tomorrow, next month or six months from now, I'm going to still cry just as hard, so you might as well go."

I couldn't help feeling guilty. "Are you sure?"

"Stephen needs both of you right now. I know he's going to make a comeback, but he probably feels like his career has one foot in the grave."

Aunt Joe pulled a red jumpsuit from the closet and held it out in front of herself. "I know what it feels like to have one foot in the grave. You need people. Go be there for him the same way you've been here for me."

She was right about Stephen and I was concerned about him, but I didn't think it was right to take Isaiah away like this.

"There's no other way, Tamar," Aunt Joe's voice broke through my thoughts like she'd been reading my mind. "Now help me pick a dress so you can leave."

I stood, closed the space between us, and wrapped my arms around her. I tried to squeeze all the love I could out of her body. She squeezed me back tight like she was doing the same. When we were done, we both had tears to wipe.

"New season, baby." She smoothed my hair. "A season with a whole lot of love in it. Go get it."

I nodded and took the red jumpsuit out of her hand. "This is it." She smiled and closed the closet door.

Isaiah and I gave her big hugs. Isaiah was excited, but I had a mess of tears streaming down my face.

We eased into Atlanta with no delay. In addition to stopping by the office and dropping the car off to Kim, I had one more thing I needed to do while I was in town. I left Isaiah at the shop with Kim and taxied to my apartment to pick up the Range Rover.

I arrived at the bank right before closing and requested my safe deposit box be opened. I reached in and pulled out the box that held my engagement ring. I pushed the lid back and stared at the 6-carat cushion cut set in a prong setting. I heard the passion in Stephen's voice all over again.

I'll wait for you. For as long as it takes.

His wait was over.

"I'm ready," I whispered. I slid the ring on my finger, gathered my important documents, and walked out of the bank with the banker happily locking the door behind me.

A flash of light reflected against the sun and blinded me for a second. No doubt it was a camera and a reporter. When I could see, I was glad to find it was a coworker from the magazine. One I didn't like much, but someone I knew.

"I thought that was you," Dedrina Akers squealed like I was a good find. "It's my lucky day."

"I doubt it." I didn't lose a beat walking to the car. She fell in step next to me.

"How do you feel about Stephen being benched

for the season?"

I stopped, rolled my eyes away from her, and resumed walking. "He's not benched for the season."

"My bad. I forgot injured reserve might be able to come off the bench. That's a new rule, right?"

"Dedrina, if you're going to ask a question about an athlete, learn his sport." I pushed the key fob for the Ranger's door.

"I see you're wearing your engagement ring. Does this mean wedding plans are still on?"

I turned and all but laughed in her face. "I'm not answering your questions."

She frowned and flailed her arms like an annoyed teenager. "Come on, Tamar. You can tell me something. Eva would give us both a raise."

I slid sunglasses on, pulled the door open, and tossed my things inside.

"I'm melting and starving out here in this heat and you're getting into that?" She put a hand on her hip. "Do me a solid. Give me a quote."

I thought about it for a moment. Eva would be happy, and I owed her. She'd been good to me while I was on leave. "Wait."

I climbed into the SUV. I removed lipstick from my bag and freshened it. I fluffed my twist-out and lowered the window. I placed my left hand over the top of the window so she could get a good shot of the ring, rested my chin on top of my hand and tilted my head. "You may print, 'Tamar Johnson is planning a winter wedding.'"

Dedrina snapped the pictures.

I pulled my hand back in the car. "Now do me a solid. Email it to me. I'm about to open an Instagram account. I'll give you photo cred, and I'll tell Eva you can come to the wedding."

Her eyes turned into saucers. I smiled and put up the window. A winter wedding was a good idea. It was time to get Saint Stephen off the market. I wasn't going to let anyone, or anything keep us apart.

***

Isaiah and I settled into our rooms in Stephen's townhouse. The house had five bedrooms, so there was plenty of space for all of us to have our own. Stephen had a realtor looking for a rental for me. There were a few luxury condominium buildings in the area with vacancies. She was confident she would find something for me in as quickly as a few days.

The closest hotel was a good distance. Stephen and I were more than capable of respecting each other and God for a few days.

Worn out from the travel and a big meal, Isaiah had already gone to bed.

Stephen and I were stretched out on a double chaise on the balcony. The Jersey heat was almost as bad as Georgia's, but an evening breeze made it comfortable.

Stephen raised my left hand. "Finally, the woman is wearing my ring."

I admired the ring with him. "It's beautiful."

"And right where it should be." He took my hand and kissed my finger. "I told you I'd wait for you. I didn't know it would be this long, though."

Once he loosened his hold, I picked up my cell, swiped the screen, and showed it to him. A little laugh escaped his belly. "Are you kidding? You have an Instagram account?"

I shimmied my shoulders. "I'm coming out like Diana Ross."

Stephen laughed again. "You're full of surprises today."

I rested my head back against his chest and let him take the phone out of my hand. "And using hashtags right." He read them:

#WinterWedding #WearYourBestCoat #LuckyGirl #Blessed #SaintStephenOfftheMarket

"You've got jokes." Stephen laughed. "You're good at this."

"I'm a writer, luv."

"Yes, you are." He kissed my forehead. "So, now that you've given us a season for this here wedding, we need to find your calendar app and set a date."

My heart was beating hard, but it wasn't from fear. It was excitement. I was ready for this. "You pick it. I don't care."

"If I pick it, it's going to be tomorrow."

I turned my head in his direction. "Maybe we should elope. That would eliminate the need for my apartment."

"Nooo…" Stephen stretched the word. "I was joking. Your father asked me to make sure we had a church wedding."

I gripped the side of the chair and sat up to face Stephen. "Did he?"

"Yes, when I asked him to marry you. He asked me not to run off with his only daughter."

"You didn't tell me that."

"I didn't have time. You were too busy dumping me."

I shoved an elbow in his thigh.

He pretended to be hurt. "Girl, don't mess with my muscles. I'm already on the injured list."

Suddenly, I felt responsibility come down on me. "Daddy, wants a wedding."

"Don't you?" He looked like he was waiting for me to shock him.

I shrugged. "I never really thought about it. I didn't think I would get married."

"Well, I want the whole big thang. A bunch of bridesmaids and groomsmen, kids bringing rings on pillows and dropping flowers, a 10-foot cake and every person who has ever cared about us in attendance." He pulled me back down and kissed my forehead again. "Can you do that for me?"

"I mean I have an IG account, man. You've got me doing things I never thought I'd do."

"It's good to know you love me enough to want to make me happy."

I scrunched my nose and turned my face in his direction. "My book contract requires me to have an IG account. All social media is in my contract."

Stephen shook his head. "I should have known there was another motive."

I laughed. "I gave that picture to a reporter from my magazine. Eva was so glad to have it. She was more than happy to tell me I could telework."

"Oh, so all this compliance is for the publishing house and Eva. I thought you were marrying me for the culture." A teasing smile spread across his lips.

I turned over and scooted higher. "That too." I looked at the calendar app on the phone. "What are we working with?"

"The second weekend in December. It's Bye week."

My eyes probed his. "That's…"

"A week we don't play. Most teams have one every season. It's that date or we're into the holidays. I want my teammates to be able to attend."

I pointed at the Saturday. "That's our wedding date then."

I hovered above him. Stephen raised his head and met me for a kiss. "It's a long way off. But I guess I've been waiting for almost thirteen years. I can wait four more months."

"Four months," I repeated. "Is that it?"

"Four and a half," he said, with his deep, sexy eyes laser-focused on mine.

God, he was fine. I did want to get married tomorrow. I fought saying it and instead asked, "Do you think we can go that long without drama or scandal?"

"I hope so," he replied. "No matter what, you have to promise me that we're going to go through it together."

I kissed him again. "Scandal ain't nothing two people in love can't handle." I returned to my supine position next to him. "We've got this."

Stephen raised my hand again and planted another kiss on my finger. "God is our strength."

Chapter 44

Happiness was my new friend. We went back to Yancy for my speaking engagement and Aunt Joe's party. I'd planned the party to be on the same day, so we'd only have to make one trip. The event was a success. There were already stories in the room about bullying and cyber sexual abuse. Afterward, I was even more sure that speaking to young women was what I wanted to do.

Later that evening, we had Aunt Joe's party. She'd gained a few pounds back. Although she hadn't lost all her hair, it was thin, so she had a wig designed that looked exactly like the hair she'd had. She looked amazing. Dr. Butler was at her side for every step she took. I'd never seen her this happy. When Isaiah told her he was staying with her for a few weeks, the joy was multiplied. She thanked me through tears and gave Stephen a hearty hug.

The next morning, Stephen and I were back in New Jersey. We met with a wedding planner and spent the day making decisions about everything that had to be done right away.

Later that evening, I checked my email and found the art department from my publishing house had contacted me. This was really happening.

"I got a few book cover options today." I removed the take-out dinner we'd ordered from the bag.

"Let's see what they sent."

I opened my iPad to the email and showed him the covers.

Stephen was dramatic with his facial expressions. "That's what's up. Do you get to pick?"

I leaned on the table on one elbow and looked at them again myself. "Not really, but I can give them feedback. I like both, so they can do what they want."

"I like your picture on the cover. That's cool."

More excitement rose up from my belly. "I've decided I want to continue the speaking. My publicist asked me if she could scout out some opportunities for me. She even mentioned a Ted Talk."

Stephen lowered the iPad and wrapped an arm around my waist. "I'm proud of you. I'm proud that you're trying to help other young people by being brave enough to get out there. You were great yesterday."

"I think it'll help. I feel like this entire thing has been healing for me." I felt warmth in my spirit that only God could give. "Anyway, the book is being released in late August of next year. They want it out in time for October, which is National Bullying Month."

"National Bullying Month." He opened the lid to a container of fried rice. "I didn't know there was a month for it."

"There's an awareness month for everything." I sat next to him at the table.

Stephen put rice on my plate first and then his. "What's the 'I'm in love with you so much I can't wait to marry you month'?"

I put a finger on my chin and cocked my head like I was thinking. "I'm guessing that's February."

"Not in this house." He winked. "That was a test. Every month is 'I love you' month."

I swooned. Could he be sweeter? I just didn't think so. "Since you put it that way. Every day is 'I love you' day." I opened another carton and put steaming Hunan Chicken on both our plates. I handed him the chopsticks, and I reached for my fork. Stephen blessed our food and we began to eat.

"How's all the wedding planning stuff coming?"

"It's crazy. There are so many details. It's even crazier because we're having two receptions. Deniece Wright has earned her reputation as one of the best wedding planners in New York City. She's great, but this is a lot."

Stephen maneuvered his chopsticks to put huge hunks of chicken in his mouth. He was giving me his undivided attention, but I knew he was not into the details of this planning.

I continued. "I'm seriously thanking God she had an opening. Believe you me, her team is earning her fee."

"I'm glad my money isn't going to waste," he chuckled. "December will be here before we know it."

We were having a private wedding and reception in Pine and then a second reception on the same day in

New York City. What had I been thinking? "I can't imagine planning a small wedding without help. This event of ours has a million moving pieces."

Hungry, we both ate for a few minutes before I said, "Speaking of the wedding. Deniece asked me about your mother. She said you were deciding who was going to stand in her stead."

Stephen's jaw got noticeably tighter, and it wasn't because he was chewing. "That's right. My mother isn't invited. Not at this time."

I placed a hand on his arm. "Babe."

He looked at me, and I saw fierce determination in his eyes. I knew I was wasting my time bringing her up. "Tay, I love her, but she went too far. She's always gone too far."

"But Stephen—"

He shook his head and took a sip of water before speaking again. "She knew what you meant to me and for her to do that…what does that say about how she loves me?"

I sighed. "I hear you, but I would do anything to have my mother at this wedding."

"Don't do that. Your mother not being able to be with us is not the same as my mother choosing not to be with us."

I dropped back in my chair. He put his arm around my shoulder and raised a hand to stroke my cheek. "I know what I'm doing. I've prayed about it. I'm not convicted to change my mind."

I knew he wanted me to stay out of this, but I

couldn't help feeling like his mother might have more resolve than he thought she did.

He continued, "I'm sure that this is how it has to go down to get her to understand that I'm leaving and cleaving for real. There's no room for her to think she's making any decisions about what I do."

I closed my eyes against his words. I didn't want him to have regrets. "But it's our wedding."

Stephen moved his arm from my chair and began eating again. "Which means it's the perfect time to get her straight. You know she's not going to want to miss a photo shoot with Essence."

I laughed. He was probably right about that. "She made a mistake."

"She manipulated a disaster, and I won't let it be another thing I let her get away with."

I stood and walked to the refrigerator for a bottle of juice. "What do you want from her?"

"An apology to you and a promise to mind her own business. I have to teach her how to treat you, or we'll keep having problems out of her. I know this seems severe, but I know what I'm doing."

I walked back to my chair and sat facing him. "Have you told her that?"

Stephen cocked his eyebrow. "Repeatedly. Is your phone ringing?"

I swallowed. "She'll come around."

"That's her choice. Until she does, she's not in this wedding." Stephen continued to eat like it was no big deal, but I could see his heart was broken.

There was always something else to pray about.

***

My hand trembled under the weight of my cell phone. I dialed the number and stared at it for a minute before pushing the call icon.

When she answered, I was relieved she'd bothered because I knew my number was unknown to her. "Mrs. Pierce, it's Tamar."

Donna cleared her throat. "This is a surprise. Is Stephen okay?"

"He's fine, ma'am." I paused and took a deep breath before saying. "I'm calling to tell you he's not going to change his mind."

She was silent. "You've made sure of that."

"I had nothing to do with Stephen's decision. I knew you two weren't talking, but the wedding planner told me you weren't participating." I had to push myself to go on. This call was harder than I expected it to be. There really was a lot of hostility between us. "Mrs. Pierce, I've been trying to talk to him. That's why I'm calling you. We're six weeks away from the wedding."

Donna continued to be mute.

"I would do anything to have my mother at this wedding, but I can't. I don't want to look at wedding pictures ten years from now and you're missing from them. I don't want to explain to my children, or even

Isaiah why Grandma Donna wasn't in the wedding."

"GlamMa," she interrupted. "My grandchildren will call me GlamMa."

"See, you want to be a part of our lives. You've already picked out your name."

"You kept my grandson from me." Her voice was filled with the same venom it held the day she found out about Isaiah, but I wasn't going to let her make this rift between her and Stephen about that.

"You disliked me long before that. I'm thinking eighth grade. You also didn't know about Isaiah when you deleted that message and destroyed the note, so please, don't make this about him."

More dead air. The only reason I knew for sure she was still there was because I could hear the low hum of the television in the background.

"What is your problem with me, Mrs. Pierce. Really, woman to woman, tell me what it is?"

I heard her sigh heavily. "He's obsessed with you. He always has been. I don't think that's healthy."

I pulled the phone away from my ear and rolled my eyes like she could see me. "But you think it's healthy to intercept voicemail messages and letters sent to your thirty-year-old son?"

"Don't you try to tell me about parenting." She snapped. "You aren't a real mother."

This time I rolled my neck. "I haven't been a mother as long as you have, but I can tell you this, I'd never do that to my child."

"But you can give him away."

I fought the urge to hang up on her. "I did what was best for him at the time. That was living with my aunt. What's best for him now is me and his father. What was best for Stephen back in March when you interfered? I doubt he'd believe it was what you did."

I heard her harrumph. "Here she is, the real Tamar Johnson."

I swallowed the words I wanted to say before responding. "The Tamar that's not going to let you talk crazy to her. The Tamar that's not letting anyone run her out of town. Yes, this is her."

I sighed and reeled my temper in. "You are family. You're always going to be family. Whether you come to the wedding or not is between you and your son and your God, but I'm on this phone today because I love Stephen. I don't want this for him. Please, work this out before it's too late."

Stubborn woman that she was, she didn't respond. I ran out of patience and time waiting for her to speak. "I have to go. My boss has called me twice since I've been on the phone."

"Tamar." Desperation filled her tone. "You have to understand. Stephen is my only child. I don't want to lose him. I've never wanted to lose him to you."

I shook my head. "You are losing him, Mrs. Pierce, but you're not losing him to me. You're losing him to yourself."

I ended the call. For the first time in all the years I'd know Donna Pierce, I pitied her.

Chapter 45

"You're ready to play."

My heart almost came out of my chest. Adrenaline surged throughout my body. I closed my eyes and rocked back on the table.

"Thank you, God!" I opened my eyes. Clyde and I raised our fists and pounded. This nightmare was over.

"Any recommendations, doc?" Clyde asked.

"Stephen is a professional. He knows he must protect every inch of his body. He knows not to take risks." Dr. Hogan's efforts at reverse psychology did not go unnoticed.

He turned his attention away from Clyde, looking me squarely in the eye. "The thing you're going to have to do now is work on your mental game. Sometimes an athlete has the tendency to overprotect the injury. That's how you get hurt again. So, with that said, I'm ordering a few more sessions with the team psychologist."

"I knew that was coming," I groaned.

"Of course, you did," Dr. Hogan stuck his hand out and shook mine. I shook the other doctor's hand.

"Good luck, Stephen. Don't hesitate to call me if you need something."

They left the room.

Clyde let out a whistle and began to dance. "Back in business."

"Not a moment too soon. I don't think I've been this scared since the accident."

Clyde took his phone out and started texting. "Make good use of the shrink," he said as he typed. When he was finished he raised his eyes to mine. "They give you tips. Good ones."

I nodded.

"I just sent a text to Gail," Clyde said referring to his assistant. "Sports Center asked me for an interview. I'm going to have her set it up, so they get the first crack at you. I told them they'd get to talk to you before the press release goes out."

I let Clyde and the team publicity people deal with this stuff. I merely nodded and stepped down from the examining room table.

We left the room and entered the training area. It was Tuesday, so the team was off. A few of the guys were here working out anyway. We greeted each other. I got high fives and pounds and congratulations.

"Glad to have you back, man. We need you."

Those words were good to hear. They didn't know I needed them, too.

Clyde and I walked down the long hall that led to the exit. I scanned the walls where pictures of all the big games were framed. There were newspaper articles that dated back to the thirties. The great players and owners and coaches had framed pictures. I knew one day, my photo would be there, because I helped make this franchise great.

Clyde stood with me. We had a moment together honoring the past before he said, "You know, Stephen, you handled this like a real pro. I'm proud of you."

"I'm not going to lie and say it was easy."

"You know, I know. I've had guys lots of guys get hurt over the course of my career in this business, so I know what that pain looks like."

We began to walk to the door and exited.

Clyde continued. "You talk about all that faith in God, and I saw it for real. You never got scared."

"I was scared plenty."

"Yeah, but it wasn't scared like what I'm used to seeing. I've had a lot of injured athletes. Some of them lose it. You kept it together like no one I've seen before." Clyde put a hand on my shoulder. "You're the kind of brother that makes this sport better. You're my hero and I mean that."

He walked down the steps and I fell in step with him on the way to the parking lot.

I got into my truck. Clyde got into his which was parked next to mine. We both put down our windows.

"You know, sometimes you make me think about this Christianity stuff."

I raised an eyebrow with interest. "Do I?"

Clyde turned up his lip like he was deciphering data. "A little bit."

"I'll keep praying for you."

"You do that." Clyde nodded. He waved and pulled off. There was a seriousness in his eyes that revealed his heart. He meant it. He was thinking about his faith.

I thought about Pastor Johnson's words about my witness during this season. Not only was the team watching, my best friend was watching and because he was so close to me, Clyde was someone I hadn't even considered.

God's plan is always bigger than ours. I knew that. I also know why we have to try to do the right thing at all times.

I arrived home to an excited Isaiah. "Dad, they're about to talk about your team."

I approached the television. I picked up the remote and turned up the volume.

"The Giants will get some much needed help next week, when Stephen Pierce comes off injured reserve. The Giants have already said they plan to activate him. He'll practice with the team this week."

The program left the studio and cut to an interview with Coach Nye.

"How's Pierce doing?"

Coach Nye replied, "Pierce is on target to return when we play the Vikings on November

18th, which would be a much-needed boost to the offense. He just has to get comfortable again. He has stayed mentally in the game by attending meetings and walk-throughs. He's been praying with the team and blessing the field. He's a regular priest out there. He looks good. I think he's lived up to his reputation during a rough year personally and professionally. I expect to see the same Stephen Pierce that left the field come back."

A better Stephen Pierce, I thought.

"Dad, you ready?" Isaiah's eyes couldn't have been brighter.

"I'm ready. I think the best thing about playing again is knowing I get to look up from that field and see you watching me."

Isaiah tossed the football he was holding to me. "I'm going to pray you get a touchdown."

I laughed. "We Pierces pray before all games." I pointed heavenward. Isaiah copied the hand signal and I knew this was going to be a great season.

Chapter 46

I opened the garage to put the trash out. My mother was standing in the driveway.

"Hello, son."

I put the bag in the can and turned to her. I could see she was dressed up a little more than usual, so I figured she was coming from one of her many social club lunches.

I looked up at the sky. The snow was coming down heavier than it had been earlier this morning when I left for practice.

"Would you like to come in?" I asked.

She nodded and stepped in the garage with me. We went into the house. My mother shed her handbag and coat, leaving them on a chair in the foyer rather than hanging them up. I surmised she wasn't planning to stay long. She always hung her coats.

"Can I make you a cup of coffee or something?" I asked, washing my hands.

"A cup of tea would be nice."

I put the kettle on. The kettle she'd purchased for me when she'd decorated my kitchen. I pulled a mug off the mug rack and dropped a bag of the tea she kept in the cabinet.

"This weather is dreadful, and it's early yet." My mother settled onto a stool at the breakfast bar.

Since we were going to open with small talk, I said, "Not too early. Thanksgiving it's always freezing."

"I'm thinking about going to Florida for a few weeks to get away from the cold. My bones can't take it anymore."

I nodded. "So, is this what we're going to do, Mom? We're going to talk about the weather."

"Don't rush me. I need to congratulate you. You're playing next week."

I crossed my arms over my chest and backed into the counter near the stove. "Thanks."

"Are you ready?"

I nodded. "I'm good. I feel strong."

My mother played with the place setting in front of her. It was more of her handy work. Tamar had been here a lot, daily, but redecorating wasn't on her list of concerns. She hadn't changed anything. She'd barely decorated her apartment. The woman was a minimalist. "I look forward to the game."

"It'll be Isaiah's first time seeing me play."

She smiled. "Good. It's a blessing you've recovered. I can't help thinking what if you weren't better. It would have been horrible for him never to see you play."

I dug deep for the patience. "What-iffing doesn't

help and now that I'm better, it doesn't matter."

My mother grunted a little. She lowered her eyes to the table setting again. "I talked to Tamar last month."

"A whole month ago." I didn't hold back the sarcasm.

My mother frowned. "She pleaded with me to talk to you about our situation. She wants me in the wedding. She acknowledges that I'm family."

"Mom, I don't think it should have taken Tamar to acknowledge that you're family."

"You're not behaving like it." She gave me a hard stare, one that would have worked when I was a child. "What son doesn't invite his mother to his wedding?"

"I don't know." I shrugged, guiltless. "One that's tired of her shenanigans."

My mother turned her head. She seemed to be focused on something in the next room. I followed her line of vision to the picture. I'd hung a 48 x 36 size photo of Tamar, Isaiah and myself over the fireplace.

"I don't know what you and Tamar talked about a month ago, but I'm pretty sure it wasn't an apology."

She rolled her neck in my direction, and our eyes locked. "So, you're going to strong-arm me into kissing up to her?"

"That's not what this is about. You did something wrong. You should want to make what you did wrong right."

The kettle whistled. I filled her cup. I handed her

a jar of honey and a teaspoon and then returned the kettle to the back of the stove.

"You owe Tamar and me an apology. And I don't think it's fair for you to think I should just behave like you don't."

"You're blackmailing me, Stephen. Like I've got to do this to keep from being embarrassed in front of the whole world."

"Mom, if you can't see you're doing this to yourself, I don't know what to say, but I want respect for my future wife. I should have demanded respect for my girlfriend back in high school. Maybe all these years and all this loss wouldn't have happened."

My mother scowled as her chest heaved up and down. "Oh, so it's my fault you didn't know about your son?"

I threw up my hands. "It's all of our fault. It's the fault of everyone who didn't give her the support she needed when that video was released. That includes you, me, dad, and her father."

My mother spooned honey into her tea and stirred. She kept her voice even, but I see she was seething. "I don't want to be forced to apologize. What happened to forgiving someone even if they haven't asked for it?"

I jerked my head back. "I'm the only one who's supposed to obey the word? You taught me the Bible verses I know about forgiveness."

She raised the cup and took a sip. She glared at me over the lip of the mug. "Maybe I raised a better Christian than I actually am."

I shook my head. "I feel like I don't know you anymore. It's not like I'm asking you to do something that's wrong. You owe my future wife an apology."

My mother raised the mug to her lips again.

"Tamar is the most important woman in my life," I continued. "That doesn't mean I don't love you. You will always be the woman who gave birth to me – who raised me – who taught me the difference between right and wrong. Which is why I know what right and wrong is."

I sighed. "So, Mom if you want to come to the wedding, come. Tamar is fine with it. She's used to being treated like trash by you. But I'm not. I'm not going to be okay with it. If you feel like you're going to be cool with being there with my disappointment, then just come and be this person."

My mother put down the mug. She raised her hands to her temples and began to massage them like she had a tension headache. There was nothing wrong with her head. It was her heart that needed work.

"I need to ask you for something."

She lowered her hands and looked into my eyes again.

"I've been a good son to you. I wish you could just love her. I wish you could just be a mother to her. She doesn't have one. She misses her mother. And I want the mother-in-law relationship between the two of you to be a blessing to her."

My mother frowned but said nothing.

"You have so much to offer. I've got dad. And

I've got Tamar's father. After all those years after the video when he was angry with me and now, he's like a second father."

Her frown deepened. I knew she didn't like hearing that because she wanted me to belong solely to my dad as well, but I needed to make this point. She was going to have to change the way she thought, or our family would not be all that it could be.

"Did you know Pastor Johnson drove all the way from Pine back in the spring to come and talk to me?"

She shook her head and raised her mug again.

"I was depressed. Really low. He was able to talk to me in a way that no one else could. I needed that from him. Tamar could use it from you. She doesn't need all this judgment. And you don't need to hold all this anger and resentment toward a woman who has a completely different relationship with me than you do. So for me, can you just love her?"

"I didn't want to lose my son." The words squeaked out like a pained whisper.

"Are you sure you didn't want to lose me, because it's taken you a long time to get back over here."

My mother laughed. I wasn't even sure why, but it released tension in her and the tension in the room.

My mother pursed her lips. "Where is Tamar?"

"She's in Georgia for a work thing."

"Okay. Then this has to happen by telephone." She pointed at my cell. "Go ahead. Call her."

My heart was pounding wildly as I walked across

the room and retrieved my cell. I pushed the speed dial for Tamar and handed it to my mother after it started ringing.

"Tamar, this is Donna Pierce. Sweetheart, I owe you an apology. When I see you, we'll have lunch, and I'll give it to you in person, but for now if you would, dear please tell me what color my dress should be."

I shook my head. That was the best it was going to get. It was better than nothing.

Chapter 47

The game started with all the usual dramatics that came with playing the Minnesota Vikings at home. The team came flying out of the tunnel loud and strong, and after the beating of a drum the fans shouted their beloved Skol chant. The Gjallarhorn sounded. It was game time.

I was nervous, but I was also ready. One of my teammates clapped me on the shoulder, then another, and another. Coach moved the second string running back up in my spot, but he'd only reached triple-digit yardage once this season and in the last game he'd lost 17 yards on 2 carries. They needed me.

But the thing I was most excited about was Isaiah. I looked to my left and spotted my family – Isaiah, Tamar, her father, and my parents. I pitched my head back and threw up a peace sign. Isaiah jumped to his feet and threw it back. Tamar's smile filled my line of vision. She blew me a kiss. We only had two more weeks until she would be my wife.

I looked up and prayed, "Thank you, God, for my family. Bless me now. Protect my body and my mind and bring me victory that gives You glory. Amen."

"That's right, man. Give Him props," one of my

teammates said as he walked by me. This guy had always been bothered by my praying, and he made it clear on several occasions. Pastor Johnson's words came back to me.

Can Stephen Pierce still walk through this locker room and around all this equipment with his busted leg and say, "God is good."

My testimony before my team meant everything. Sure, I was on the field to play, but I was also on the team to be light. Football was a hard sport. It was violent. We needed light because sometimes it was dark. I was glad I'd had that talk with Pastor Johnson. It turned me around and gave me what I needed to hold my head up high as a Christian on this field.

The coin toss fell in our favor. We had the ball. In the third quarter of the game, I scored a touchdown. I dropped to my knees and thanked God again. The applause from the crowd was insane. I was back. I was better. I was the Stephen Pierce I was created to be.

Chapter 48

"This cold is so disrespectful it's blasphemous." Kim's teeth chattered on every word. "I can't believe black people live up here."

The other bridesmaids, two of my cousins, rolled their eyes at her back. They'd been living a few towns over from Pine, with the rest of my father's family, their entire lives.

"The snow is pretty. It's the perfect backdrop for our pictures." I shifted into the place the photographer's assistant instructed me.

"Why can't we take pictures inside?" Kim cried again. It had only been five minutes since her previous protest.

"We just came from inside." I laughed. "Stephen and I grew up with snow. We want pictures with snow, so stop tripping."

"I'm from New Orleans," Kim said to the assistant. "Y'all hurry up."

I laughed again. "Girl, you ain't been out here ten minutes. Pull yourself together."

"We're ready," the assistant said speaking into a lapel microphone. She moved off camera and the photographer took a set of group photos. When he was finished, he said, "All done for now."

The assistant directed us inside. We hustled into the church and were met with a blast of warm air from a large heater that had been set up in the rear vestibule.

The skirt that had been clipped under my dress to protect it from the snow was removed. All of our faces were powdered again and one of the hostesses offered us warm cider.

"The next time you have an event up here, you make sure it's late spring or summer," Kim insisted.

I laughed. "You were one of the people encouraging me to get married where and how I wanted."

"Well, if I had known you were going to do it on a glacier, I would have encouraged you to do a wedding moon in Jamaica."

"We're done with the bride, but we'll need the rest of you to come back out for photos with the men when they're done."

I looked at Kim. "Do not curse in this church."

After the men took their photos, my party went back out to join them for more pictures. In the presence of the men, I noticed Kim didn't appear to be complaining as much. She seemed to be dealing with the temperature just fine.

"Girl, you a mess," I whispered.

"Those two are interested in each other." My father's voice came from behind me.

I turned. "I didn't know you were there."

"Watching," he said. "I love weddings. They're the highlight of being a pastor."

"So, who are the two you think are interested in each other?" I asked, looking at the small group.

"Your friend and Stephen's best man."

I squinted for a better look. "Kim and Clyde?"

"Oh yes," my father said. "I'm an expert. I can always see when there's a spark in the wedding party."

I looked at the two of them. Kim was adjusting Clyde's tie. Sixty-four teeth were showing between them. They had been flirting at the rehearsal dinner last night. Kim had asked me who he was.

"Hmmm…" I murmured. "I guess we'll see."

My father took my arm and looked me up and down. "You are a beautiful bride, baby girl." His eyes were misty. "Your mother would be so proud."

I wagged a finger at him. "Don't make me cry."

He chuckled. "I wanted to talk to you for a moment." He reached into his pocket and removed a small pearl broach. He raised it eye-level and turned it back and forth in his hand. "Your mother wore this on our wedding day."

I reached for it. "I remember seeing it in pictures. It's beautiful."

"It's made from paste," he said matter-of-factly. "Your mother's dress was plain. We didn't have any money. We stopped in Belk's Department store and went to the jewelry counter to find something to dress it up with. They had a lot of fancier stuff, but it wasn't in the budget." He tilted his head. "Her family had lost all their heirlooms in a house fire when she was a teenager."

"The one that killed her father."

Daddy nodded. "And her mother. I mean, she was heartbroken. She didn't live much more than a few years after he died. Heartache is poison, Tamar."

I knew what he meant.

Struggling to wrangle his emotions, he cleared his throat. "We've all had our fair share of it. I'm glad you're home. I'm glad you and Stephen and Isaiah have reunited. I'm glad you're happy, baby."

My eyes filled with tears. "I'm not supposed to cry."

"I know. I'm not going to say anymore. I'll save it for a toast. But I wanted to give you this. Something old." He smiled again. "Love each other. Fight for the love. Never run."

I nodded. "I promise, daddy."

"That's my girl." He reached for a tissue from the nearby holder and handed it to me. "I think you're okay, but just in case."

I took it and wrapped my arms around him. "I love you."

"I love you too, baby girl. I'll see you in a few."

Chapter 49

My chest filled with love and pride as Tamar's father walked her down the aisle. Save for the few flicks to the left and right at the guests, her eyes connected solidly with mine. Tamar and I were already joined as one. We had been since we sat on the backsteps of this church, eating Jolly Ranchers, at the age of six. I knew she was special. I knew she would be in my life forever, even then. This ceremony was important, but it was a formality. We moved through it seamlessly with me saying my vows first.

"I vow to share my life with you as both a lover and a friend, I promise to support your dreams. To share and help you achieve all your goals. I promise before God and this company that I will never allow anything to break the bond between us and God. I will live a life completely submitted to God and to our covenant. I will love and cherish you in good times and difficult times and honor you always until death separates us."

Her eyes sparkled like the ring I slid on her finger. "I love you, Tay, today and forever. Thank you for agreeing to be my wife."

Tamar blinked and a lone tear escaped and slid down her cheek. I raised my hand and wiped it. Tamar raised a hand to cover mine. She leaned into my hand, kissed it, and pulled it down to hold it while she said her vows.

"Stephen, you still haven't given me my two dollars."

I chuckled and so did a few other people in the sanctuary.

"But I owe you so much more. You are an amazing man. You're more than I ever could have hoped for, dreamed for, or had the wisdom to ask God for. I promise to love you, respect you, honor you, and partner with you through the good days and the tough days. I will humbly and happily submit to your leadership because I know God is the head of your life. He will never fail you, and you will never fail me. We will succeed in faith together. I promise to be your biggest cheerleader. Your greatest fan, a gentle critic, and loving support to you. I will spend every day of our lives appreciating our journey together. I vow to never give up on our love."

Tamar slid a ring on my finger.

I clasped her hands, raised them to my lips, and kissed them. A murmur of appreciation swept through the sanctuary. There were more words. Words I barely heard and then the assistant pastor pronounced us man and wife.

God, she's my wife. "You're my wife," I whispered.

Tamar smiled and I leaned in for my "welcome to my world forever" kiss.

Our guest clapped and whistled. I pulled her into my arms. We walked up the aisle into our future.

Chapter 50

The limo ride from Pine to New York City wasn't long enough for Stephen and me. We made love with our hearts and words and kisses. We napped and briefly and woke up aware that we were wearing each other's rings and beginning our lives together.

Our arrival at the Legacy Hotel was met with a complete court press. Lights from cameras popped and bounced off the impressive rock on my finger. The large diamond earrings Stephen had given to me as a wedding present were like glittering glacial rock in the lighted tunnel we stepped through from the car to the entrance. I could see them gleaming in my peripheral vision.

Clad in a form-fitting gown in my favorite shade of deep purple, I walked down the long, white, carpeted foyer of the venue with my husband. Once inside, thousands of gold balloons and confetti fell from the ceiling and our crowd of guests applauded.

Stephen and I greeted countless people, took pictures, accepted congratulations, and we danced. There was a decadent menu. Deniece and her crew had made sure we had the best of everything. Most of the remaining cake, a pretty confection with an elaborate gold and purple trim, had been cut into pieces and boxed up for the guests to take home.

Stephen and I had just finished taking some photos for *Essence* magazine when one of his teammates moved to the area in front of the stage.

"Can I have your attention," he bellowed into a microphone. Ten other players joined in around him.

He looked in our direction. "Tamar, we welcome you to the family. Let me tell you, we love you already because we can see you have made him a better man. So as part of this here Giant's family, you have to get used to surprises."

Stephen let go of my hand. He smiled and joined his teammates.

"What are you doing?" I mouthed the words.

He shook his head. Kim appeared behind me with a chair.

"Sit down, girl." She was in on whatever was about to happen, so I took my seat. A member of Deniece's staff pushed a chair next to me, and Kim sat too.

"What is happening?" I asked through clenched teeth.

"Just wait for it," she responded.

The stage to the left rotated and the curtain opened to a large piano. John Legend and a band were on the stage.

"Oh, my goodness!" I shrieked and popped to my feet. My favorite artist.

John greeted everyone. Then he said, "This is a

special version of one of my songs that I would only do for a brother as righteous as Stephen Pierce. Tamar, our congratulations on your marriage. I pray you and Stephen have every happiness."

I covered my mouth and sat down. He was going to play for us. My heart was pounding out of my chest.

The music to "Tonight Will Be The Best You've Ever Had" began, but instead of using the words best you've ever had, John sang, "blessed you ever had." Stephen and his team began to dance.

I hollered. They had choreographed an entire routine to the words. And they had it together - complete with all kinds of props and smooth moves.

Kim leaned over and whispered, "If you don't introduce me to one of those Giants, I'm going to kill you."

I laughed without taking my eyes off the show. "Are you sure you haven't met your Giant? You seemed pretty friendly with Clyde."

I cast a quick glance in Clyde's direction. He was standing right near the area where they were performing.

Kim puckered her lips before speaking. "He's good looking, and if he's getting a percentage of Stephen's bank, I know he's rich, so I gave him my number. But if it doesn't go anywhere, I'm coming for you."

The music keyed down. Stephen and his team were done dancing. Most of the guests were standing, but the few who weren't now were, and everyone applauded their performance.

Stephen and John shook hands, and John came down the stage to me. I stood. He gave me a hug and congratulated me. I nearly melted. I loved his music so much.

"This was such a sweet surprise," I cried.

Stephen raised an open hand, and I took it. Breathless he asked, "You liked?"

"I loved," I said. "And John Legend?"

"Only the best for you," he said with his whole heart. "I promise you you'll never have a dull moment with me."

I dropped my head back and squinted. "Don't work too hard at it. I could use a dull moment with you, sir."

He chuckled. "Well, you're not going to get it tonight. This party is officially over for us. It's time for the honeymoon."

Stephen turned into the crowd. He waved. I waved. The wedding coordinator told everyone to wish us well and they did. We exited the room and the hotel through the tunnel we'd entered through. Once inside the limo, Stephen knocked on the glass partition that separated us from the driver. The music to John Legend's "Best You Ever Had" filled the speakers. A darkened privacy glass lowered. My husband took me in his arms and whispered, "All right, Mrs. Pierce, game on."

The End

Look for the "Winter Baby" December 2019, and have you read the first book in the Restoration Series? The Winter Reunion is available now. Read the excerpt after the Reader Discussion Guide.

Sign up for my **NEWSLETTER** for updates.

Reader Discussion Guide

1. Tamar had her reasons for not telling Stephen about her pregnancy. Anger, fear, and shame played a big role in her choices, but ultimately, she was protecting his football scholarship. What do you think about her decision?

2. What did you think of Aunt Joe's role in keeping Isaiah from Pastor Johnson?

3. Stephen's injury revealed a form of pride that he didn't know he had. I originally named the character Stephen because I intended for him to be persecuted for his faith. Although he was in some respects, his character's emotional reactions were based on the Job in scripture. Specifically, the revelation that Job was prideful found in chapters 38 and 42 of the Book of Job. Have you had a time in your life where God took you through the refiner's fire and you discovered something about yourself that you didn't know?

4. Tamar's father was a strong spiritual voice in the book. What was your favorite scene of his and why? Did he make you think about your own heart and situations in your life?

5. Donna Pierce was messy. Stephen was firm

with her, stating he was teaching her how to treat Tamar. What did you think of the decision he made to not allow his mother to be in the wedding until she made peace with his future wife?

Scriptures On Healing

"By your stripes I am healed," – Isaiah 53:5.

"Have compassion on me, Lord. I am weak. Heal me, Lord, for my bones are in agony," – Psalm 6:2.

"God you heal all diseases, you redeem my life from the pit and crown me with love and compassion," – Psalm 103:1-5.

"You will restore health to me and heal my wounds," – Jeremiah 30:17.

"Lord, these bones can live," Ezekiel 37:1-14.

The Winter Reunion

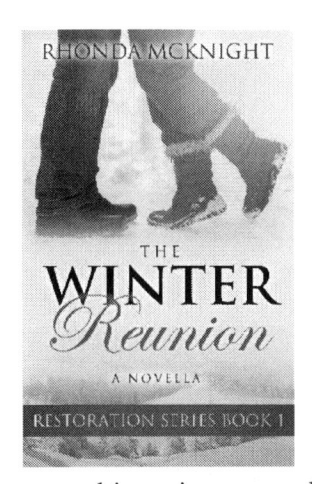

Everyone knows the woman in the famous 'viral" video that hit two million views on YouTube. Humiliated, *Tamar Johnson* changed her name and disappeared behind the embarrassing video that captured her losing her virginity on prom night. But who was the guy?

NFL Running Back *Stephen Pierce* is football's darling. He's spent his entire career doing community service work with at risk kids, and endeared fans as a devoted Christian, even claiming celibacy. It's time for his high school reunion. Stephen is determined to get his EX, Tamar, to come out of hiding, even going as far as posting their prom picture on Instagram in hopes that she would accept the challenge to show up.

Tamar isn't interested in the reunion, but her boss is. She writes for a small magazine. Stephen Pierce is a big story. Tamar is going to the reunion whether she wants to or not.

With reunion activity in full swing, tension between Tamar and Stephen reaches an unbearable high. Before it's over will the world find out who the real Stephen Pierce is? Will Tamar survive spending time with the only man who's ever had her heart?

Chapter 1

"You're fired."

I frowned. "You can't fire me."

"Actually, I can." My boss, Eva Stanford, dropped into her chair. She folded her arms over each other on the desk. That position meant business. So did the steely glare in her eyes.

"You can't." This time my voice held the question. *Could she?*

"I'm the managing editor. I can fire whomever I want."

"But I have a contract."

"You sure do. Have you looked at it since you signed it? There's a part in the legalese that says you have to do the stories that are assigned to you."

I hadn't looked at my contract in years. I never had a reason to. I was happy doing the stories that came across my desk. I didn't have aspirations of becoming some big time reporter. All I wanted to do was pay my bills and keep pecking at the novel I'd been revising for three years. But now paying my bills might become an issue.

"I can't do a story about Stephen Pierce. I don't know anything about sports."

Eva picked up her cell phone and shoved it in my direction. "You may not know sports, but you know him. I'm pretty annoyed that you kept that from me."

I took the phone and looked down at an

Instagram photo of myself and Stephen. The blood drained from my face. Pain constricted my heart. He was going to be the death of me. "This is my prom picture."

"That's obvious." Eva rolled her eyes. "One of the interns brought it to my attention. He recognized you."

I squinted at the picture. My head got light. I was glad I was sitting. "I can't believe he posted this."

"He's on his way to your reunion. I guess he's feeling nostalgic."

I continued to stare at the picture – at him really. I hadn't seen this picture in years. I didn't even have my yearbook or any of the memorabilia anymore. My exasperated sigh filled the momentary quiet. "It's not my reunion. It's a thing they do. It's for all classes."

"Small school stuff. I get it." Eva unfolded her arms and pressed her back into her plush, leather chair. "You're thirty, right? So it's been eleven – twelve years since prom?"

I nodded.

"Did you go to this thing last year?"

"I don't go to my reunions." I pushed the offending phone across the desk to her.

Eva cocked her head. "I'm sure there's a story there. Does it involve Pierce? Do you ever talk to him?"

I fought hard to keep my face from telling my truth. "He was a prom date, Eva. It was a lifetime ago. I have no idea what he's doing now."

Eva extended a manicured fingernail and tapped the screen. "Hmmm…the caption over his Instagram is evidence that he's curious about what you're doing. He put the same thing on Twitter."

I sighed again. I could tell by the look in her eyes that I was not getting out of this. I harnessed my irritation. "I can't believe you're going to make me do this. I haven't been to Pine since I finished high school."

Eva reached for a lipstick-smeared, latte cup. "Stephen certainly seems to love it. It looks like he spends a lot of time there."

Easy for him to do. I resented that.

"Do you have family there?" Eva probed.

I shifted in my chair. "Some."

"They'll be glad to see you." She pushed the button to boot up her laptop. "People get old. They die. I can't stand my family either, but I visit every few years or so."

I stood. The booting up of her laptop meant I was dismissed. "Eva —"

"It's settled, Anne. I need a good story. We're going to run this for February. Try to find out if he's dating someone. Something romantic for a Valentine feature."

I shook my head. "You know how private he is. He's not going to tell me that."

Eva cocked an eyebrow. "I won't push. You know what I need for a cover story."

I turned to leave the office.

Eva called to me. "Any truth to that rumor about him? The one about the video."

I swallowed. "That old story?"

"Nothing is really old. I'll have to see if we can dig up that video. Ask him a question or two about it."

"Asking him about the video is not going to endear him to me. He really won't talk to me then."

"You're right, but you can ask. I know this isn't what you normally do, so I'll send you a few questions. You always ask the hard stuff after you get the easy stuff."

"I know how to do my job, Eva."

She lowered her eyeglasses and peered down her nose at me. "You're acting like you don't."

I resisted the urge to fight with her. She always won. "I need to take the afternoon off. I wasn't planning to go, so I don't have anything to wear."

"Fine. Expense it. Expense a trip to the hair salon, too. You need it. Donna has your itinerary and some other details."

I walked to the door, grabbed the handle, did a half turn and looked back at her. "I guess this is just as good a time as any to tell you this, because it'll probably come out now that I'm going to the reunion."

A disconcerting look came over Eva's face. "Spit it out."

"Anne Ferguson isn't my real name."